SHADOWLAND

P. L. HAMPTON

Published in North America, Australia, and Europe by RIZE. Visit Running
Wild Press at www.runningwildpress.com/rize Educators, librarians, book clubs
(as well as the eternally curious), go to www.runningwildpress.com/rize.

ISBN (pbk) 978-1-955062-80-0
ISBN (ebook) 978-1-955062-81-7

OTHER NOVELS BY P.L. HAMPTON

Picking Chrysanthemum

Dedicated in loving memory to Lynda D. Jackman

To India and Phalen.

PART I
OPENING THE DOOR

"Let the child in search of his mother
    Sprinkle his eyes with lustral water,
    Then shall the dead be visible to him.
    Let the child in search of his mother
    Follow the shadows' noiseless footsteps,
    So, shall he reach the land of the dead."

—Excerpt from a Yoruba Fable

PROLOGUE

FEBRUARY 29, 1976

It was perfect. Each fold, each crease, of the paper airplane was exact. Aaron meticulously made sure each wing was precisely the same length and size. He turned up the tips to give the plane lift and prevent unexpected nose dives. When he threw the plane in the air, it dipped and dived just like the paper planes his father made.

Eager to show his father his handiwork, Aaron said, "Look, Dad!" He proudly held the plane up for his father to see.

"I really can't look right now, son. I'm driving."

"Ooo, Ray, turn it up! That's my jam!" his mother shrieked.

Aaron's dad turned up the volume. "Anything for you, baby."

Aaron marveled at his creation, while Denise Langford snapped her fingers and sang along with Marvin Gaye, while his father drove his majestic Lincoln Continental down Georgia Avenue, there were plenty of reasons to be joyous this particular Sunday. It was Aaron's birthday. It was February 29th, 1976, a leap year, one of the few times his birthday fell on an actual day. There was no need to celebrate on February

28th or March 1st. In 1976, February 29th was an actual day, and it was an unusually warm and sunny day in Washington, D.C.

Aaron sat in the backseat of his father's car admiring his paper plane as his mama sang along with Marvin Gaye. To Aaron, his mother was beyond approach. No woman in the world compared to her. Her copper-toned skin shined like gold, and the constellation of freckles that straddled the bridge of her nose glittered like the stars in the Milky Way. Her hazel brown eyes were hypnotic. To Aaron, his mother was more than a social worker. She was the center of his universe.

Aaron smiled as she serenaded him and his father. Often, Aaron would boast that his mother was a better singer than Diana Ross and ten times finer than Pam Grier. That led to many schoolyard fights. In 1976, you were a fool to question Diana Ross' voice and the thickness of Pam Grier's thighs.

Aaron hummed along with his mother as he toyed with the paper plane. From the expression on his father's face, Aaron could see how hearing his mama sing made him happy as well. She had a way of making him feel like a king, which Aaron assumed, was very much appreciated. Aaron's father was a tall, slender man, standing roughly around 6'4". He was as dark as midnight, blue-black as some would say, with a dusty afro, sprinkled with gray flecks. Despite the weight of the world that his son sometimes sensed seemed to sit on his shoulders, judging from his constant complaining, there was no one in the world he wanted to be more like than his dad. To family and friends, Raymond Langford was a loving husband, a loyal friend, and a solid family man.

Aaron held the paper airplane next to the ivory seats of his father's 1963 Lincoln Continental. The plane matched the color of the seats perfectly. Sitting behind the wheel of that car was another reason why his father was so happy. When he drove that car, no one could tell his father anything. Life couldn't dampen his spirits. He once told Aaron, "A Continental is a black man's chariot." Aaron took that as being the truth, judging by the countless black men who drove Lincoln Continentals in 1976. Yet, his father's Lincoln was special. It was a 1963 snow-white with suicide-doors Lincoln Continental. Aaron was always mesmerized by how the pearl white flakes in the paint made the car change colors. There were occasions when the car appeared white, sometimes cream or even a purplish white. The ivory leather interior, milky white carpet, fat white wall tires gave Aaron the impression that he was floating on a cloud every time he rode in the car. His father only drove the car on special occasions.

"Why isn't Mother Dear coming to eat with us?" Aaron asked.

"Your grandmother had to attend a Missionary meeting after service today," his father said.

It was Sunday, which meant church in the Langford household. Religion did not come easily to the Langfords. Aaron especially hated early Sunday mornings, getting dressed to simply hear the reverend go on and on about the same ole thing. Then have the nerve to ask for money after boring him half to death. Only the exuberant singing of the choir managed to keep his attention. His mother grew up in the church. His father, on the other hand, didn't take to church right away. Sundays were reserved for the Redskins or the Bullets, not for sitting in the pews. Yet, he made an effort to attend church after Papa Joe passed away. Aaron's father knew the only way he was going to be able to fill the hole in his wife's heart and satisfy her concern for Mother Dear after Papa Joe's passing was to go to church. That was where Mother Dear spent most of her time.

Mother Dear was a devout Christian. She measured a

person's worth on how they chose to serve the Lord. How often they went to church was not the measuring stick. Rather, she measured an individual's worth by what was in their hearts. Often, she would tell Aaron, "Scooter, if you're looking for the devil, you'll find him sitting in the first pew." She would then laugh until Aaron reminded her that she sat in the first pew from time to time.

"I can't help but rejoice after being served a heaping teaspoon of the Lord's blessings!" his mother shouted.

Aaron figured that maybe he too could help himself to some of those blessings when the offering plate came to him that morning. He figured God wouldn't mind him taking a couple of dollars for penny candy. It was his birthday. More importantly, Aaron wanted to hurry up with lunch so he could find out if his mother and father had gotten him the bicycle he had been begging them for the past year.

As if he had read his son's mind, his father said, "I don't want you to get your hopes up about getting a bike, son. A postman doesn't make a lot of money."

Aaron was tired of hearing about how much money a postman made. Just once he wanted to get what he had asked for. Santa Claus always seemed to miss his house or mess up his Christmas list. He was tired of always receiving underwear and socks. Discouraged, Aaron tossed the paper plane in the air. The plane lifted upwards towards the top of the cabin, then was captured by the wind blowing in from his mother's window to crash land in between his father's legs.

Denise Langford's duet with Marvin Gaye came to an abrupt end. "Aaron Langford!" Whenever his mother called him by his full name, or incorporated his middle name, Jebediah, it usually meant he was in trouble.

"Be easy on the boy, Dee Dee. It is his birthday. It only comes around every four years." Ray peered at Aaron through the rearview mirror. "I'll get the plane for you this time, son. Just hold on to it."

"Okay."

"He was supposed to be paying attention in Sunday school and not making paper airplanes. I wonder where he gets that from," his mother said, cutting her eyes at Ray.

"I don't have a clue," Ray said.

"I heard you snoring during the sermon."

Ray chuckled. "That wasn't me, snoring. Besides, God was the one who declared the seventh day to be the day of rest." Denise glared over at her husband.

Aaron's father reached down in between his legs in search of the plane, trying his best to locate it without taking his eyes off the road. Not having much success, he decided to look down. That was when Aaron saw the blue pickup truck barreling at them.

The sound of twisting metal, accompanied by the bite of shattered glass cutting Aaron's cheeks, was immediate. A sense of weightlessness overwhelmed him as his body was catapulted forward. Marvin Gaye continued to sing, yet he was distant, far away. Voices all around him sounded frantic and afraid. They gradually built-in intensity until they became the crashing of words and sounds all intermingled into a mountain of gibberish. Piling up into mounds, followed by a voice, screaming, "Scooter." Then, everything was gray. Gray sand dunes seemed to roll on as far as the eye could see.

WRESTLING

40 YEARS LATER

Morning arched its back and stretched itself out across the sky. Its soft blush danced on Donna's skin. Sinewy strands of muscle pronounced themselves upon her mahogany thighs. The sun accentuated every curve of her body: from her muscular legs to her firm backside. Aaron laid his hand on her waist, his eyes tracing the curvature of her hips, and the symmetry of her breasts.

Their eyes met.

Aaron smiled.

It had been so long since they had shared an intimate moment. Since the move, life had gotten in the way, unpacking, arranging, and of course rearranging. Seattle did very little to create the ideal circumstances for them to connect.

"I love you," Aaron whispered.

The corners of Donna's mouth turned up like eucalyptus leaves reaching for the sun. She rarely smiled, for it exposed her crooked bottom incisor.

"I love you, too."

In their little bubble, their souls rejoiced. Donna kissed

Aaron's tourmaline lips, then eased her way out of bed, letting Aaron's hand fall haplessly onto the mattress. He watched as she walked over to the dresser. The kids were in the kitchen. It was their arrival downstairs that put an end to their lovemaking.

"What are you doing?" Aaron asked. "Come back to bed."

"The kids are awake."

"Ah yes, the kids."

Aaron could feel the gears of the world slowly grinding back into place. Life returning to its slow, steady death march.

"Can you walk Imani to school? I want to get a run in before it starts to rain. The weatherman said it's supposed to rain today," Donna said, pulling her sports bra down over her head.

Rain. It was never a matter of "if" rather "when" in Seattle. The weather had been bearable since their arrival, but the long summer was coming to a close. Mist-filled mornings were gradually becoming the norm as clouds rolled in and out over the Sound as if on a conveyor belt. Aaron had heard all the horror stories about Seattle, like how you could tell the difference between day and night depending upon the shade of gray. He didn't particularly care for the city. It just so happens this was where he landed.

"Yeah, I got her," Aaron said. "Aren't you going to take a shower?"

"Nah. Why should I? I don't see the need if I'm going to get sweaty jogging. I'll shower when I get back."

"I don't see how you can run around in public without washing up after sex. That's nasty!"

"Are you going to take Imani to school or what?"

"I said yeah."

"I'll walk Asher to the bus stop before my run."

"Why?"

"Because I want to. Is there a problem with it?"

"Yeah, there is. Why are you walking him to the bus stop? We've lived here for two months. Asher knows where the bus stop is. He is in the ninth grade. He doesn't need 'Mommy' walking him to the bus stop, so he can catch the bus. You need to stop babying the boy."

"If I want to walk him to the bus stop, then I'll walk my son to the bus stop!"

And just like that, everything grinded to a halt. Without saying a word, Donna stormed out of the room. The euphoria of sex was gone. Aaron threw on his sweatpants and tried to catch her before she barricaded herself in the office. She was overly protective of their son. At fourteen years old, Asher was diminutive in stature. He couldn't help that he was a late bloomer like his father. He was also the child of two parents who carried the sickle cell anemia trait. Aaron knew Donna meant well, but she was putting a target on their son's back for every bully to see.

Aaron was too late. Donna had already locked herself in the office. She would remain there until it was time to take Asher to the bus stop. In the kitchen, Asher and Imani sat eating cereal.

"Good morning," said Aaron.

"Good morning," Imani said, smiling.

Asher only grumbled, "Hey."

"What's up with the big smile?" Aaron asked his daughter.

Imani giggled. "We heard you and Mommy wrestling this morning."

"How many times do I have to tell you they weren't wrestling?" said Asher.

"Yes, they were! Daddy told me! That is why Mommy is always grunting and groaning!"

Aaron interrupted before Asher could reply. "We were wrestling!"

Asher smirked. "Whatever."

Imani looked like she felt vindicated. "See! I told you!"

Aaron looked over at Asher and nodded his head before going into the bathroom. As he turned on the water, he considered consoling Donna but decided against it. The sound of the water rushing into the basin filled the bathroom. He pulled up the lever to redirect the water through the showerhead. The water sputtered before a steady stream cascaded down from above. Pulling off his sweats, he stepped into the tub and pulled the shower curtain shut. As the water beat down on him, Aaron made a note to himself to keep his voice down the next time he and Donna decided to "wrestle."

SEATTLE

"Have you seen him?" Imani asked, interrupting Aaron's thoughts.

"Seen who?"

"Mr. Palmer."

"No, baby. I can't say that I have other than briefly." Aaron peered over at the Palmer house.

"Don't you think that is weird?"

"What is?"

"That we haven't seen him since we've lived here?"

Imani had a point. They had lived in their new home for two months and had yet to see Mr. Palmer more than once. Aaron mainly heard about him from the other neighbors. He also had yet to meet their neighbor who resided in the large yellow Victorian house on the corner. His neighbors assured him he would recognize her when he saw her, for she was an albino.

"Johnny at my school says that Mr. Palmer is a serial killer," Imani said.

"Is that right? How would Johnny know?"

"He said he saw Mr. Palmer's picture on the Internet."

"That really doesn't mean he's a serial killer. I mean, my picture is on the Internet. Does that make me a serial killer?"

"No, that's because you're my daddy."

Aaron smiled. "Yes, I am. That doesn't mean I can't be a serial killer."

"Stop being silly, Daddy."

"Just because Mr. Palmer's picture is on the Internet doesn't mean he is a bad guy. Do you think the police would just let a killer wander around the neighborhood?"

Imani paused. She looked perplexed. "Maybe."

"Maybe?" Aaron said.

"I don't know! Are you sure?"

Aaron smiled. "I'm positive."

In spite of her father's attempt to assuage her fears, Imani did not seem convinced. "Well, Asher said he's seen Mr. Palmer watching me when I walk to school."

"Asher told you that?"

"Uh huh."

Aaron glanced over at the Palmer house. "I think your brother is trying to scare you. How would he know if Mr. Palmer is watching you when you walk to school? Asher is already on the bus by that time.

"And if he was watching you, it's probably because he doesn't want you stepping on his lawn."

"Do all old men always yell at kids and tell them to stay off their grass? You're old, I don't see you yelling at the kids playing outside."

Aaron laughed. "That's because I'm not that old. You wait and see. One of these days, I'm going to be sitting outside on the porch with nothing on except my underwear and galoshes yelling at every little kid that walks past the house."

"Eww, that's nasty. I don't think anybody wants to see you in your underwear," Imani said.

Aaron laughed. "Neither do I."

Imani grew silent. "Are we ever going to go back home?"

"I don't know. Maybe."

Aaron gazed out onto the arbor lanes, the junipers, spruces, and big leaf maples. They were a departure from the concrete of their neighborhood back in D.C. Their new home was close to Imani's elementary school, Aaron's job at the University of Washington, the Arboretum, Lake Washington, and Lake Union. It was a lovely Tudor rather than a cramped brownstone. They were able to get more for their money in Seattle. The only drawback was that Donna and the kids hated it.

Aaron decided to change the subject. "So, do you like your new school?"

"It's okay."

"It's just, okay? Why is it just okay? It sounds like you've made friends. I mean, it sounds like Johnny is a friend?"

"No. Johnny is always bothering me. He is always talking to me and getting me in trouble."

"Oh. Are you sure that it's Johnny getting you into trouble, and it's not you getting you into trouble?"

"It's Johnny."

"Okay, if you say so. Well, do you have any friends at school who are not getting you into trouble?"

"I talk to Daphne sometimes."

"What about your brother? Has he said anything to you about his new school?" Aaron asked.

"He hates it. No one likes him. He has no friends. Don't tell him I told you. But he said he was going to run away. He said he's going to go back home and live with Grandma and Grandpa."

"He said that?"

"Yeah. I promised him I wouldn't tell. You can't tell him I told you," Imani said.

"I won't."

"Swear?"

"I swear."

"So, Daddy, who wins?" Imani asked.

"Who wins what?"

"When you and Mommy wrestle?"

Aaron chuckled. "Your mama. Your mama wins every time."

After accompanying Imani to school, Aaron returned home to prepare for work. The commute to the university was pretty much the same every morning. The usual bottleneck into the U-District at the Montlake Bridge over the Montlake Cut brought traffic to its customary stop and go. The University of Washington was not Aaron's first choice to continue his research. Moving his family from the East Coast to the West Coast was the farthest thing from his mind. Yet, he had very little choice if he wished to maintain control over his work. The University of Washington was willing to provide him with the necessary funding to continue his sickle cell anemia research. The fact the university's medical center was one of the best in the nation was an added bonus. Also, the hospital's staff was skilled in treating complications that arose from the illness.

Aaron's obsession to find a cure for sickle cell anemia went beyond simply his son. He grew up with the disease. His grandmother, Mother Dear, suffered for some time from the disorder. Without a cure, possibly the same fate awaited Asher. So, Aaron was determined to crack the code on gene HBB, which was responsible for whether or not a person's red blood cells formed into sickles. Aaron's research allowed for him to temporarily convince a patient's bone marrow to produce normal-shaped hemoglobin. Yet, the difficulty came in making the switch from sickle-shaped hemoglobin to normal round cells permanent.

Once inside his office, Aaron set his briefcase down and looked out the window at the countless homes dotting the hills around Lake Union. He looked at the reams of papers stacked on his desk, like they have been every day, except today; rather than stacks of papers, he saw paper airplanes.

THE HOUSEWARMING GIFT

"There. How's that?" Donna pushed the couch into its new location, then looked over at Aaron.

Donna was obsessed with rearranging the furniture. She tried so desperately to recreate the warmth and feel of their brownstone in D.C.

"Aaron!" Donna screamed, pulling Aaron away from his thoughts. "For one second can you please focus and tell me what you think about the sofa being here rather than over there?"

Aaron envisioned the couch in its previous location. "I kind of liked it where it was."

"What do you mean you liked it where it was?"

Aaron had apparently hit a nerve. There was some lingering resentment from that morning. Aaron wished he had stuck to his customary response of "It looks great."

"Look, baby, it's fine. Okay?"

Socrates, the family cat, had taken a front row seat to the looming argument.

"That is not what you said." Aaron acted like he did not

hear her. "Don't stand there like you don't hear me talking to you, Aaron Langford."

"What do you want me to say?"

"I said, what do you mean you liked it where it was?"

When the doorbell rang at that moment, Aaron was relieved to know he didn't have to explain himself right away. "Look, there's Otis and Teri. Can we talk about this later?"

"Oh, we're going to talk about 'this' later. You're not going to get off that easily." Aaron hastily made his way to the door.

This was the first time, since arriving in Seattle, Aaron would have a chance to spend time with his old college buddy. Aaron and Otis were more like brothers than friends. Otis was there for every major milestone in his life. He was the best man at Aaron's wedding. He was Asher and Imani's godfather. He consoled Aaron when Mother Dear died.

Otis ushered Teri in from out of the rain. "Hey, we're not late, are we?"

"Nah, you guys are right on time." Aaron embraced his old friend. "Thank God you're here."

"I heard you, Aaron," Donna said from somewhere behind him. "You guys are right on time. Dinner should be ready in a few minutes."

Otis had forewarned Aaron he was bringing a date, which was rare for him. It took a lot for Otis to be serious about a woman. Right away, Aaron could see why Otis was attracted to her. She was a light-skinned, curvaceous woman. Otis had a penchant for light skinned, shapely women. A direct contrast to his tall, lanky, features.

Donna took Teri by the hand and led her into the living room. By the expression on Donna's face, it was clear she was pleased to have another woman in the house.

As Donna and Teri made themselves comfortable, Otis whispered, "What's going on?"

"Donna's on the warpath."

Otis seemed to find humor in that tidbit of information. "What is it, PMS?"

"Hell, I wish. It's this whole move. It's not sitting well with her. I mean, she has rearranged the living room furniture five times this week. She's testy and ornery. The slightest thing sets her off."

"She rearranged the furniture five times?"

"Five times."

"She's that depressed?"

"Depressed is not the word; it's more like antsy. She misses being back in Washington, D.C. Not to mention, the chilly, overcast days are not helping."

"I know the weather takes some getting used to. Rest assured, when spring and summer roll around, and she sees how beautiful Seattle can be, she'll warm up to the city. There is no place more beautiful than Seattle in the summer. In the meantime, maybe you should consider taking her to a lodge in the Cascades, or even better, Whistler in British Columbia."

"Maybe she needs to get a job or start seeing patients again, so she can stop jumping down my throat," Aaron said.

"How is that going?"

"There are a few more pieces of paperwork she needs to submit to the state, but she is taking her sweet time. She also has an opportunity to do some adjunct work at the university. She has an interview with the chair of the psychology department, but she keeps putting it off. A few community colleges have expressed an interest in her possibly teaching as well. Honestly, I don't think she will have any problem teaching or reviving her practice. The question is, does she want to?"

"Well, if she doesn't like it here, and she doesn't have much to do during the day, what does she do to occupy her time?" Otis asked.

"She spends most of her time on the phone with her mother and rearranging the damn furniture."

"I surely hope you have a good cell phone plan."

"I'm not worried about my cell phone bill. I'm worried about my sanity!"

"I hear ya. I hope you don't mind. I brought a little something for Teri and me to drink." Otis held up a Cabernet Sauvignon, Aaron's favorite blend of wine.

"That's fine. Just because I've taken an oath of sobriety doesn't mean everybody around me has to." Aaron realized he was closing in on nine months without a drink.

"I didn't want to make you uncomfortable," Otis said.

"I appreciate the thought. What is that?" Aaron said, pointing towards a wooden tray tucked beneath Otis' arm.

"Oh! Isn't it beautiful?" Otis held up the piece of wood like it was a treasure. "It's a handcrafted divination tray," he said. "I bought it at the house down the street. I thought it would make a wonderful housewarming gift."

"The house down the street?"

"Yeah, the big yellow house on the corner. It appears as if one of your neighbors has kicked the bucket, and her kids are having an estate sale." Otis held out the tray, to let Aaron marvel at the exquisite carvings.

"The craftsmanship is impeccable, isn't it?" Otis asked.

"Yeah, I guess. Do you know what these symbols mean?" Aaron asked, pointing to the images along the edges.

"I don't have a clue. Marc, an anthropologist at the university, possibly could tell me. He showed me one of these a few years back when he returned from a trip to Lagos. These boards are one of the ways West Africans communicate with the dead. Sort of like an African version of an Ouija board. I thought it would give us something to do later."

"Otis, you know how I feel about Ouija boards. I don't mess around with those things."

"First of all, it is not an Ouija board. It's a divination tray. It is a tool West Africans use to speak with their ancestors and spirits. Besides, who said you had to believe in it? I'm talking about having a little fun. I thought after dinner when the kids are asleep, we whip out the board and entertain ourselves," Otis said.

He handed the oblong wooden tray, along with a small satchel and a statuette in the shape of an elderly man with an elongated hat, to Aaron.

"What is this stuff?"

"That is the tapper," Otis said, pointing toward the sculpted figurine. "And the small sack contains the cowrie shells."

"What do we need cowrie shells for?"

"I'll show you later."

"That is what I am afraid of." Aaron begrudgingly took the wooden plate.

"Where are Asher and Imani?"

"They're upstairs."

Aaron gazed at the piece of wood, taking note that the carvings were arranged in a pattern that repeated itself on both sides. At the top of the tray, there was an etching of a face, and at the bottom, a serpent.

Once dinner was over, and the kids had gone to bed, Otis suggested they amuse themselves with the divination tray. His nagging eventually led everyone to relent and let him retrieve the artifact off the coffee table.

Otis laid the housewarming gift down. "Okay, who wants to go first?"

"What is that?" Donna asked.

"It's the West African version of an Ouija board," Aaron said.

"It's not an Ouija board. It's a divination tray. It's how some West Africans communicate with their ancestors," Otis said.

"I don't like the sounds of that," Donna said.

"How does it work?" Teri asked.

"From what I've been told, the tray helps a seer receive advice from the spirit world. Supposedly, the oracle taps this thing, the tapper, against the board after a person has asked the spirits a question." Otis held up the statuette. "The seer then tosses the cowrie shells onto the tray three times. The way the cowrie shells land relay the spirits' answer to the individual's question, similar to the Geechees down in the French Quarters in New Orleans who throw the chicken bones on a table and tell you your fortune based on how the chicken bones are arranged," Otis said.

Donna frowned. "That doesn't sound like a game to me. It sounds like something we shouldn't be messing with."

"Exactly!" Aaron said.

"Ah, come on you guys. Which one of you is brave enough to go first?" Otis asked.

"Why don't you go first? You want to play with the damn thing so bad," Aaron said.

"Look, I bought the tray as entertainment for us, not me," Otis said. "What about you, Donna? I know you want to go first."

"I think I'll pass. That thing scares me."

"Fine. Teri?" Otis stared willfully at his date.

"I think I'll watch."

Otis looked at Aaron and smiled. "I guess that leaves you and me."

"Otis, you know I don't play with those things. I am quite sure the fortune teller or seer always responds to the gullible individual's question with a generic answer that could be the answer to a dozen similar questions."

"Why are you such a killjoy? Can you, for once, stop thinking so damn analytically and humor us by pretending to enjoy yourself?"

"If doing so will make you shut up, then yes!" Aaron said.

Otis situated the divination tray in front of Aaron. He grabbed the cowrie shells from the small sack. Along with the cowrie shells, there was a chicken bone and a small black pebble. What was even more peculiar was that all the shells, except two, had been shaved, allowing them to have two openings. The natural opening, and another one where the shells had been filed flat at the top.

Otis gazed at the chicken bone and pebble. "What are these doing in there?" He quickly put them aside.

With the cowrie shells in one hand, and the tapper in the other, Otis looked at Aaron. "Are you ready?"

Aaron sighed. "Get on with it."

"Now ask a question."

Aaron paused.

"Come on."

"Give me a second, will you?" Aaron closed his eyes. "Will I live a long life?"

"What type of question is that?" Otis grimaced before tapping the tray with the statuette and throwing the cowrie shells.

"What do you mean? It is the question I wanted to ask."

"Couldn't you have offered up a better question?"

"Look, you told me to ask a question! That is the one I

wanted to ask! If you don't like my question, then maybe you should ask one of your own!" Aaron got up from the table and went into the kitchen.

"Let's play something a little more fun, and all of us can play together, rather than this African Ouija board," Donna said.

Teri agreed. "Yeah, that sounds like fun. Plus, everyone can play."

"Oh, come on you guys," Otis cried.

Aaron poured himself a cup of coffee. "Otis, please. I tried playing your stupid game, and you told me I was playing it wrong. So, let's do something else."

"I think you could have asked a better question. Aren't there deeper things in life you'd much rather know the answer to besides 'How long am I going to live?'"

"I think wanting to know if I am going to get hit by a bus tomorrow morning is a pretty damn good question."

"Why don't you guys try one more time? This time, let Otis ask his quote-unquote philosophical question," Teri said.

"Yeah, let's give it one more try?" Otis asked.

"Okay, you're asking the question this time."

"Fine," Otis said.

Reluctantly, everyone headed back into the dining room. "Here, take the tapper." Otis handed the small figurine to Aaron as he took his seat.

Otis looked at Aaron and smirked before saying, "Are there spirits amongst us?"

Aaron glared at Otis. "Tap the horn of the tapper on the board, and then toss the shells," Otis said.

Aaron tapped the tapper on the divination tray and threw the cowrie shells. The cowrie shells danced upon the wooden plate before coming to rest. As Otis examined the arrangement of the cowrie shells, a look of dread spread across his face.

Despite his claim of not being superstitious, Aaron feared the cowrie shells foretold of something ominous. "What do the shells say?"

Otis sat there silently studying the shells before bursting out into laughter. "I don't know."

Donna rolled her eyes. "Aaron, you need to get your friend."

Otis' insistence on playing the farce out had annoyed everyone, including Teri. Aaron figured he needed to rein Otis in before he made a complete ass of himself.

"Otis, that's enough."

"What do you mean, that's enough?"

"I'm serious."

He looked around the table before sliding the divination tray over to Aaron. "Sorry."

Before grabbing the tray to put it away, though, Aaron noticed the cowrie shells had landed at the base of the tray—near the serpent.

THE AWAKENING

Aaron saw the paper airplane glide upward, then dip. He could hear his mother calling his name, her voice lilting amongst the haze similar to how lily pads dance upon the ripples of a pond. Aaron could not discern if the voice was that of his dream calling out to him or reality beckoning him back.

"Aaron! Aaron, wake up!"

He opened his eyes to find Donna standing over him. "Are you awake?" she whispered.

"I am now."

"I think somebody's in the house."

Aaron sprung up trying to collect his thoughts. "How do you know?"

"Because I got up to use the bathroom, and I saw the shadow of a man in the living room."

"Are you serious?"

"Yeah."

"What made you go into the living room?" Aaron asked.

"I heard something."

"Is the alarm activated?"

"Yes."

"Then I seriously doubt anyone is in the house. They would've tripped the alarm." Aaron promptly rolled over.

"God damnit. I know what I saw! Now what are you going to do about it?"

Although framed as a question, it was fully intended to be an ultimatum. Donna wanted him up and out of the bed inspecting the living room.

Aaron propped himself up on his elbows. "I guess I'm going to go into the living room, so the man in there can kill me."

"That is not funny."

Aaron eased his way out of the bed. "Be careful," Donna warned.

"Yeah, I wish somebody had said that to me before we got married."

"What did you say?"

"I said, I will."

Aaron looked at the clock. It was 2:26. He had hoped for a decent night's sleep since he needed to be in the lab early the next morning. There was no telling how long he would be forced to search for the boogeyman.

Aaron was certain the so-called shadow in the living room was nothing more than a figment of Donna's imagination. All the talk of ghosts and African Ouija boards had ignited Donna's imagination. Aaron shuffled clumsily into the living room. He tried to be quiet–in case someone really was in the house. Regrettably, he lacked the grace to be light on his feet.

The living room floor was freezing. Aaron suspected a window was left open. A quick scan of the room showed the windows were closed. Aaron turned on the lights. Other than him, there was Socrates asleep in his recliner.

"Git!" Aaron shouted, shooing the cat out of his chair. The

tabby hissed before scurrying off. The last thing Aaron wanted was to have his favorite chair lined with cat hair.

"Is anybody in there?" Donna called from down the hall.

"Nope."

"I swear to you, I saw the silhouette of a man in there as plain as day."

"Well, if that is the case, he has up and disappeared like a fart in the wind."

"There was a man in the living room."

"Okay, I believe you. Now, go back to bed. I'll be there in a minute."

Donna walked back towards the bedroom while Aaron scanned the room one last time before turning off the lights. As the room faded to dark, something caught Aaron's attention out of the corner of his eye. Intuition told him that it was the cat, but he had already seen Socrates dart off into the kitchen.

"Socrates, is that you?"

Aaron held his breath, hoping it was the cat. He figured all the talk of spirits and conversing with the dead had caused his own imagination to wander.

Fucking Otis.

Donna must have sensed something was amiss because she asked him if everything was all right.

"Yeah, everything is fine," Aaron answered.

"Come to bed."

"I'm on my way."

It was difficult to identify the shadows cast throughout the room. He had definitely seen something move, exactly what he did not know. He looked at the fern on a stool in the opposite window. The shadow cast by the fronds did resemble arms, while the legs of the stool could have been mistaken for a person's legs.

Wanting to feel certain, Aaron went to the front door to

make sure it was locked. He unlocked the door, opened it, then shut the door, and locked it again before testing the doorknob. Aaron then unlocked the door, opened the door, shut it, and locked it again a second time and even a third time before feeling confident the door was indeed locked. Next, he checked the windows to see if they were locked shut. He unlocked them, then opened them, and then locked them again. As with the door, Aaron repeated this routine with each window three times until he was satisfied nothing bad would happen. Walking back to the bedroom, Aaron realized that was the first time since the move that he felt the compulsion to triple-check the door and the windows.

THE WOMAN IN THE MINISKIRT

Otis barged into Aaron's office out of breath. "What's up?"

Aaron was having a hard time concentrating. The events of the past hour had him dazed. "Did you jog down here from Savery Hall?"

"Yeah, I wanted to see if you wanted to go up on the Ave and grab a bite to eat."

"Couldn't you have called or texted? I could've met you."

"I guess so. I don't know. Who cares? Besides, I can use the exercise. So, do you want to go?"

"Yeah, I guess so."

"You guess so? What's up? Are you busy?"

Aaron motioned for Otis to shut the door. He did not want his assistant to overhear their conversation. Otis tried to shut the door discreetly but failed miserably. "What's going on?"

"I just came from my lecture in Bagley Hall."

"And?"

"Well, today one of my students decided to come to class and sit in the front row in a bright red floral miniskirt."

"And?"

"And she just sat there. She just sat there staring at me."

"What's so strange about that?"

"It was the way she looked at me. It was like she wanted me to see her. She didn't take notes or anything."

"Are you sure she wasn't high?" Otis asked.

"I don't know. Plus, how can you tell?"

"Who knows? She probably ate too many edibles before class. Be glad she didn't puke right there in class."

"Maybe. I just found her behavior strange. She threw me off. I fumbled through my lecture for the better part of an hour. I doubt I had one coherent thought the whole time. I tried to find her after class to ask her if she was okay, but she was gone."

"Let it go. There's nothing you can do about how these kids chose to spend Mommy and Daddy's money. These kids are experimenting with so much wild shit nowadays. Synthetic marijuana and the likes. One kid told me he smoked potpourri once. I mean come on."

"Yeah, you're probably right."

"Anyway, I didn't come over here to talk about your students. I thought you might want to grab a bite to eat. I'm in the mood for Thai. I thought we could go to the Thaiger Room."

"Sounds good, I've been meaning to talk to you about last night. We can talk over lunch."

* * *

When they had finished eating lunch Otis leaned up against the brick wall at their table, which was tucked away in the back of the restaurant close to the exit and restroom. "So, what's on your mind?" Otis asked.

"Huh?"

"What is it you wanted to talk to me about back at the office?"

"I want to know what the hell got into you last night?"

"What do you mean?"

"I'm talking about the little performance you put on with the African Ouija board."

"I may have had a little too much to drink."

"Tell me about it. The whole ordeal with the Ouija board scared Donna to death. She had me creeping around the house looking for little green men last night."

Otis laughed.

"That's not funny. I have to live with this woman. Like it isn't bad enough I have to come home every evening to find my living room furniture rearranged, now I have to investigate every creak the house makes."

"Okay, first of all, for the record, it is not an 'African Ouija board.' It's a divination tray," Otis said. "Secondly, I'm sorry. I was having a little fun. If it makes you feel any better, Teri was spooked, too."

"All of us were disturbed by the tray and the way you were acting. All of that mumbo jumbo about spirits. You know you need to stop that."

"What is it with you? Why is it so hard for you to believe that maybe there is more than this? Is it that hard to believe that maybe, our essence, our energy, lives on once our bodies have perished?"

Aaron was sorry he had even brought up the subject. Religion was always a touchy conversation between the two of them. "Ah, here you go!"

"Yes, here I go."

"I'll tell you why it is so hard for me to believe in such places as Heaven and Hell," said Aaron.

"Why?"

"If you give me a chance to spit it out, I'll tell you."

"Excuse me. I didn't mean to interrupt."

"The reason it is hard for me to believe in Heaven and Hell is because neither place exists," Aaron continued. "Stories of this utopia filled with trumpeting angels, or this fiery inferno filled with cloven-hoofed demons are nothing more than stories made up so people will accept their suffering. People are convinced to believe their suffering will be justified with a seat in the kingdom of God after death, while others enjoy their heaven right here on earth.

"Religion is nothing more than a tool used to divide and conquer, make people accept the inequity and injustice they're forced to endure at the hands of those in power. That's all it is. To be quite honest with you, I'm sad to hear such talk coming out of your mouth. You're professing a belief in something that cannot be seen, heard, touched nor quantified," Aaron said.

Otis looked at Aaron. "Our ability to think on a conscious level and openly ask ourselves pointed questions sets us apart from animals. Whether the question is 'Why am I here?' or 'Is there a God?' we seek the answers to things we cannot see nor quantify. You cannot see gravity. Yet, you feel its effects every day. You cannot see, hear, touch, nor quantify love. Nevertheless, everyday people profess to be in love.

"I don't know what happened to you. After Mother Dear died, you lost faith in everything."

"I stopped believing in God a long time ago. Way before Mother Dear died."

* * *

At home, Aaron was pleased to find all the furniture in its rightful place. However, Donna was in the kitchen staring out the window. He contemplated just continuing on to the bedroom, but instead, he eased up next to her and kissed her on the cheek. "Hi, baby."

The kiss seemed to break her from her trance. "Hi," she said.

He really didn't care to know what was troubling her; however, Aaron knew he had to ask. "What's wrong?"

"I've had a weird day."

"What was so weird about it?"

"I don't know. Everything seems to feel slightly off. Plus, I cannot find Socrates." Aaron was glad to hear Donna's fretting had only to do with the family's mangy cat.

"When was the last time you saw him?"

"Yesterday morning when I fed him."

"Well, I chased him off my recliner last night. I also saw him this morning when I went downstairs in the laundry room to grab some socks. He was holed up in a corner hissing."

"Hissing?"

"Yep."

"Was he hissing at you?"

"Who knows? You know that cat and I do not get along. The cat is crazy if you ask me."

"You know Socrates doesn't like you."

"And I don't like him. I'm starting to believe you've given the cat way too much catnip, and it has fried his brains."

"Please."

"I'm telling you that cat is a catnip junkie. I wouldn't be surprised if he isn't outside right now trying to score some catnip from the neighborhood cats."

Donna looked panicked. "Do you think he got out?"

"No, not at all. That cat is probably hiding somewhere in the house. You know how Socrates is. When he doesn't want to be bothered, he disappears for the better part of a day. He probably found a nice, secluded place somewhere in the house where no one can find him."

"Skipping a meal is not like him. I hope he didn't sneak outside. He's in a new, unfamiliar environment. He could easily get lost." Donna's voice cracked.

Aaron did not understand his wife's affinity for the feline. Asher was the one who had found the stray pilfering through the garbage. Nonetheless, it was Donna who adopted the cat and claimed the tabby as her own. Her love of philosophy prompted her to name the cat Socrates. Regardless of Aaron's personal feelings for the feline, he knew how much Socrates meant to her, particularly after the move.

"Look, if the cat doesn't show up by tomorrow morning, we'll send out a search party to find him."

Donna appeared relieved, yet she abruptly went into the living room and started rearranging the furniture. As Aaron watched her move the coffee table and a chair, he couldn't resist counting the strands of cat hair he saw on the floor. He figured if he counted at least twenty stray cat hairs, then everything was going to be okay.

PAPER AIRPLANES

"I want to go home! Why can't I go back home?" Asher
yelled as Aaron walked in the house.

Donna stood at the bottom of the stairs. "Asher, will you
please listen to me?"

"Why? Moving here was bullshit!"

"Hey! I'm your mother! You don't talk to me that way!"
Donna screamed. But that statement was met with the sudden
sound of Asher's bedroom door slamming shut.

Aaron put his briefcase down in the office and walked into
the kitchen. He stopped dead in his tracks when he saw a paper
airplane sitting on the breakfast table. A chill ran its way down
his spine.

"What is that?" he asked Imani.

"What is what?"

"That," Aaron said, pointing at the paper plane.

"Everyone made planes in class today. Since it was raining
outside, we went to the gym and measured to see whose paper
airplane flew the farthest."

"Whose paper plane went the farthest?"

"Daryl's."

"Hmmm ... What is going on with your mother and Asher?" Aaron asked, keeping his eyes on the plane.

"I don't know. I think Asher has girl problems," Imani said.

"Girl problems?"

"Yeah, Mom had to go to school and pick him up because some girl said he looked like a leprechaun."

"A leprechaun?"

"Yup, that's what I heard. All I can say is be careful, Daddy. Mommy is not happy."

"Thanks for the advice, baby."

"No problem."

"Take that off the table. Put it away somewhere," Aaron said, pointing at the plane. He walked down the hall and rapped softly on the bedroom door.

"What?" Donna yelled.

"Can I come in?"

"I don't see why not! It's your room, too!"

Aaron eased the door open to find Donna sitting on the edge of the bed in tears. "Are you alright?"

"I can't keep doing this, Aaron!"

Aaron shut the door behind him. "What are you talking about?"

"I'm talking about Asher! I'm tired of being the one to deal with him! You need to talk to your son!"

Aaron wondered how all this was his fault. "Why, what happened?"

"There is a girl at school that Asher likes. Another boy at school, a senior, embarrassed him in front of her. He called him a 'leprechaun.' From what your son tells me, words were exchanged, which in turn led to the fight. He is suspended for the next three days. After that, he has three days of detention."

"Well, if he is suspended, did he at least make it worth his while?"

Donna glared at Aaron. "That is neither here nor there! Your son needs you. You need to talk to him."

The thought of wringing Asher's neck crossed his mind. "I will. Though, I think I will wait until everyone has had a chance to settle down."

"That is always your excuse," she grumbled

Wishing to not antagonize her any further, Aaron silently took off his clothes, slipped on his sweats, and quietly left the room. He went into the kitchen and made himself a peanut butter and jelly sandwich. Depending on Donna's mood, that might be the extent of dinner for the evening. The paper airplane was gone. So, with the peanut butter and jelly sandwich in hand, he sat down next to his daughter.

"See, I told you it was about leprechauns," Imani said.

"Yeah, you were right."

Aaron looked up just in time to see Socrates' tail disappear around the corner. He felt the urge to chase after the cat, but stopped himself.

"Your mom found the cat?"

"Maybe. I'm not sure"

THERE IS NO SUCH THING AS MONSTERS

Aaron opened his eyes to find Imani staring at him. "What are you doing up?"

"There are monsters in my room."

"There is no such thing as monsters. How many times do I have to tell you that?"

Imani frowned. "Yes, there is; I've seen them. You need to come into my room and chase them away."

Aaron looked over at the clock. It was 3:34. The idea of going upstairs and pretending to chase monsters out of his daughter's room did not excite him. "Baby, can Daddy chase the monsters away in the morning?"

Suddenly, a sharp pain laced its way up the back of Aaron's leg. He looked over his shoulder to see Donna glaring at him. Apparently, his conversation with Imani was not a private one.

"If you don't chase them out tonight, then I'm going to have to sleep with you and Mommy. I don't like sleeping with you and Mommy because you snore," she complained.

"I do not snore."

"Yes, you do."

"That's your mama who snores," Aaron said.

"No, it's you."

Aaron grinned. "Okay, baby, I'm on my way." The kick in the leg had made it clear he did not have a choice.

Aaron wiped the sleep from his eyes and took his time putting on his robe and house shoes. He led Imani by the hand upstairs. Anxiety was the monster in the house for numerous reasons. Tension between Donna and Asher earlier might have also made it difficult for Imani to sleep.

Light trickled out of Imani's room into the hallway as Aaron pushed open the door and looked inside. "I don't see any monsters."

That's because you are the monster.

"You can't see them with the lights on. You can only hear them," she told him.

"Oh."

"Listen." Imani stood still. Following his daughter's lead, Aaron did not move.

"Did you hear that?" she whispered.

"Hear what?"

"That noise. It's gone now. You got to pay close attention, Daddy."

Aaron giggled. "Okay, baby, I'm sorry. Well, I guess the monsters are gone. Don't you think it's time to go to bed?"

"Maybe? You're going to have to stay here with me in case they come back."

Aaron was not eager to share his daughter's twin-sized mattress. "All right, I'll lie here with you for a little bit. Then Daddy has to go back and get in his own bed."

"Okay."

Aaron crawled onto the bed next to his daughter. Once they had gotten comfortable, Aaron reached over to turn off the light. "No, Daddy! You have to leave the lights on! They come out when it's dark!"

Clearly, Aaron had forgotten the monster rules. "Okay, baby, I'll leave the light on."

Dawn crept into the room. Aaron's plan to wait until Imani had fallen asleep and slip out undetected had backfired. Unwittingly, he had dozed off. Aaron eased his way off of his daughter's bed, doing his best not to wake her. He turned off the lamp and slipped out of the room, hopeful he'd get in another hour of sleep before having to get ready for work.

"Aaron, wake up!"

Startled, Aaron bolted upright. "What! What's wrong?"

"I can't find Socrates! I thought he might be hiding like you said, so I searched the house!" Donna said.

Aaron could not believe he was awakened by the cat. "You what?"

"I said, I cannot find Socrates!"

"Donna, I cannot believe you woke me up for the cat!" barked Aaron, lying back down. "I thought I saw the cat yesterday!"

"You what? Where did you see the cat?"

"I thought I saw Socrates when I was eating a peanut butter and jelly sandwich in the kitchen with Imani. I thought I saw his tail dart around the corner."

"I've been in this house for the past two days, and I have yet to find the cat," Donna said.

Aaron closed his eyes and shook his head; all he wanted to do was get some rest. "Maybe I imagined seeing him."

"Well, while you're imagining, Socrates is gone! The same food I put in his dish yesterday morning is still there!"

"Socrates is a cat! He can fend for himself!" Aaron threw the sheets up over his head.

"I can't believe you! I've moved clear across the country! I've given up my practice for your research, and all you can do is lay there under the covers!"

"That cat can take care of himself! He is an alley cat. If anything, the cat is out robbing somebody's garbage."

A hush fell over the room. Aaron assumed the conversation was over, but the sudden sound of drawers slamming shut caused him to pull back the covers to see Donna dumping her clothes out of the dresser drawers onto the floor.

"What are you doing?"

"I'm packing."

"Packing?"

"Damn right! I'm packing!" Donna sobbed.

"Why the hell are you packing?"

"Because I'm going back home to D.C., and I'm taking the kids with me. I don't like it here, and neither do they. It's cold and rainy all the damn time, and you act like you don't give a damn about me!"

"What? Wait a minute; I never said that."

"You didn't have to."

"Look, if you want me to look for Socrates, I will. Simply because we had a disagreement about the cat doesn't mean you need to go off the deep end."

"Aaron, this is not about the cat!" Donna threw more clothes onto the floor. "Did you not hear what I said? I do not like it here! I hate Seattle! I don't know anybody! I have no family here, and the kids have no friends, so they wear on my fucking nerves!"

Aaron sat up. "I don't understand why you have such a distaste for Seattle! Pretty soon you'll be able to resume your practice, and your time will be occupied. I don't think you are looking at the positives here."

"Not one damn thing about this place is positive!" Donna took a deep breath. "Look, I know what your research means to you. I'm not asking you to abandon it. While you search for a cure, the kids and I will be in D.C."

"While I search for a cure? You make it sound like I am doing this all for myself!"

"Sometimes, I wonder."

"Are you serious? I'm doing this for our son!"

"Are you? Or are you doing it to rid yourself of your own demons?"

"Do you truly believe that?"

Donna looked at the pile of clothes on the floor. "I don't know. I don't know about much anymore. Sitting in this house all day drives me crazy. I miss my mother. I miss being around my family. I miss my girlfriend, Felicia." Tears streamed down her cheeks.

Aaron climbed out of bed and embraced his wife. "Look, I know the transition has been rough. All I'm asking is for you to do is give it some time."

"I've given it time."

"I don't think two months constitutes giving the city much time to grow on you."

"What constitutes enough time?"

"Give it six months."

"Six months?"

"Six months is not as long as it sounds. I guarantee, if you are feeling this way after six months, we can pack everything up and head back home. I'm certain I can get my old job back."

"I don't know."

"Look, I can't do this without you."

"I don't know."

"Please, Dee. I promise, if your feelings have not changed in six months, we can pack up and head back to Washington, D.C., I swear."

"Six months and not one day more."

"Six months and not one day more," he repeated.

"You got six months."

"Thank you. Now, how about we find the cat?"

FAVORITES

Aaron spent the better part of a week combing the
neighborhood for the cat before concluding that
Socrates had slipped out of the house undetected. Donna took
the loss very hard, so Aaron avoided mentioning the cat's name
in her presence. He knew she blamed him for Socrates' disappearance.

After a brief morning rain on Saturday, the sun had broken
through the clouds. Perfect timing for Imani's soccer match,
which he and Donna were looking forward to. It provided a
much-needed excuse to get out of the house. The field was a
mess, but the girls did not seem to mind. They actually seemed
to take pleasure playing in the mud.

"I'm going to have to wash that girl's hair tonight," Donna
said.

Imani looked over at her father and waved. Aaron waved
back. "I see ya! Now, let's score!"

Donna looked over at Aaron. "That girl adores you. She
worships the ground you walk on."

"I don't know about all that."

"You know she does."

"Whatever. I wish I could reach that one down there." Aaron nodded his head in Asher's direction.

Donna gazed at their son. "You start by talking to him."

Asher bobbed his head to the music playing through his ear buds. He intentionally sat apart from his parents. The distance was a good reflection of the gulf Aaron felt existed between them. Even though Aaron tried to close the gap, Asher's belligerence made it impossible for him to connect with him.

"You are way too hard on him. He feels as if he can't do right by you."

"That's not true."

"Then tell him that. I mean, really, when was the last time you sat down and talked to him? Other than lecturing him or telling him how to be a man? I mean, when have you had a conversation with your son? Listened to what he had to say? Listened to what's going on in his life? I bet you didn't even talk to him the other day about what happened at school like I asked. Did you?"

Aaron didn't respond.

"He is your son, and he needs you."

"I'm here for my son."

"No one is questioning that. However, you need to talk to him about more than being a man," Donna said.

She knows how hard it is for me to talk to him. I'm the bad guy, the evil one.

"Don't look at me like that! Go talk to your son," she insisted.

Aaron peered down the bleachers at Asher. Heeding Donna's advice, Aaron ambled down to where his son sat. "What are you listening to?" he asked.

"Nothing."

"So, you're bobbing your head back and forth to dead air?"

Aaron sat down next to him, sneaking a peek at his cell phone. He was posting on Instagram.

"What are you posting?"

"Nun ya."

"Nun ya? What is that?"

"None of ya business," Asher said. "Wow! I can't believe you fell for that. Wasn't that joke around when you were a teenager in the Stone Ages?" Asher chuckled.

I really want to snap your neck right now!

Silence settled in between them as Aaron looked out onto the field trying to manage his frustration. He saw Imani darting into a scrum. The floral pattern on a parent's blouse briefly caught his attention. He had seen that floral pattern before somewhere else.

"So, how is school?" Aaron asked.

"Sucks."

"Does everything always have to 'suck?' Isn't there at least one thing about school that you like? Like a girl?" Aaron thought mentioning a girl might get Asher to talk about the incident at school.

"Nope, pretty much everything about school sucks."

Aaron looked back out onto the field. He saw Imani and smiled; she waved, and he waved back.

Aaron tried to look at Asher's cell phone again, but he pulled it from view. "Why are you here? Did Mom send you down here to 'talk' to me? Did she tell you to 'connect' with me?" There was one thing Aaron could say about his son. He wasn't stupid.

Aaron lied. "No, she didn't. And don't talk to me like that. I'm your father. Since you have better things to do, I'll go back and sit with your mother."

"Whatever. She's your favorite anyway," he said, without even taking his eyes off his phone.

At first, Aaron didn't think he heard him right. "What? What did you say?"

Asher ignored him.

"I said, what did you say?"

"Nothing. I didn't say anything."

"No. You said something. If you got something to say, you need to spit it out."

Asher looked up at him. "I said, 'she is your favorite.'"

"What do you mean by that?"

"Imani. She's your favorite."

"What would make you say something like that?"

"I see it in the way you fawn over her. It's obvious you love her more than you love me. When it comes to me, it's like you could care less."

"That's not true."

"Whatever."

"What is this all about, Asher?"

Asher pulled his buds out of his ears. Aaron could hear the music blaring and wondered how his son managed to hear him over the noise. "I want to go home! I hate it here! I have no friends! It's always so gloomy! I mean, fuck! Does the sun ever shine?"

"Whoa, watch your mouth! I'm not going to remind you again to remember who you're talking to! Do you understand me? Unfortunately, son, going back home to D.C. isn't an option."

"Why?"

"I got a job here."

"Well then, why don't you let me and Imani go back to D.C. and live with Grandma and Grandpa?"

"That's not going to happen. You are my kids. We stick together. I refuse to let you go back to Washington, D.C., and be a burden to your grandparents."

"Why didn't you talk to us about moving to Seattle before you moved us out to this crappy ass city?"

"Boy! I'm not going to tell you again to watch your mouth! I'm not one of your friends!"

"Sorry," Asher muttered. "Sometimes, I wonder if I would be better off dead."

Aaron felt his eyes growing wide. "You don't mean that."

"Yes, I do."

"Why would you say such an asinine thing?"

"Because it is the truth! It's how I feel."

Aaron buried his face in his hands and exhaled. He didn't understand how the conversation had gone awry so fast. Dragging his hands away from his face, Aaron said, "I'm sorry if I make you feel that way, son. Maybe we need to talk to somebody about these feelings you're having?"

"I'm not crazy! I don't need to see a shrink!"

"I'm not saying you are crazy. I think it might help if you were able to talk to someone about how you are feeling other than me or your mother."

"I want to go home!" Asher placed his buds back in his ears.

Rather than make a scene, Aaron somberly walked back down the bleachers towards Donna.

The look on Donna's face said it all. Aaron sat down next to his wife without saying a word. He pretended to be watching the soccer game.

"Our son thinks I don't love him. He believes he is better off dead." Aaron could not believe he was uttering those words.

Donna's eyebrows raised. "He said that?"

"Yes."

Tears swelled in her eyes. "And what did you say?"

"I told him that was an asinine thing to say."

Suddenly, there were cheers. The other team had scored.

Aaron searched for Imani. A scowl graced her face. "It's okay! We'll get it back!"

Donna clapped and shouted, "It's okay!" She then looked over at Aaron and whispered, "I doubt telling Asher it was asinine for him to say that made him feel any better."

"What am I supposed to say? I told him we can see someone, and he told me he wasn't crazy. He said he wanted to go back home to D.C."

Donna shook her head. "Aaron, there is a reason why he is feeling this way. These feelings he's having aren't coming out of nowhere."

Aaron tried to keep his voice down. "Donna, what do you want me to do? I do everything in my power to make sure that boy has everything under the sun."

"You're not providing him the one thing he absolutely needs right now: his father."

A bright red skirt crossed Aaron's field of vision when he looked up to see Imani racing down the field. It seemed completely out of place, yet familiar, and though it was sunny, he felt a cold rush of air, on his skin as he shouted, "Go!" to Imani. Bringing his voice back down, he turned to Donna. "I know 'at times' I avoid talking to him because I want to avoid an argument; that does not mean I don't love him."

"He doesn't know that."

Aaron peered down the bleachers at Asher. "He's so damn rebellious."

"He's a teenager."

The sound of parents screaming caught Aaron's attention. He looked up to see Imani weaving in and out of defenders. "Go, baby! Go!" Aaron screamed.

Donna chimed in. "Go, Imani!"

One defender stood in her way. "Go, Imani!" Aaron yelled.

Imani feigned kicking the ball, then passed it to a teammate for the goal.

"That's what I'm talking about!" Aaron screamed.

"Good job, baby!" yelled Donna.

Aaron watched Imani joyously trot to the center of the field.

"How can Asher think I do not love him? We moved here so I would have a better chance at finding a cure for him," he said, leaning over towards Donna.

"I know this may sound strange, but Asher doesn't need a cure right now. He needs you."

Aaron sighed. He looked down the bleachers at his son only to see a bright red skirt, fluttering upwards and take on the shape of the woman he saw in the front row of his lecture hall the other day. She was sitting at the far end of the bleachers, looking dead at him.

TRYING TO CATCH A KILLER

I *would've been better off not having children, especially Asher.*

Was coming to Seattle worth it? Maybe my research is doing more harm than it is good.

Blood transfusions and hours of kidney dialysis did not stop the inevitable when it came to Mother Dear. The sickle-shaped blood cells in Mother Dear's body lacked the flexibility like normal red blood cells to pass through her blood vessels. So, not only did the sickle-shaped hemoglobin not carry an adequate amount of oxygen, but they also, because of their shape, got stuck in Mother Dear's blood vessels reducing the flow of oxygen-rich blood to her organs, causing them to eventually fail. Even with that said, sickle cell anemia saved Aaron's life.

As a domestic worker, Mother Dear's wage did not allow for her to live luxuriously. It was already difficult of her to support herself, let alone add a child to the equation. She could not afford the video games many of Aaron's friends enjoyed. To keep Aaron occupied, Mother Dear encouraged him to solve the daily riddles and crossword puzzles in the newspaper. She started off innocently asking for his help. After a while, Aaron completed the crossword puzzles on his own. For Aaron, the crossword puzzles and riddles fed his intense curiosity. They were the precursor to the ultimate Riddle Aaron wished to solve: the human genome. The fundamental building blocks for every human being. The quantity of information stored on a minute enzyme, in the nucleus of every living cell, was infinitesimal. The simple change in the protein makeup of a single gene could transform a human being into something completely different. People looked to the heavens to answer life's pressing questions, overlooking the answers to those same questions locked away within every single cell inside us.

The photo of a familiar feline greeted Aaron as he pulled into the driveway. It seemed Donna had spent the better part of her day plastering fliers of Socrates up on the telephone poles throughout the neighborhood. The flier was not the only thing that caught Aaron's attention. Every light in the house appeared to be on. Aaron's heart skipped a beat. Visions of Asher in crisis, struggling to breathe and in pain danced in his head. Often, it didn't take much to trigger a crisis. Aaron hurried to the front door. Inside, he could hear Donna. He recalled that moment, when his wife told him their newborn child's fever was not breaking.

Aaron followed Donna's voice down to their bedroom. There, he found Donna reading to Imani. Asher lay on the bed, playing with his cell phone. None of them noticed Aaron standing there. Eventually, Donna looked up. "Hey you."

"Hey."

Imani squirmed over to her father's side of the bed. When she was close enough, she leaped off the bed into his arms.

"What is everyone doing up?"

"We're scared of the monsters in our rooms," Imani said, gently caressing her father's cheek.

"Imani is scared of the dark. So, we turned on all the lights," Donna said.

"That's because they don't come out when the light is on; it hurts their eyes," Imani said. It appeared Donna had a better understanding of the monster rules.

"Well, you're not going to be as scared of the dark as I'm going to be of the electric bill," Aaron said.

"The kids think the house is haunted," Donna said.

"It is haunted!" Imani barked.

Aaron looked over at Asher. "Asher, why are you down here?"

"I asked him to come down here and be with us. I thought it would ease everyone's nerves if I read a book."

Aaron's arms grew tired. He set Imani down on the edge of the bed, sat down next to her, and removed his shoes. Imani rested her head on her father's shoulder.

"Long night?" Donna asked.

"Yeah." Aaron looked over at Imani. She flashed him a crooked, snaggletooth grin. "Looks like you're having a long night, too."

"Not really. To tell you the truth, I enjoy the kids' company."

"Yeah, Mommy likes us sleeping in your bed," Imani said.

"Well, I don't know if that is a good thing or a bad thing. Regardless, it is time for you two to get in your own beds."

"Aww, Daddy!"

"It is time to go to bed. Both of you have school tomorrow, so you need to be well-rested."

"But the monsters will get us," Imani griped.

"No, they won't, little lady, because I'll get them first."
Aaron tickled her belly.

When the giggling stopped, Imani stared solemnly at her
father and asked, "Do you promise?"

"I promise. I'll get them first. Now, go get in the bed."
Aaron looked over at Asher. "That means you, too."

Asher said good night to his mother but conveniently forgot
to give the same pleasantry to his father before marching
upstairs. Unlike her brother, Imani gave her father a big kiss
and a hug before climbing off the bed and following Asher
upstairs. When he heard the doors shut to the kids' rooms,
Aaron breathed a sigh of relief.

"What is bothering you? Something is eating at you. It is
written all over your face?"

"Nothing is bothering me."

"That sigh didn't sound like nothing to me. Did you think
something was wrong?" Donna asked.

Aaron nodded his head.

"Asher?"

"Yeah."

"Did you think he was in crisis?"

Again, Aaron nodded.

"Thank God that was not the case. Knock on wood."
Donna rapped her knuckles against the nightstand.

"Yeah, tell me about it."

"You really need to lighten up on him. Did you hear
anything he said to you yesterday? Our son is lost right now.
You are being way too hard on him. Even the tone you take
with him is harsh. He's fourteen. He's entitled to be scared.
He's at a difficult, awkward time in his life."

"You're right. Sadly, life is going to be a lot harsher on him
than I ever will. Asher must learn he can't run to the comfort of
his mama every time life gets rough. He has got to learn to

stand on his own two feet because there is going to come a time when we're not going to be around."

"The boy is fourteen. Didn't you not hear him yesterday tell you he wished he was dead? You talk about him like he is a grown man. He is not you. He has not had to endure the hardships you had to endure as a child. We need to be there for him. I admit that I agree with the kids: our lives have not been the same since we've moved here."

"What do you mean?"

"I mean, nothing is the same. The kids are having a hard time adjusting. You're working so much we hardly get to see one another. When was the last time we ate together as a family? Or had date night?"

"It's been a while."

"Exactly. We're always tense and stressed. We hardly talk anymore."

"I don't intend to be distant. You've made it clear to me that you're not happy. Add to that the disappearance of Socrates, and you've been pretty unapproachable lately. I figured it was best to stay out of your way."

"Not talking to me is not how we handle the situation better."

"I don't want to compound my issues here at home with mine at work."

Donna corrected him. "Our issues at work."

"What?"

"Our issues. We're a team. Your issues are my issues. Sure, I'm upset about Socrates and, yes, I'm not too fond of Seattle. Regardless, we're a team. We came here together."

"You sure didn't make it sound like we were a team the other day when you were dumping your clothes out onto the floor. You made it sound as if I was doing this solely for me."

"I was angry." Donna slid over to her husband's side of the

bed and wrapped her arms around him. She tenderly kissed the nape of his neck. The convergence of her lips upon his skin caused his body to melt back into her embrace. Donna gently massaged the cords of muscle around his neck.

Aaron turned to face her and found himself floating in the shimmering lagoons of her eyes. Their lips touched.

"That felt good," she said.

"I need you." Donna placed her index finger in between their lips. "What?"

"Go check on the kids."

"Why?"

"To make sure they are in bed."

"I'm quite sure they're in bed." Aaron attempted to push his way past Donna's finger.

"Please. For me?" Donna removed her finger, allowing their lips to meet again.

"You keep doing that, and I'm not going anywhere," Aaron said.

"Please?"

"Okay, you better be awake when I get back."

"Don't fret. I'll be here when you return, Romeo."

Aaron ran up the steps to the children's rooms. He ventured into Imani's room only to find it empty. Aaron quickly remembered Imani often slept with her brother when she was scared. Sleeping with Asher made her feel safe.

Aaron turned the light off in his daughter's room and stepped across the hall to Asher's bedroom. As he had suspected, Imani was huddled up next to her brother. Aaron pulled the cover up over his son and daughter before reaching over to turn off the light.

"Don't turn off the light!"

Startled, Aaron turned to find Asher staring at him. "Don't turn off the light," his son repeated.

"Why are you not asleep?"

"I can't sleep."

"Well, you better get to sleep."

"I will. Can you leave on the light?"

"Why?"

"Because."

"Because of what?"

"Because, if Imani wakes up and finds the lights off, she's going to freak out."

"Are you sure the light is for her?"

"It will help me sleep, too."

Aaron was certain Asher wanted the light on so he could continue to play on his cell phone he was trying to conceal. "Okay. You know there is no such thing as ghosts, right?"

"Yes, there are!" Imani said.

"And how long have you been awake, little lady?"

Imani smiled. "Since you came into the room."

"You've been laying here the whole time playing like you were asleep?" Aaron started tickling her.

"Dad, are you sure there is no such thing as ghosts?" Asher said, interrupting the horseplay.

How did he explain the difference between the ghosts that were imaginary and those that were real?

"I'm certain, son. Why?"

Asher appeared to give his father's words some thought.

"Tell him, Asher. Tell Daddy, about the monsters."

"Shut up!"

"Hey," Aaron said.

"You're scared! You're scared to tell Daddy!" Imani teased.

"I am not!"

"Yes, you are!"

"No, I'm not!"

"Uh huh!"

"That's enough!" Aaron shouted. It took a minute for the arguing to cease. He was losing precious time with Donna.

"Asher, tell me about these monsters?"

Eager to talk, Imani intervened. "They're not really monsters; they're ghosts!"

"Ghosts?"

"Yeah, and they talk to us," Imani said.

Aaron looked over at Asher. "Is this true?"

Asher shrugged. "I guess."

"What have they said to you?"

"They asked me, what is my name, and how did I get here. One lady ghost asked if I could help her get back home."

"How to get home?" Aaron asked.

"Yeah."

"Is that right?"

"Yep."

Aaron contemplated telling Imani again that there was no such thing as ghosts but decided against it. "The next time these monsters or ghosts try to talk to you, you tell them to leave you alone because you have to go to bed."

"Okay," Imani said.

Asher did not look too thrilled with his father's advice. "Can you leave the light on?"

Aaron examined his son closely. "You're not having any problems, are you? Are you feeling okay?"

"I'm fine."

"Are you sure?" Aaron wondered if the ghosts Asher spoke of were in his head.

"Yes, Dad."

"Alright, I'll leave you alone."

"Now, give me a kiss good night," Aaron said to Imani.

Aaron left Imani in her big brother's room to return downstairs. "Donna, have the kids said anything to you about talking to ghosts?" he asked.

There was no reply because Donna was fast asleep.

As he walked over to Donna's side of the bed and pulled the covers up over her, he stood there for a moment and watched her body rise and fall with each breath. He kissed her tenderly before undressing and turning in for the night. As he hit the light, and the room faded to black, he swore he saw something move out of the corner of his eye.

GHOSTS

"Aaron!"

Aaron awoke to find Donna hovering over him.

"Are you alright?" she asked.

Aaron hesitated before answering. Was he in the backseat of his father's Continental? Was that Donna or his mother screaming his name? His forehead was wet. Was it blood? Or perspiration? Aaron dragged his hand across his forehead and gazed into his palm. Sweat.

"Yeah, I'm fine."

Donna examined him closely. "Did you have another nightmare?" Aaron did not answer her. Instead, he climbed out of bed and slipped on his sweats.

"You hear me talking to you. Did you have another nightmare?"

Aaron walked out of the bedroom without saying a word. He was tired. He had been lying for too long. He no longer knew where the truth began, and the lies stopped. He lacked the energy necessary to dream up another story that would placate her.

Five months ago, Aaron had pronounced himself cured. The nightmares had ceased. He was certain he had conquered his demons. He stopped seeing his therapist. Ghosts from the past no longer tormented him. Intrusive thoughts no longer disrupted his life. Regrettably, their absence was only short-lived. Rather than alert Donna to their return, Aaron said nothing at all. Instead, he chose to keep their return to himself.

Aaron walked into the bathroom and locked the door. The bathroom was his only place of refuge from Donna's onslaught of questions. Aaron listened for her footsteps. Silence. He stared in the mirror. The image that glared back was in stark contrast to the little boy trapped in the backseat of his father's car. His heart pounded against his chest as the last vestige of adrenaline coursed through his veins. The tension within him was twisted ever-so-tightly, similar to a rubber band, just before it breaks. He closed his eyes and started to hum the Marvin Gaye tune his mother sang on the day of the crash.

I killed them.

That is why they haunted him, tortured him, because he killed them. There wasn't enough alcohol to rid Aaron of the remorse. He felt their torment was the price he had to pay for throwing that paper airplane. So, rather than fight them, Aaron decided to form a pact with them. He permitted them to perse-cute him at night as long as they allowed him to function during the day. It was meant to maintain his sanity. The accord had worked out nicely.

Aaron turned on the water. He cupped his hands beneath the faucet and let the water pool in his palms. Rivulets of water dribbled through the seams of his fingers before he splashed the cold water onto his face. As the water dripped from his chin, Aaron could hear, "Scooter!" Then came the brute force of the pickup truck slamming into his father's Continental. The weightless feeling of his body sailing. Then silence. The force of the impact threw his mother's body into the dashboard doing irreparable damage. She sustained fractures to her left eye socket, cheekbone, nose, as well as a punctured lung, and a crushed larynx. Despite the extent of her injuries, his mother clung to life. His father was not so lucky. He was impaled by the steering wheel, dying instantly.

His father's prized Lincoln Continental became a tomb. A mangled metal death trap. Bystanders tried to rescue his mother from the wreckage but were fearful that freeing her might hasten her death. Her body was pinned against the dashboard. Each breath was a struggle until she no longer had the strength. Denise and Ray Langford were pronounced dead at the scene. And like that, everybody, everything of value in Aaron's life was taken away from him.

Mother Dear always told him, "It was by the sheer grace of God that you were spared that fateful day God called your mother and father home."

Where Mother Dear saw divine intervention, Aaron saw a curse. February 29th, 1976, was seared into Aaron's brain like a wildfire sweeping across the plains. All that stood in its wake was scorched earth. New memories took hold. However, they were rooted in blood-stained soil. A once rambunctious, outgoing kid shied away from life for fear the people he loved would leave him.

Aaron turned off the water. He stared at his reflection.

You are a killer.

Aaron went to live with Mother Dear. They were two heartbroken misfits in desperate need of one another. The way Mother Dear thought they could steer their way through the grief and sorrow was by going to church. So, Mother Dear forced a steady dose of the Lord's grace down Aaron's throat. She constantly preached about the splendor and divine mercy of the Lord. Yet, Mother Dear's God never inspired divine providence within him. Aaron saw God as nothing more than a sick, sadistic bastard. His attendance at church was out of respect for his grandmother. He tolerated Mother Dear's ranting about the scriptures out of deference. Aaron already knew everything he needed to know about Mother Dear's God. Besides spending every waking moment in church, Mother Dear worked day and night cleaning houses. She shuffled around for politicians and dignitaries so she could put food on the table and eventually send Aaron to college.

Aaron turned the light off and walked out into the hallway. He expected Donna to be waiting. He looked down the hall to see the dim glow of her lamp. She wasn't going to let him off easy. To postpone the inevitable, Aaron drifted into the kitchen. Right away, his eyes fixated on Otis' bottle of cabernet. Otis had forgotten to take the bottle of wine home. It was highly unusual for liquor left behind to survive a night in his household. Donna diligently disposed of any alcohol. What was even more highly unusual was that Aaron had walked past that bottle of wine several times and never noticed it.

"Relapse begins with one sip," his rehab counselor would say. Aaron contemplated how much damage one drink could possibly do.

I dare you to take a sip. You are not a shining example of a husband or father anyway.

Aaron reached for the bottle of wine. There was the soft pop of the cork as he pulled it free from the mouth of the bottle. A crisp, sweet aroma filled his senses. Aaron examined the bottle, taking in the burgundy coloration. A fleeting moment of guilt passed over him, but quickly evaporated.

Who cares? You're no good anyway. You killed your parents.

Aaron brought the bottle to his lips. He let it linger there. He wanted to enjoy the aroma before sipping. The cabernet's bouquet of flavors created a warm sensation against his palate.

The velvety feel of the liquor washing over his tongue and down his throat was intoxicating. Instantly, the tightness in his chest vanished. The tendons around his neck were set free. Aaron looked at the bottle and smiled. He felt like he had been reacquainted with an old friend.

I always felt good about myself when I had a drink in my hand.

Aaron took another sip. This time, he was startled by a harrowing scream. It was Imani. He could hear Donna scurrying to get out of the bed. Aaron set the bottle down and ran upstairs. He opened Asher's door and turned on the light. Imani was not there. Aaron dashed across the hall to Imani's room. He pushed open the door and turned on the light. Panic set in when he saw that the room was empty. Then he saw her, cowering in a corner. Her face was flush, her eyes were the size of saucers, and she was out of breath.

Before Aaron could say a word, Donna barged into the room past him. "Imani, what's wrong, baby?"

Imani was in stupor.

"Imani, baby, talk to me?"

"What's going on?"

Aaron turned to see Asher behind him. "I don't know, son. Why don't you go back to bed? Your mother and I got this handled."

Aaron turned his attention back to Donna's pleas. "Imani, talk to me, baby!" She grabbed Imani by the shoulders and shook her.

Aaron contemplated calling 9-1-1. He was close to retrieving his cell phone when Imani seemed to break free from her daze. A stricken look of fear gave way to tears. "Mommy!" she cried.

Donna, too, started to cry. "Don't you ever scare me like that again! What happened?"

Imani stared at Asher. Donna repeated the question. "Imani, what happened?"

"There was a ghost! She woke me up and forced me to follow her into my room!" she yelled.

"A ghost?"

"Yeah, I told her what Daddy told me to say. I told her, 'Leave me alone because I have to go to sleep,' but she kept bothering me."

"She?" Aaron asked.

"It was a woman. She wanted me to go with her. When I told her, 'No,' that is when she got mad and grabbed me."

"Where was she trying to take you?" Donna asked.

"I don't know." Imani looked at Asher. "Mommy, can I sleep with you tonight?"

Donna stared at Aaron. "Sure." She then looked at Asher and asked, "Do you want to sleep in our bed, too?"

Asher looked at his father. "No, I'm fine. I'll sleep in my room."

"Asher, there is nothing wrong with you sleeping in our bed with me and your sister."

"He said he was fine with sleeping in his own room," Aaron said.

"That is because he is more worried about what you'll think if he says yes."

Aaron opened his mouth to reply but caught himself. Instead, he turned to Asher. "Asher, go to bed, please." He then looked over at Imani. "Imani, go downstairs and get in my bed."

As soon as Asher and Imani had left the room, Donna laid into Aaron. "I don't like this! I don't like this at all! You are more intent on teaching your son on how to be a man rather than making sure he is safe!"

"You heard what Imani said. It was a ghost. Something concocted by her imagination."

69

"This move has really affected the kids! Imani's running around here claiming she's seeing ghosts! Asher's homesick! I'm ready to go! And I get the impression the kids are, too! I am ready to go home now!"

"What do you want me to do?"

Donna opened her mouth to respond, then paused. Her eyes narrowed.

"What?"

"What's that on your tongue?" she asked.

"What do you mean what's on my tongue?"

"You know exactly what I am talking about. Have you been drinking?"

"Why are you asking me that?"

"Because your tongue is purple. There is only one thing I know that can turn someone's tongue purple. On top of that, I can smell it."

Donna brought her index finger an inch away from Aaron's face. "I knew I should have poured that bottle of wine out this morning when I saw it sitting there on the counter!

"Don't even bother giving me an explanation because there is no justification! The way you're acting right now is convincing me moving here was a mistake! Was that your plan all along, get us out here then revert into the old Aaron?"

Donna stormed out of the room. Tired and dejected, Aaron turned off the light in his daughter's room. Then, he went across the hall to Asher's room. His son pretended to be asleep, but Aaron knew he had heard everything, so he shut his door and headed downstairs.

Downstairs, Aaron peeked into the bedroom to see Imani resting comfortably on his side of the bed. He quietly shut the door before heading into the kitchen to pour out the wine. Afterwards, he walked into the den and removed the cushions from the couch. As he reached for the handle to pull the hideaway bed from the basin of the sofa, the phone rang. Aaron stared at it. It was 3:52 in the morning, precisely the same time when he received the news that Mother Dear had passed away. He contemplated letting the call roll over to voicemail, but ultimately he dared himself to look at the caller ID. It read, "Out of Area."

Not knowing what to expect, Aaron's hands trembled as he reached for the phone. "Hello?"

Static filled the line. Aaron could barely make out a voice. Then, he heard a woman say, "Scooter." Aaron's heart skipped a beat. No one had called him "Scooter" since he was a child.

He tried to talk over the static. "Hello!"

"Scooter, it's—" her voice faded out.

"Who is this?" Only a handful of people referred to him by his childhood nickname, and all of them were dead.

Then, for a split second, the call was clear. "Scooter it's the—." Then the line went dead.

Aaron stared at the phone in disbelief. The caller on the other end sounded eerily like Mother Dear. Aaron reviewed the caller ID log. It read "Log empty." There was no call logged for 3:52 a.m. Slamming the phone down, he concluded that it had to be broken.

"Did the phone just ring, Donna?" Aaron asked, barging into the bedroom.

"What? Be quiet. She's trying to sleep." Donna pointed at Imani.

"Did the phone ring?"

"Why are you asking me about the phone at four in the morning?"

"Can you answer the question? Did the phone ring?"

"No, okay? Now, can Imani and I get some sleep?"

"Are you sure?"

"If you ask me one more time about the phone, I'm going to throw it at you! I told you no! It did not ring!"

Not believing her, Aaron walked over and checked the caller ID. Like the phone in the den, it read "CID Empty." Donna glared at him. Not wishing to feel Donna's wrath, Aaron gently placed the phone back in the cradle and made a hasty retreat out of the room. Not totally convinced, Aaron checked the phone in the kitchen. It too read, "CID Empty."

Baffled, Aaron went back into the den. Was he hallucinating? Was he so exhausted that he thought the phone had rung? None of the phones in the house had registered the call.

"Scooter, it's the -"

It's the what?

FALLIBLE

Trees and cars whirled past during the drive to Garfield High. Asher missed his bus. So, Aaron was tasked with driving him to school. The ride was quiet, since both of them were exhausted. Asher attempted to take advantage of the silence by squeezing in a nap.

However, Aaron felt the need to ask his son a question. "Hey."

Asher did not respond.

Aaron nudged him. "Hey!"

Asher looked over at his father. "Yeah?"

"Are you awake?"

"I am now."

"I'm curious to know, what was up with you and your sister last night?"

"What do you mean?"

"I'm talking about the way the two of you looked at each other when your mother asked Imani what happened."

"It was nothing."

"It didn't look like nothing to me."

73

"Imani was scared. That's all it was."

Aaron looked over at his son.

"I'm serious!"

"The two of you wouldn't have conspired to cook up some story about the house being haunted in order to pressure me and your mom into moving back to Washington, D.C., would you?"

"Believe me, Mom doesn't need to be pressured into moving back home."

"You sure?" Aaron asked.

"I'm sure." Asher leaned his head against the window. "Can I ask you something?"

"Sure."

"Why do you hate me so much?"

"What? What in the world would make you say that?"

"You're always on me. According to you, I never do anything right."

"That's not true. That's not true at all."

"You know, Dad, I'm sorry I was born with sickle cell. I'm sorry I'm not the star athlete on the basketball team. I'm sorry to be such a burden. Sometimes, I wish I was never born. That way, you wouldn't have to always worry about me."

"Don't say that! Where is all of this coming from? I love you." Aaron looked over to see Asher staring out the window.

"Could've fooled me."

"I'm tough on you because I want you to be ready for life. I don't want you to think life is easy. Life is rough. And to be honest, you've had it easy. I want you to be prepared."

Asher turned towards his father. "Really? I mean, really? I'm the one living with an illness, not you! I'm the one living in fear of the next crisis, not you!"

"You know, you're right. I'm not giving you enough credit."

Tears ran down his son's face as Aaron parked the car. "I

want what is best for you. I'll admit I don't want you to suffer like I did. Now, I know I can't shield you from everything, so I want you to be prepared.

"I'm aware I am not the best dad in the world. When I became a father, no one gave me a manual and said, 'Now that you're a father, here's what you need to know.' My father died when I was a child. I'm winging this as I go. I may not always hit the mark, but I want you to know I'm trying my damnedest. And regardless of what you think, I do love you."

Asher wiped his eyes with a napkin he found in the glove compartment.

"Please remember that I love you, son," Aaron said. "I'll see you later this evening."

"Okay."

"You better hurry inside. You are already late."

"No doubt."

Asher bounded out of the car and up the steps into the school while Aaron watched his son disappear behind the doors.

AN UNEXPECTED GUEST

Doors. The secrets people lock away behind them, sheltered, hidden from view. Seeing Asher disappear behind those school doors made Aaron think about another door. The basement door at Mother Dear's house. It was an old rickety door whose hinges squeaked loudly whenever opened. It was a door that hid its own secret.

Growing up, Mother Dear had encouraged Aaron to play football. She wanted to keep him busy. This particular afternoon, football practice had ended early, and Aaron contemplated hanging out with his friends rather than heading straight home. He was in no rush to go home because he had forgotten to do the dishes. Rather than get into trouble hanging out with his buddies, Aaron decided to go home. That was when he discovered the secret the basement door concealed.

Upon arriving home, Aaron believed he had fallen upon a stroke of good luck. The house was empty. There was no sign of Mother Dear. Aaron called out to his grandmother a few times. No answer.

He then made his way into the kitchen. To his surprise, he

found the dishes clean and drying in the rack. Mother Dear had been home; Aaron looked over at the refrigerator. There was no note. Typically, she left a note on the refrigerator door if she went to the store or to a friend's house to play cards.

While he was thinking about all the places Mother Dear might've gone, he heard what sounded like yelping coming from the basement. Aaron feared someone had broken in and was in the basement torturing his grandmother. It wouldn't have been the first time a junkie had broken into the house searching for money or merchandise they could pawn or trade for drugs. I need Papa Joe's gun, he thought, looking at the cellar door, but he did not know where Mother Dear hid Papa Joe's gun.

Aaron pressed his ear against the door. The weird noises continued. Fearing the police may take too long, Aaron decided to see what was going on downstairs for himself.

The door squeaked loudly when he opened it. He feared the shrill screech from the hinges would alarm the intruder downstairs. It didn't; the squealing continued. Aaron tiptoed down the stairs. The scents of jasmine and mint, intermingled with the smell of mildew, filled the air. Shimmers of light danced on the concrete walls. At the bottom of the staircase, the bicycle Aaron was to receive for his eighth birthday collected dust. The shrieks morphed into grunting and groaning, accompanied by someone banging on a drum.

Over the din, Aaron could hear Mother Dear chanting. What his ears did not recognize, his eyes filled in for him. He saw his grandmother, along with their neighbor, Gladys Yates, chanting and dancing topless around Eva Barksdale, while another one of Mother Dear's friends, Ethel Miller, banged on a bongo. Miss Barksdale lay prone on the floor, topless. Each woman's face and torso were painted in either some shade of white, blue, red, or green. Mother Dear's chest was a vibrant green and her face blood red. Mrs. Yates and Ethel Miller were a ghostly white, and Ms. Barksdale was a deep shade of blue. Mrs. Miller feverishly banged on the bongo, quickening her pace as Mother Dear danced around Miss Barksdale with a sprig of thyme she waved while chanting: "Enemy mine, your power is gone. The hex is broken, the spell undone. The eye has been turned away. Enemy mine, you've gone away. So shall it be, from this day."

Seeing half-naked elderly women dancing around, especially one being his grandmother, was a jarring sight. The apparent pagan ritual made the situation even more worrisome. However, the women were so preoccupied with their chanting and dancing that they didn't notice Aaron standing there.

"What the hell is going on?" Aaron shouted.

Everything stopped. Seeing Aaron, Mother Dear, and the others, scurried to find their clothing. Mortified, Aaron ran upstairs.

In the kitchen, Aaron could hear his grandmother and her friends gathering their belongings. Mrs. Yates, and then Mrs. Miller, with her bongo tucked underneath her arm, were the first ones to make their way up the steps; then came Miss Barksdale, still wiping remnants of paint from her face. None of them said a word. None of them even looked Aaron's way. Mother Dear took her time making her way up the stairs. Aaron assumed she was trying to figure out how she was going to explain to him what it was he saw. Mother Dear calmly ascended the staircase, locked the basement door, and walked over to the cabinet and put a skillet on the stove.

"Are you hungry?" she asked.

Aaron couldn't believe how nonchalant she was acting. "What was that downstairs?"

Mother Dear cut her eyes in his direction and repeated, "Are you hungry?"

"Yes, ma'am."

"I see football practice ended early," she said.

"Yes, ma'am."

"By the way, don't think I didn't notice you didn't wash the dishes this morning before heading off to school," she added, opening the refrigerator door, and grabbing a packet of pork chops.

The only acknowledgement of what Aaron had seen in the basement was when Mother Dear said to him, "Also, you know better than to be swearing in my house."

THE VANISHING ACT

The pitter-patter of the rain danced upon the hood of Aaron's coat as he scoured the neighborhood searching for Socrates. Searching for the cat had become an evening ritual. Aaron really was not looking for the feline. He knew Socrates was not coming back. There was no need to voice the obvious. Everyone knew it.

A week had passed since Imani had seen "the ghost." Life had returned to some form of normalcy, albeit tenuous. Aaron's dabbling in Otis' bottle of wine remained a wedge between him and Donna. At least, they were talking. Every evening, Aaron pretended to go out and look for Socrates, hoping it would create a soft spot in Donna's heart to forgive him. He usually trekked down to the Arboretum. The tranquility of the park was always welcoming. In a city that seemed to be growing upwards and becoming more condensed, Aaron was grateful for the green expanse of the park. It brought with it a measure of peace.

A menagerie of colors announced fall's arrival. Bright reds, vibrant yellows, deep auburns, and brilliant oranges dotted the landscape. Small clearings, tucked away amongst the trees, allowed his mind to wander beyond the entrapments of city life. One meadow, nestled deep amongst maples and junipers, had become Aaron's favorite place of refuge.

The clearing, though, was not without its imperfections. Two large stones, marred in graffiti, marked the clearing's entrance. Cigarette butts, empty dime bags, beer cans, and used condoms littered the ground. The clearing's seclusion made it a perfect place for cutting class, feeding one's addiction, not to mention lovers copulating in haste, but even others' trash did not dissuade Aaron's admiration for the place. That evening, as he sat there, a light mist hugged the treetops and coated the grass in a carpet of dew.

* * *

"Aaron, wake up! Wake up!" Donna shook Aaron awake.

"What?"

"Have you seen the kids?"

"What kind of question is that? I've been asleep." Aaron laid his head back down on the pillow.

Donna's voice cracked. "I can't find them!"

"What do you mean you can't find them?"

"I mean, I can't find them! I've looked everywhere. Asher and Imani are nowhere to be found!"

Aaron sat up. "They're in the house. They must be in the house. Where else could they be? They're probably pulling a prank on you."

"I thought the same thing. So, I looked everywhere and there was no sign of them!"

"That's not possible." Aaron struggled to pull himself up off the hideaway bed. He had yet to be let back into his own bedroom. His back ached from the metal frame protruding through the flimsy mattress.

"I wish it was, but I kid you not, I cannot find Asher or Imani!"

"Is the alarm activated?"

Tears escaped the corners of Donna's eyes. "No, I turned it off."

Aaron climbed out of bed. "Stop worrying. When did you turn the alarm off?"

"I turned it off before coming in here to wake you."

"Then Asher and Imani have to be in the house."

Aaron yelled out Asher and Imani's names.

No response.

"It is time to stop playing games! You guys have got your mom down here worried sick! You need to get ready for school!"

Nothing. Instinctively, Aaron marched upstairs to the children's rooms.

"I've already searched the entire house!" Donna screamed.

"Well, we'll search it again."

"I'll check the basement again," Donna said.

Upstairs, Aaron entered Asher's room. The bed appeared to have been slept in. Yet, the sheets were cold.

"Asher! Imani! It's time to come out! This isn't funny!" Aaron yelled.

Aaron peered underneath the bed: Snickers' wrappers, along with an assortment of dirty socks. No Asher or Imani. Intuition told Aaron the next logical place they could be was the closet, so he walked over and opened the door.

He pushed the garments aside, hoping to find his children hiding behind them. No luck.

Where the fuck are they? Did I do something to them? Did I hurt them?

Aaron walked across the hall to Imani's room. His daughter's room was in shambles: books were strewn about, her lamp lay on the floor, shards of glass from the shattered light bulb were everywhere. His daughter's mattress was halfway on the floor and halfway on the box spring. Dresser drawers were open with clothes dangling out. It looked like Imani had left in a hurry, but that was impossible. Donna had deactivated the alarm right before waking him. The thought of an intruder entering the house seemed far-fetched, but crept into his mind.

Did I do this?

You did.

I couldn't have.

He wondered if Asher had made good on his threat to run away. He scanned Imani's room. Then, he went back across the hall to Asher's. There was no note.

See. No note means you did it.

Not necessarily.

Then why is there no note?

Good point.

Aaron rushed downstairs to find Donna sitting at the bottom of the steps. "Did you see Imani's room?"

"Yeah."

"How could they get out of the house without us knowing?"

Because they didn't leave. I killed them.

I have to refuse to believe that.

"They're in the house. Otherwise, we would've heard them leave."

"I hate to think about where they are or what is happening to them," Donna cried.

"Don't think like that!" Aaron said.

"Did you find a note anywhere, like in Asher's room or on the kitchen table?" Aaron asked.

"No. Why? Do you think they ran away?" A fresh stream of tears ran down her face.

See? No note.

There's got to be a reason.

"Did you check the basement?"

"Twice. They're not down there. I don't think you understand. I checked the entire house three times before I woke you."

"We need to check again. It doesn't make sense. Asher and Imani couldn't have gotten out of this house without us knowing."

That's it. Check again. Keep checking. The more you check, the safer everyone will be.

Aaron went to the front door. He tested the doorknob. It was locked. He opened the door, then shut it and locked it again. He opened the door again, then shut it and locked it a second time.

"What are you doing?"

"I'm making sure the door is locked." Aaron opened and shut the door a third time.

"I told you. I turned off the alarm before I awoke you. If they went out the front door, the alarm would've gone off," Donna said.

In spite of what Donna said, Aaron opened the door again, shut it, and re-locked it two more times before he felt certain the door had been locked.

"Baby, the kids are not here!"

Aaron refused to listen to her. There was no way Asher and Imani could just vanish. "They've got to be here!" Aaron charged into the kitchen and down into the basement.

Don't do this to me. Don't do this to me again.

In the basement, he tossed aside empty boxes. As Donna

had stated, the basement was empty. Aaron trudged back up the stairs.

"What do we do?" Donna asked, in tears.

"We got to keep looking!"

"Aaron, we've looked everywhere. They're not here."

"They're in this house! There is no way they could've gotten out of this house without us knowing!"

I couldn't have done this. I couldn't have.

Donna held her hands to her face and wept. Unlike Donna, Aaron refused to believe Asher and Imani were gone. He walked into the den.

"What are you doing?" Donna asked.

"We didn't look in the den."

"Aaron, you were asleep in the den," Donna reminded him.

"They probably snuck into the room while I was asleep." Aaron got on his hands and knees and looked under the pullout bed.

Donna stood in the doorway. "Aaron, listen to yourself."

"We have to check everywhere." Aaron threw open the closet door.

"Asher and Imani are not in there."

Then where could they be?

I don't know, I don't know, I don't know.

The closet was empty. There was nothing but board games and the divination tray. Aaron eyed the tray before shuddering and shutting the door.

HOLDING ON

This must be a dream! I'm going to wake up!
Rubbing a sobriety medallion did very little to ease the sinking feeling consuming him. Aaron needed a drink to stay afloat. To make it through the day. However, a pledge of sobriety had left the house dry.

He fought to control his emotions while the police canvassed the house, scanning for prints and searching for points of possible entry.

"Did anything strike you as odd about the kids last night?"

"Huh?"

"I said, did anything about your children strike you as odd last night?" the officer repeated.

"No," Aaron said.

Should I turn myself in? I know I did something to Asher and Imani. That's why they've disappeared. Only problem is I have no proof.

"Did you hear or suspect anyone in the house?"

"No."

The questions felt redundant, the same question was asked differently.

A droplet of blood was found in Imani's room on the floor next to the bed. There was no telling whose blood it was. It was classified as evidence and sent to a lab for DNA testing. When they finished searching the house, the police gathered what they felt was relevant and left, telling Aaron and Donna that someone would contact them. That was it.

Aaron called Dr. Whitten, the dean of the school of medicine, informed him of the situation, and requested a leave of absence. He specifically asked for the dean to keep the matter private. Despite seeking privacy, curious neighbors came to the house, and calls from Donna's parents kept the phone ringing and someone consistently at the door. Aaron found himself consoling others, rather than having the opportunity to process his own feelings. He needed the world to stop spinning just for a second, so he could catch his breath.

Eventually, the incessant chiming of the doorbell became too much. "LEAVE US ALONE!" Aaron screamed as he ripped the doorbell off the wall and stormed off to the bedroom.

"Fine, I'll answer the door," Donna said. Aaron responded by slamming the bedroom door shut.

* * *

Aaron heard footsteps coming down the hall and stopping at the bedroom door, followed by a gentle knock.

"What?"

"Hey, man, it's me," Otis said.

"Otis, I'm not in the mood right now."

"I understand. I want you to know I'm here if you need anything."

"Thanks. I'll keep that in mind."

"Call me when you're able."

"Yeah, whatever."

There was silence. Then Aaron could hear Otis' footsteps receding down the hall, followed by some whispering between him and Donna. Then he heard the front door slam shut. When Donna came into the bedroom, Aaron could see her eyes were puffy from the steady stream of tears.

A WARNING

Five yards. Aaron's life had been reduced to five yards. That was the distance from the bathroom to the bed. There was no need to frequent the kitchen because hunger rarely pained him. A peanut-butter-and-jelly sandwich here and there, along with a glass of water, usually sufficed. Rather, it was time that tormented him. Minutes turning into hours. Hours evolving into days. Days seeming to slip away from him. The passing of every minute, every hour, and every day, in silence was pure hell. The house suddenly lacked life. It was devoid of laughter, of his children's voices. Every so often, Aaron thought he heard Asher or Imani somewhere in the house. But they were nothing more than mirages conjured up by his imagination.

Crawling out of bed, he searched for his sweats and T-shirt. They were nowhere to be found. So, he put on his housecoat and slid on his house shoes. He grabbed his wallet and car keys. Where he was going, he did not know. Nor did he care. He simply needed to break the monotony of those five yards.

Visits from the neighbors had stopped. People had gone

back to living their lives while his sat in suspended animation. When he got in the car, Aaron simply sat there staring at the steering wheel as if it was a foreign object. He wanted to drive. Drive until the car ran out of gas. Settling on no particular destination, Aaron started the car and backed out of the driveway.

Eventually, he found himself sitting outside of Imani's elementary school. Aaron watched as parents chatted amongst themselves as they gathered to escort their children home. Yellow buses lined the block to ferry kids off to their respective neighborhoods. The sound of the school bell announced the end of the day. Children filed out into the loving arms of their parents. Seeing the kids joyfully exit the building brought tears to his eyes.

I killed them. I killed Asher and Imani. Just like I killed my parents.

A soft tap against the window startled him. A mother and her child peered inside the car. "Are you okay?" the mother asked.

Aaron wiped his eyes. "I'm fine."

"Are you sure?"

"I'm fine! Thank you!" Aaron started up the car and sped away.

Grief is a slow, efficient killer, gently squeezing the life out of you, one breath at a time. Aaron yearned for a drink, so he went to Mont's, the local neighborhood store. They only sold wine, but at that point, anything would do.

He disregarded the stares from the store's patrons and clerks when he entered. One clerk greeted him warmly, but Aaron ignored him and walked straight to the wine section. The prices were steep, but that didn't matter.

Not sure what to pick, Aaron grabbed both a red and a white. With bottles in hand, he was preparing to stand in the checkout line, when he saw the woman in the miniskirt walking towards him. She smiled as she drew near.

She walked right up to him and said, "You're in danger" before turning around and walking away.

Aaron didn't understand what she meant. Bewildered, he chased after her only to find that she had disappeared. He searched the entire store, but she was nowhere to be found.

"Hey, are you okay, man?" the clerk asked.

"Huh."

"Are you cool?"

"Um, yeah. I'm just wondering where she went?"

"Where who went?"

"The woman in the floral red miniskirt. You saw her, right?"

"I haven't seen anyone in a red miniskirt in here today, bro."

Aaron stood there confused. He could feel everyone's eyes on him, so he decided it was best to stand in line. It was clear he was making a woman in line ahead of him nervous, judging by the way she fidgeted. After paying for her groceries, she made a hasty exit out of the store.

When it was Aaron's turn to check out, a nervous giggle escaped the young checkout clerk. "It's a little chilly to be dressed in a bathrobe, don't you think?"

"I'm starting a new fashion craze."

"Sure, whatever. $25.15."

After paying, Aaron walked out of the store, just in time to see a plane disappear into the billowing clouds. He thought about how he had folded the paper airplane's wings just right, turning up the tips to give it the right amount of lift. How he had taken the time to fold each crease precisely. His nerves rattled with each thought, each fold, as a sick feeling settled in his stomach—right about the same time that he looked down to see the patrol car blocking him in.

FALLING DOWN

Aaron watched the patrol car's headlights in the rearview mirror. The officer decided not to arrest Aaron. Rather, he gave him a warning and followed him home. Aaron fit the description of the man in a bathrobe at Montlake Elementary. So, the officer must have known he had the right guy when he saw him walk out of Mont's.

When Aaron pulled into his driveway and parked, he took his time getting out of the car. "This your house?" the officer asked.

"Yes, it is."

The officer examined the house before looking back at Aaron. "Nice home."

"Thanks."

"You should be careful traipsing around town in your bathrobe. You might get more than you bargained for."

Aaron was not sure what to make of that comment, but decided to offer an answer anyway. "I guess."

"See you around."

"I hope not," Aaron said, under his breath as he walked to the front door, while fishing his keys out of his housecoat.

When the police car was out of sight, Aaron grabbed one of the bottles of wine and twisted off the cap. He downed a quarter of the bottle before opening the door. He held up the bottle to inspect the label: a tasty white from a vineyard in the Russian River Valley of Sonoma. Aaron took another greedy swig.

As soon as he stepped in the house, he immediately didn't want to be there. *Why did I come home?*

Stumbling down the hallway towards the bedroom, he found Donna lying in bed, staring vacantly up at the ceiling. He was prepared to turn around and head into the kitchen when he noticed the sleeping pills on the nightstand. Fearing the worst, Aaron called out to his wife, but got no answer. So, he called her name again.

"What?" she said.

"Nothing, I was wondering if you were -"

"What? Dead?" she said. "Don't think it didn't cross my mind. I took every one of those pills out of the bottle and counted them. I wondered how many I would need to go to sleep and never wake up. The only problem was, I couldn't do it. I didn't have the heart to do it. Do you want to know why?"

"Why?"

"Because of the kids. What if the kids came home, and I wasn't here?"

Aaron stared at her, then teetered away. He had his own demons to contend with. He didn't have the time or capacity to deal with Donna's.

The house was eerily quiet. Other than the sound of Aaron's house shoes scuffing across the hardwood floor, and the tick of the kitchen clock, there was very little of anything else.

Aaron plodded into the dining room with his bottles of wine in hand. He took a seat at the dining room table, twisted off the cap of the white wine, and drank. He wondered why the woman in the red miniskirt felt the need to tell him he was in danger.

MOURNING

I t had been at least a century since Savanne had mounted. It always took a little while to get used to new skin. He looked at himself in the mirror. Not bad, middle-aged white guy, sort of average looking. He rummaged through his pockets until he found his wallet. Pulling it out, he looked at the ID.

"James Mourning," he said. He looked at himself in the mirror. "Well, hello, James Mourning. You're not the most handsome fucker, but you'll do."

He pulled the badge clipped to his waist off and gazed at it. "Detective James Mourning." He looked at himself in the mirror again. "You have no idea how many assholes I had to possess just to get to you."

Savanne chuckled. "Never mounted anyone in law enforcement before. I guess it is like they say; there is always a first for everything."

He tucked the wallet back in his back pocket and clipped the badge to his belt. He glanced at himself one last time before walking out of the bathroom.

The television was on, blaring the nightly news. Nothing

had changed; the world was still in chaos. The Chinese food Detective Mourning ordered sat on the kitchen counter. The delivery driver had provided the demon a way to get to the detective. Savanne opened the bag and grabbed an egg roll. He shoved the egg roll into the detective's mouth.

"Oh my god, that is so good." He was always famished after a jump.

Savanne searched through the cabinets for the plates and utensils. Finding what he needed, he helped himself to the detective's fried rice. Next, he combed through the refrigerator in hopes of finding something to wash the food down. The demon conveniently happened upon a six-pack of beer. Grabbing his plate and a bottle of beer, Savanne sat down in the recliner in front of the TV. The newscaster went on and on about conflict and war, but the demon was too preoccupied with feeding his hunger to pay attention.

"Kill 'em all," the demon yelled.

Once he had cleaned his plate, he eased back to relax. He had been spending so much time jumping from one unwitting soul to the next in hopes of getting closer to the divination tray, that he had very little time to reflect on being back amongst the living. Then, he noticed a roach sitting on the TV tray next to a manilla folder.

"Detective, is that what I think it is?" Savanne grabbed the small nub of a joint and inspected it. "Why, Detective Mourning, you are a naughty boy. I see I am going to have some fun with this body."

Grabbing a lighter, he burned the tips of the detective's fingers as he inhaled what little was left of the joint. He exhaled a plume of smoke and immediately erupted into a coughing fit.

"This is some good shit," the demon said.

Savanne grabbed the detective's case file and examined the

papers. Two missing children were taken from homes. There were no signs of forced entry. No note. The alarm was activated until the following morning.

"Bingo! This is the reason I went through all this trouble to find you, Detective Mourning," he said, throwing the folder back onto the TV tray.

The demon gulped down the beer and slouched down into the recliner. Now, all he had to do was get the divination tray and keep the door open.

SINKING

"Aaron! Get up!" Donna's voice rang in Aaron's ear. Aaron opened his eyes to see Donna staring at him. "Get up, you need to clean yourself up. You stink."

From what Aaron could tell, it was morning. His head was pulsating. He dug his fingers and toes into the rug, hoping it would stop the world from spinning. When he inched his way out from underneath the dining room table, he noticed a huge purple stain on his bathrobe and the rug. Judging from the empty Cabernet bottle lying next to him, he either spilled the red wine all over himself and the rug, or he vomited it back up. From the stench, he assumed it was the latter. Aaron grabbed the bottle of Cabernet and tipped it up, hoping to savor any remnants of wine left. He was clueless as to how he had gotten under the dining room table. The last thing he remembered was polishing off the white wine and reaching for the cab.

Slowly, Aaron rose to his feet, bracing himself against the table. Walking would need to be slow and deliberate. He did not want to reacquaint himself with the floor.

He looked at the purple-colored stain on the rug.

"Don't worry about it. I'll clean it up. The stain remover should be able to get it out. You need to go wash up," Donna said.

Aaron lumbered into the bathroom and carefully peeled off his robe and underwear. The puke was caked onto his clothes. He turned on the water and waited for it to warm up. When it reached the desired temperature, he sent the water to the showerhead. He gingerly climbed into the tub, making sure not to fall. He was standing there, letting the water run down his back, when his stomach started to churn. That was the only warning he got before throwing up.

Weak, Aaron sat down. He watched as the water did its best to wash the vomit down the drain. He sat there until the water turned bitterly cold. Not until then did he grab the bar of soap and wash up. Too exhausted to do much of anything else, Aaron dried off and staggered out of the bathroom and into bed.

* * *

Somewhere, the telephone was ringing. He could hear Donna talking. By the time Aaron opened his eyes, Donna was already back in the bedroom.

"Who was that?" Aaron asked.

"A Detective Mourning. He and his partner are handling Asher and Imani's missing persons' case. He wanted to know if we were going to be around. They want to come by and ask us some questions."

"About time. We were supposed to get a call over a week ago. What happened to that? By this time, Asher and Imani could be halfway to D.C. Did they say anything else?"

"Nah. That was it," Donna said.

"What time is it?"

"It's 1:54. Almost two o'clock."

"Why did you let me sleep so long?"

"You were out cold. Besides, you weren't hurting nobody."
She was right about that.

Aaron lay there in bed trying to piece together the night
before. He recalled his student and her warning, but that was
about it. Aaron hopped out of bed.

"Where are you going?" Donna asked.

"I'm going to get some work done on my laptop. Try to
think of something else other than the kids."

Aaron walked out of the bedroom and down the hall to the
office, where he opened his laptop and pulled up his class
rosters. He scrolled through the names, hoping to figure out
who the woman in the red floral miniskirt was.

20 QUESTIONS

Krabinay, a demon who had mounted Detective Smith, pulled the cruiser up to the Langford household. Alongside him rode Savanne, as Detective Mourning. It was important they found the divination tray. Savanne found Detective Smith's flesh much more appealing than Krabinay's usual hideous appearance. As he examined the Langford household, he contemplated simply going inside and mounting everyone until he got the information he needed. Of course, that was reckless and unwise.

"Are you ready?" Krabinay asked.

"Yeah, let's get this over with."

* * *

The second Detectives Mourning and Smith walked in, Aaron sensed the visit was more than just an update on the progress of the investigation.

Detective Smith validated his assumption when he said, "We know you believe your children may have run away.

However, in order to identify and be able to rule out either you or your wife, we will need DNA samples from the both of you."

This made sense. The need to eliminate all possibilities. Even so, the request rubbed Aaron the wrong way. "Why?" he asked.

Detective Mourning interceded. "As a precautionary measure, it's necessary to distinguish between strands of hair or flakes of skin that do not match you or your wife's, particularly since blood was found in your daughter's room. If possible, we will need DNA samples from your children as well."

"That will be hard to do if they are not here," Aaron said.

"We may be able to collect DNA samples from a brush or recently worn clothing," Detective Smith said. "If possible, I would like to inspect your children's rooms and make sure I understand the events of the morning the two of you discovered your children were missing. Have the two of you been in your children's rooms since they disappeared?"

"Yes," Donna said.

"Have you done any cleaning or rearranging of furniture?" Detective Smith asked.

"I've straightened up their rooms," Donna said.

"Why?" Detective Mourning asked.

"I saw no reason to leave them a mess." Donna looked over at Aaron. "Did I do something wrong?" she asked.

"No. Was there some reason for tidying up the room so soon after their disappearance?" Detective Smith asked.

"She said she didn't see any reason why she should leave their rooms a mess," Aaron said.

"I didn't see any harm in it."

"Were we supposed to keep my daughter's room in shambles until you guys showed up?" Aaron quipped.

"Like I said, it's no big deal," Detective Smith said.

"Then why does it sound like you're making it a big deal?"

"Don't worry about it. We're only here to help, Mr. Langford. Do you think you can show me to their rooms?" asked Detective Smith.

"Sure, this way," Donna said, accompanying Detective Smith upstairs.

Aaron watched them leave the room before turning to Detective Mourning and asking, "What kind of detective are you again?"

"Homicide."

"Why is a homicide detective working a missing person's case?"

"We want to make sure there wasn't any foul play involved in your children's disappearance."

"Why? Do you suspect there is?"

"Not currently. However, we want to make sure."

"I see," Aaron said.

"So, Dr. Langford, you say you moved here from Washington, D.C.?"

"Yes. That's correct. We've lived here for almost three months."

"How is that going for you?" the detective asked.

"How is what going?"

"The move here. Life in Seattle. Has everything gone okay with the move? I mean, you're moving from the nation's capital to the land of espresso, granola bars, composting, and tech companies. I think that would be quite a culture shock."

"Up until the disappearance of my children, everything had been fine," said Aaron.

"The rain can be a bitch. Plus, all the damn Californians who moved up here. The hypodermic needles everywhere. Junkies shooting up in broad daylight. Tents up and down the sidewalks. This city has really gone to hell in a handbasket. Then you got all of the immigrants with their H-1B visas and transplants coming to work for the tech companies making it impossible to afford to live in the city or find a decent parking space. The high-rise condos have made the place look like San Francisco. It's hard to find a good ole dive bar anymore. The Socialists in the city council have turned the city into a fucking mess."

Aaron wasn't sure if the detective was talking to him or complaining out loud.

Detective Mourning glanced around the house. "You know that son of bitch, Perry Como, had the nerve to sing, 'The bluest skies you'll ever see are in Seattle.' That bastard obviously had never lived here. The weather can get downright dreary from November to June. Did you know Seattle is the suicide capital of the United States?"

"I've heard that."

The detective laughed. "People say the weather is so damn miserable that it causes people to lose their minds. Anyway, that is neither here nor there. Honestly, there is no truth behind the city being the suicide capital of the country. It's an urban myth."

An awkward silence fell between them. "Did surveillance cameras at the train station or bus station turn up anything?" Aaron asked.

"I'm not sure. I'll look into that." Detective Mourning then quickly pivoted to a question of his own. "I'm curious to know if there have been any issues going on at home, I need to be made aware of?"

"What do you mean?" Images of Donna tossing her clothes onto the bedroom floor ran through Aaron's mind.

"You know, have you and your wife been having any problems that may have affected your children? Were there incidents at school they may have spoken to you about? Or maybe strange events of some sort."

Aaron thought about Asher's fight. "There was an incident at my son's school. A senior was teasing him, calling him a leprechaun. It led to him getting into a scuffle and subsequently suspended."

"How did your son act afterwards?"

"He acted like his typical self."

"What's that?" asked the detective.

"My son is somewhat of a reserved, quiet young man. An introvert."

Detective Mourning jotted notes down before moving on to his next question. "What about drugs? Do you know if your kids take drugs?"

"Detective, my children are fourteen and six. I doubt my daughter is doing drugs."

"You'd be surprised. I know a couple who made their six-year-old smoke pot. They didn't see the harm in it since it was legal. They thought it relaxed the child. What about prescription drugs like Ritalin, Zoloft, or Prozac?"

"Nope, they don't take any of those."

"What about your wife?"

"What about my wife?

"Is she on any medication? Or has she noticed anything strange around the house?" Aaron's mind went to the sleeping pills.

"No."

"Did your wife mention anything about there being anything different about the kids the night before their disappearance?"

Aaron recalled the exchange between Asher and Imani the night Imani saw a ghost. "No."

"Are you sure about that?"

"My daughter did scare the hell out of us about seeing a ghost," Aaron said.

"What was so scary about it?"

"We found her hyperventilating in her bedroom. She said the ghost tried to take her away."

"Take her away where?"

"She didn't say."

"And where did this happen?"

"In her room."

"Upstairs?"

"Yes."

"Hmmm." Detective Mourning jotted more notes down in his notepad.

"Other than your daughter claiming to have seen a ghost, had there been any other occurrences in the house that might've seemed odd?"

"None that I'm aware of."

"You are certain you never heard or saw anything strange? Like strangers, they may have encountered in the neighborhood?"

Aaron recalled Imani's story about Mr. Palmer. "No."

"Did your daughter, son, or anyone bring anything home that may have looked peculiar?"

The divination tray crossed Aaron's mind. "No. Can you tell me what you are writing in your notepad?"

"Nothing, I'm writing down a few notes. Tell me, doc, would there be any reason for your kids to make any of this up?"

"Not that I can think of. Why would you ask that?"

"I just want to make sure your kids wouldn't have a reason to lie to you," said Detective Mourning.

"My kids did not particularly like us moving here to Seattle. However, I doubt that would be a solid reason for them to lie."

"I take it your son or daughter told you they did not like it here?"

"My son voiced his dislike of the city. He much preferred we stayed in D.C."

"He told you that verbally?"

"Yes."

Detective Mourning scribbled something in his notepad.

"Do you have children, Detective Mourning?" Aaron asked.

"No, I don't."

"Then you have no idea what it is like to see your children come home every day and breathe a sigh of relief as soon as they walk through that door. The self-doubt that consumes a parent when you question if you are doing the right thing when it comes to raising them, deep down hoping you don't mess them up somewhere along the line."

"Dr. Langford, please try to understand I am doing my best to locate your children. In doing so, I need to ask you some very pointed questions. It is all necessary in understanding your son and your daughter's frame of mind."

"Asher and Imani," Aaron said.

"Excuse me?"

"Asher and Imani. Those are my children's names. Not once since you have been here, have you called my children by their names."

"I'm sorry. I know these are some very unsettling questions," Detective Mourning said.

"Yes, they are. I'm curious to know their relevance. Are my wife and I suspects?" Aaron asked.

"As to whether you and your wife are suspects, I have no reason to believe so at this time."

"That is a very evasive answer."

Before Aaron could get any further, Detective Smith

suddenly interrupted, calling out, "Jimmy, can you have the doctor activate the alarm?"

Detective Mourning looked over at Aaron. "Sure thing! Can you turn the alarm on, doc?" Aaron looked at the detective before walking over to the security panel and activating the alarm. He waited for an explanation for why he should turn on the alarm but wasn't given one. Instead, he received another directive from Detective Smith to open the door.

"You want him to open the back door or the front door?" Detective Mourning asked.

"It doesn't matter!" screamed Detective Smith.

"If I open the door, the alarm will go off," Aaron stated.

"Steve, if he opens a door the alarm will go off!" Detective Mourning yelled.

"That's the point!"

Aaron opened the back door as instructed. Right away, the keypad chirped. Aaron needed to input the security code within thirty seconds, or the alarm would sound. "Should I turn it off now?" Aaron asked.

"Should he turn it off?"

"Not yet!" Detective Smith said.

As expected, after thirty seconds, the deafening sound of the siren filled the house. "Good! Now, turn it off and reset it!" yelled Detective Smith, trying to be heard over the blaring siren.

Aaron deactivated the system and reset it.

"Jimmy, tell the doctor to reset the keypad. I'm going to open a window up here!"

"Gotcha! You heard him, doc?"

Aaron nodded. Like before, the keypad began to chirp. Again, after thirty seconds, the aggravating siren sounded.

"Okay, turn the alarm off!" Detective Smith instructed.

Aaron entered the code, deactivating the alarm. "What was that all about?"

"I couldn't tell ya," Detective Mourning said.

The phone rang. It was the security company following protocol and calling the house. Aaron answered, giving them the code and assuring them that everything was fine before hanging up.

Meanwhile, Detective Smith and Donna made their way downstairs.

"What was the purpose of opening and shutting the door and the window?" Aaron asked.

"The police report stated there were no signs of forced entry. I wanted to make sure the windows and doors were properly wired to the alarm system," Detective Smith said.

"All you could've done was ask, and I would have told you the system worked. I do not understand what opening the door and the window proved?"

"It proves that if anyone had tried to enter your house that night, they would have activated the alarm. We checked with the security company, and they stated the alarm system was armed the entire night," said Detective Mourning.

"So? Are you inferring that Asher and Imani never left the house?" Aaron asked.

"I'm stating a fact, Dr. Langford," Detective Mourning said.

When Detectives Mourning and Smith left, Aaron asked Donna what she had disclosed to Detective Smith upstairs. He suspected Detective Smith had quizzed her in the same manner Detective Mourning had interrogated him. His suspicions were right. It was clear the detectives were fishing for something.

Do they know I might have killed Asher and Imani?

WHISPERS IN THE DARK

"Daddy. Daddy, wake up."

Imani?

Aaron opened his eyes. "Wake up, Daddy," Imani whispered.

"Imani, is that you?"

"Help me, Daddy! Help me!"

"Help you? Help you do what! Where are you, baby? Why do you want me to help you?"

"Help me, Daddy! Help me!" she urged.

"Oh, baby, tell me what you want me to do? Where are you?" Tears swelled in Aaron's eyes. "I'm so sorry. I miss you, baby."

"Daddy."

"Imani!"

"Aaron! Wake up! You're dreaming!" Donna said, nudging him awake.

Aaron sat up and looked around the room. It was 2:08 in the morning.

Why was she asking for help?

Aaron forced himself out of bed. He wandered into the kitchen and grabbed the bottle of vodka on the counter. A few weeks ago, Donna was pissed at him for drinking Otis' wine. Now, she no longer cared. Aaron grabbed the bottle and went into the living room. He brushed the cat hair off the recliner before sitting down and breaking the seal on the bottle with a quick twist of the cap. The vodka smelled flammable. It was cheap. It burned the instant Aaron brought the bottle to his lips.

As he drank, he heard Donna in the kitchen. "Donna?"

No response.

Aaron got up and walked into the kitchen. "Don't you hear me calling you?" Aaron's voice trailed off when he noticed the kitchen was empty.

Figuring he was hearing things, Aaron returned to the recliner. Before sitting down, he heard chatter coming from the kitchen again. Aaron glanced over into the kitchen. This time, he got up and turned on the lights. Again, there was no one. Aaron surveyed the room before turning the light off and making his way back to the chair.

He brought the bottle of vodka to his lips when someone whispered, "Potent stuff, huh?"

Aaron jumped out of the recliner. "Who's there?"

Frightened, he turned on the lights. Other than himself, the room was barren. He had distinctly heard a man's voice, but that was impossible because there was no one else in the room. Refusing to believe he was hearing things, Aaron rushed to the bedroom. In the bedroom, Donna appeared to be asleep.

"Were you in the living room?" Aaron demanded to know.

"What?"

"You heard me; were you in the living room?"

"What kind of question is that? What is wrong with you? You see I'm in the bed," she said.

"Don't play games with me. You were in the living room and whispered in my ear!"

"What are you talking about? How could I be in the living room if I've been in bed?"

"You were in the living room. I know you were. I want you to know that was not funny!"

"What the hell is wrong with you? Did you hear me? I have not been in the living room! Are you drunk?"

"Nothing is wrong with me! I don't think your joke was funny!" he said, before storming out of the room.

Back in the living room, Aaron decided to drink his vodka with the lights on.

* * *

The sound of cupboard doors slamming shut drew Aaron from his slumber. Morning peeked in through the blinds. Aaron pulled himself out of the recliner and walked into the kitchen. There, he found Donna pouring herself a glass of orange juice.

"What are you doing?" he asked.

"What does it look like?"

"Why are you drinking orange juice?"

"Because I want to. I didn't know drinking orange juice was a crime?"

Aaron grumbled, "Well, good morning to you too."

Donna shook her head in bewilderment while Aaron walked into the bedroom and flopped down onto the bed. He had gotten very little sleep the night before. Every little sound the house made startled him. Donna came into the bedroom. Instead of climbing back into bed, she placed clothes out to wear.

"Where are you going?" asked Aaron.

"What is it with all the questions? You really need to stop

drinking. I'm going to go take a shower. Do I need to get clearance from you for every little thing I do?

"And if you must know after I shower, I'm going to work in the garden. It's halfway decent outside, and I'm tired of being cooped up in this house."

"When did you take an interest in gardening? If I recall you hated getting dirt under your fingernails."

"Yeah, I do. That is why they invented gloves," she said, walking out of the room.

When Aaron woke up, it was 10:45. He had drifted in and out of sleep throughout the day. Donna, on the other hand, was fast asleep.

Restless, Aaron dragged himself out of bed and into the kitchen where he found his fifth of vodka. He grabbed the bottle and took a sip. As the liquor lingered on his tongue, he heard a noise upstairs.

Walking over to the staircase, he stared at the steps, contemplating if he should go up the stairs. He faintly heard what he thought were people talking, so he followed the voices, cautiously. He had only gone upstairs once since Asher and Imani had disappeared: to look for Donna. He found her sitting in Asher's room staring off into the distance. The voices came out of Imani's room. Aaron slowly approached his daughter's bedroom door, realizing he had come upstairs ill-prepared. With nothing to protect himself, he gripped the neck of the vodka bottle like a club.

He slowly swung his daughter's door open. "Who's there?"

The room was empty. The appearance of the room was quite the opposite from how he remembered it the last time he had seen it. Imani's bed was made. Her favorite sky-blue dress was laid out on the mattress as if waiting for her to get dressed. On the floor beneath the dress were his daughter's favorite white, belt-buckled shoes. Imani used to dance around the house in the dress and shoes proclaiming she was a princess.

He heard something in Asher's room. Aaron walked across the hall to a similar sight in his son's room. Asher's clothes to lay out on the bed: his favorite jeans, with the holes in the knees, along with his dingy Nike T-shirt and favorite sneakers. The way Donna had meticulously arranged their children's clothes was bizarre. He missed Asher and Imani; however, Aaron doubted he would've gone to such lengths in their absence as Donna. Feeling like he had desecrated something sacred, Aaron turned off the lights and returned downstairs.

Seeking to pass the time, Aaron went into the den and turned on the TV. He flipped through the channels before settling on the news. He really wasn't paying much attention until he saw her, the woman in the red floral miniskirt. Aaron turned up the volume.

"Tragic news tonight," the newscaster said, "the coroner has confirmed the remains found buried in a shallow grave in Snohomish County as those of missing University of Washington student, Jennifer Taylor."

Aaron couldn't believe it.

The newscaster continued. "If you recall, Jennifer Taylor went missing six months ago when she did not return to her dorm room after telling her roommate she was going to the library to study..."

Aaron turned the TV off. Dead? He had seen her the other day at Mont's. She had told him he was in danger.

Aaron walked down the hall to the office. In the office, he opened his laptop and scrolled through his class rosters, but he didn't find a Jennifer Taylor. He typed Jennifer's name in the search engine and clicked on the first article that appeared.

Aaron read the story regarding her disappearance and death. If she was dead, then who was that he was seeing in his class and at Mont's?

There was only one possible reason why Aaron was seeing her. *I must've killed her.*

Aaron was ashamed. He didn't know what to do. He sat there in amazement when an internet ad caught his attention. The ad showed a disheveled blonde with the words, "Check the criminal record of anyone." Aaron clicked on the ad. He followed the prompts until it brought him to a map. Clicking on Washington state brought him to a page where he had to enter the first and last name of the person he wished to search. Not knowing whose name to type, Aaron entered his own name and date of birth in the search field. The site took a minute before coming back without any results. Then he remembered something Imani had said to him. He thought about it for a moment before typing Jacob Palmer.

JAKE PALMER

J ake Palmer stood in his kitchen rinsing off his plate when
he saw a light, darting across his backyard. At the time, he
had been debating whether to head up to the dispensary
and stock up on some Blueberry Kush. Enjoying a joint before
getting laid sounded like the perfect way to end the night.

Uncertain who it was in his backyard, Jake waited to see if
the light would reappear. It did. This time, the light darted to
the other side of the yard. Jake walked over to the back door
and eased it open. He hoped by turning on the porch light, it
would scare away whomever it was. Jake squinted over at the
bush where he last saw the light. He could see the silhouette of
a man trying to hide behind the bush.

"This is private property! You are trespassing!" he yelled. "I
know you're over there by the bush! I see you!"

A tall, slender black man eased his way out from behind the
shrub. He looked familiar, yet Jake couldn't quite remember
how he knew him.

"Hey, man, I don't know what you are doing snooping
around my house, but this is private property! You're lucky I

don't have a gun or something because I would be in my right to shoot you!" He thought that would be enough to scare the guy away.

The man shined the flashlight in Jake's eyes. "I know what you are," he said, walking towards him.

Jake tried to shield his eyes from the glare. He assumed the guy must be on a bad trip. He could sympathize, for he had been there a few times himself. "What are you talking about? And will you please stop shining that flashlight in my face?"

"I know what you are, Jacob Palmer."

"Look, man, I don't know who you are, or who sold you some bad shit. Nonetheless, you're going to have to tweak someplace else. I don't have time for this. If need be, I can call you a paramedic and have them come and get you. They can pump your stomach or something."

"You're a pedophile."

"What?"

"I saw your criminal record online. You're a registered level one sex offender."

The man drew closer.

"Look, it's not what you think. I'm not a pedophile. Now, will you please turn that flashlight off before I call the cops and tell them that you are harassing me?"

"You got my children in there," the man said.

Then it hit him. Jake had heard of two kids in the neighborhood going missing. Jake didn't really associate with any of his neighbors. Since inheriting his mother's house after her death, he mainly kept to himself. The clerk at Mont's kept him abreast of the neighborhood gossip. He was attractive, so he and Jake hung out from time to time. It wasn't serious. The clerk was younger, and Jake really wasn't into getting serious with younger guys. Most of them lacked the maturity to maintain a relationship. Regardless, the clerk was good in a pinch. That evening, Jake's date flaked on him, so it just so happened that Jake was in a pinch.

Jake tried to think of how he could explain to his neighbor that he wasn't a child molester, even though his name was in the national sex offender registry. "Look, buddy, I sympathize with what you're going through. That sex offender stuff is one big misunderstanding. Why don't you stop shining that light in my face and let me talk to you? Let me get you some help?"

"You got my son and daughter in there, and I want them back."

Jake's patience was wearing thin. "Look, put the flashlight down so we can talk! Believe me, everything isn't as it seems!"

"I don't want to talk! There isn't anything you can say to me! You are the worst kind of filth on the face of the earth. You're scum preys upon children. Now give me back my son and my daughter!"

Jake didn't understand how many times he had to tell this guy he wasn't a pedophile. "Buddy, I said I'm not a fucking pedo -" Before Jake could finish his sentence, the man struck him with the flashlight.

IMANI'S ROOM

Aaron sat in the back of the patrol car staring out the window. A cadre of people had gathered around Jacob Palmer assessing his wound and listening to his version of events, including Donna. The officer spoke with Mr. Palmer and his guest. Aaron recognized the young man from Mont's. He was the clerk who joked with him about wearing a bathrobe in the store. He pulled him off Mr. Palmer and called the police.

Having gathered enough information, the police officer sauntered over to the car. "Well, you're lucky. It appears the guy doesn't want to press charges, even though I told him he should. You put a nice knot on his forehead with that flashlight," the officer said, peering at Aaron through the steel mesh that separated the front seat from the back.

Aaron glanced over at Mr. Palmer. There was a nice-sized lump on the left side of his forehead.

"Did you check his house?" Aaron asked.

"Why? I have no reason to check that man's house."

"That man is a known sex offender!"

"Mr. Langford, Mr. Palmer is a level one sex offender."

"So! What does that mean? He's a pedophile."

The officer sighed. "He's not a pedophile, okay? I ran a background check, and he's not a pedophile. The state usually gives level one sex offender classification to someone if they get caught taking a leak in public."

Aaron was confused. "Doesn't being classified as a sex offender mean you're a pedophile or a rapist?"

"Not really. Like I said, Washington state classifies people who get caught pissing in public as sex offenders. The state figures a person must expose themselves to the public in order to take a leak. Thus, someone might see their pecker.

"Look, even though he is not going to press charges, I got to take you down to the precinct. I need to fill out some paperwork, and then I'll have to place you in a holding cell. You'll more than likely be released on your own personal recognizance. Do you have anyone that can come down and pick you up?"

"Yeah, my wife," Aaron said.

"Where is she?"

"Right there." Aaron nodded his head in Donna's general direction.

"Are you referring to the woman right there, staring at the car?" the officer asked, pointing at Donna.

"Yeah."

The officer got out of the car and walked over to Donna. He said a few words. She nodded. The officer then came back to the car. Donna looked at Aaron, then walked away.

"She said she is going to meet us at the precinct," the officer said, getting in behind the wheel.

Donna didn't rush to pick Aaron up. She let him languish in the holding cell for a while. More than likely punishment for the spectacle he had caused at Jacob Palmer's house.

When she did arrive, she didn't say much. Not until she pulled into the driveway did Donna speak at all. "Aaron, what is going on?"

"Nothing," Aaron said, walking into the house.

"I don't call you sitting in the back of a patrol car for everyone in the neighborhood to see nothing!" Donna followed him into the house.

"I went over to Jacob Palmer's house to talk to him, that's all!"

"Is that right? Well, how Jacob Palmer and the cashier from Mont's tell it, you were trying to beat the man. The man was screaming at the top of his lungs for help! I heard him half a block away!"

"He's a pedophile!" Aaron shouted. "I saw his name in the national sex offender registry online!"

"So, you go over to the man's house and accuse him of abducting our children?"

"He had something to do with Imani and Asher's disappearance! I know it!"

Donna sighed. "Are you listening to yourself? Do you even hear what you're saying?"

"I know exactly what I am saying! And how are you so certain he didn't abduct our children? Kids are usually abducted by someone they know!"

Donna sat down on the bed with tears in her eyes. "Who even said Asher and Imani knew the man?"

"What?"

"You heard me. What I am trying to figure out is how did we go from Asher and Imani running away to now being abducted? Do you know something I don't?"

"There is no other logical explanation. The state of Imani's room. No sign of Asher or Imani at the train or bus station. No sign of the kids turning up at your parents' house in D.C. and, finally, the blood. If nothing else, the blood at least tells of a struggle."

"What is going on with you?" Donna asked.

"What do you mean?"

"I'm talking about you barging into the bedroom late at night claiming I am sneaking up on you in the dark. That was bizarre, to say the least. Then this. You've been acting really strange lately."

"I'm fine!"

Aaron walked out of the room and into the den. He could hear Donna crying. Rather than deal with her, Aaron pulled out the hideaway bed and shut the door.

* * *

What was that?

Something had jarred Aaron awake. He had unknowingly dozed off. He got up and walked across the hall to the bedroom. Donna was asleep. Aaron quietly closed the door. Then, he heard it again. It was upstairs.

This time, Aaron was not going upstairs empty-handed. He thought about Papa Joe's .38. The only problem was, he instructed Donna to hide it from him, so he didn't harm anyone or himself. So Aaron went into the kitchen. He had also asked Donna to hide all the knives. Yet, he knew where she hid one large cutting knife, which she used when cooking. Aaron retrieved the knife from underneath the spatula and rolling pin in the kitchen drawer where Donna hid it. With the knife in hand, Aaron proceeded upstairs. The faint sound of people talking emanated from Imani's room. The closer Aaron got, the louder they became. There were three distinct voices. However, they seemed to talk as one.

Brandishing the knife, Aaron slowly opened the door to his

daughter's room. The room was frigid. "Who's there?" he said, turning on the light.

There was no one. A putrid, nauseating smell permeated the air. The low glow from the lamp illuminated Imani's blue dress and white buckle shoes. Then, out of the corner of his eye, something moved.

"Who's there?"

There was no one.

Suddenly, the room began to crackle and pop as the shadows peeled away from the walls. Twig-like fingers reached out from the dark. Pointy heads spiraled down from the ceiling. Not certain what he was seeing, Aaron slashed wildly at the wraiths, but his blade glided through them effortlessly.

Terrified, Aaron tried to back his way out of the room. Then, he heard them, their voices filling his head, words crashing together in a noisome of chatter.

"Oh my God, Aaron!"

Donna?

"Oh my God!" she screamed. "Why, Aaron? Get up, baby! Get up! Aaron, you got to get up!" Donna pleaded.

The shadows were gone, and Aaron found himself on the floor. "Hang on, baby! I'm going to get some towels!" Donna disappeared.

"Donna!"

Something is not right. What's wrong?

Donna came back into the room with towels. She took one and tried her best to fashion a tourniquet around Aaron's wrist. That was when Aaron saw the blood. Donna diligently tried to stem the flow. However, the manner in which Aaron's wrist had been cut made it difficult. There was both a vertical and horizontal laceration.

"Oh my," Aaron gasped.

Donna did her best to stanch the flow of blood, but every

towel turned crimson red. "Stay with me, baby! Stay with me, god damnit!"

I'm dying.

Donna's pleas grew faint until Aaron couldn't hear her anymore. Her voice was washed out by the sound of water. Aaron found himself walking amongst trees until he wandered out into a field of thigh-high grass. He waded through the thicket down to a riverbank. He ambled along the riverbank to a point where the grass gave way to a rocky shore. Standing there, he admired the scenery. Birds sang in the distance. The air was crisp and clean. Pure. From his vantage point, he could see the stream meander around a bend at a slow, rhythmic pace.

He looked down the shoreline to see a beached innertube; he felt a devious grin twist up the corners of his lips. He had always fantasized about inner tubing down the Potomac. Aaron ran to the innertube and gleefully pushed it out into the slow-moving current. He waded out into the water until it lapped at his armpits; then, he hoisted himself up. Delight burst within him as his backside rested comfortably in the donut hole. As if on cue, a soft breeze swept over the river and gently pushed the innertube downstream.

HOME AGAIN

"Scooter!"

Mother Dear's voice jolted Aaron awake. He opened his eyes to find himself in his childhood bed. The sun beamed through the bedroom window. Sitting up, he searched for Mother Dear. Then it hit him.

Where's the innertube, the river?

Aaron had always imagined what it would be like to be a grown man sleeping in his childhood bed. Time had not changed his room one bit. It continued to be an atrocious green color. Growing up, Aaron had tried to conceal the disgusting paint by putting up posters. Regrettably, Mother Dear was not going to let "half-naked women who fermented thoughts of fornication," and "young men who talked like they didn't know God," to adorn her walls. Mother Dear allowed Aaron to have only one picture on the wall: a blonde-haired, blue-eyed Jesus. She hung the picture directly over the headboard. Whenever Aaron looked up, Jesus was staring down on him. Aaron glanced up.

Yep, still there.

He didn't like that picture. It made him feel uncomfortable. He couldn't rightfully argue with Mother Dear over a picture of Jesus. That was blasphemy. Why couldn't it at least be a black Jesus? The white, doe-eyed embodiment of God peering down on him every night was creepy. Many nights, Aaron would take the picture down and hang it back up in the morning.

The smell of hotlinks drifted into the room from underneath the door. It had been a long time since Aaron had smelled the spicy aroma of pork links. He could hear someone singing "Go tell it on the Mountain," Mother Dear's favorite gospel hymn. Gospel music was the only music played in Mother Dear's house.

The singing grew closer before stopping outside the door. It had been over thirty years since Aaron had seen his grandmother, so when the door swung open, he was stunned. Mother Dear sashayed into the room with a big smile on her face and a plate of eggs, grits, and a juicy hotlink. Now, the woman who stood before him was a far cry from the woman he remembered in the latter days of her life. The hump in her back was gone. The woman before him stood tall. She held her head high. She had both feet and all her toes.

"Is this heaven?" asked Aaron, eyeballing the hotlink with delight.

Mother Dear laughed. "Not quite."

Aaron examined his grandmother closely as she sat the plate on his lap.

This is not real.

"Why can't it be?" Mother Dear said.

Aaron looked at his grandmother in disbelief.

Mother Dear smiled. "I can hear you, Scooter."

"How? Am I seeing a ghost?"

"That depends upon what you classify as being a ghost."

"It doesn't matter if I am seeing a ghost or not. I sure am glad to see you," Aaron said.

Mother Dear kissed Aaron on the forehead. "Not as much as I am glad to see you."

"Is this real?"

"What is your definition of real? Does it feel real to you?"

"It feels real."

"Then it is real. Now, stop talking and eat before your food gets cold. You're going to need your strength."

Aaron bit into the link. The spices set his taste buds ablaze. "What do I need my strength for?" Aaron huffed, trying to cool his mouth off in between bites.

"Boy, didn't I teach you any manners? Don't talk with your mouth full!" Aaron quickly closed his mouth. "You need your strength for what's to come," she said.

"What do you mean by 'what's to come?'"

"You got to go back, Aaron. You can't stay here. It's not your time."

"My time? Why are you talking in riddles?"

"You always loved riddles, didn't ya? There is no need to jump right into it. Right now, you need to eat, so you can have the energy to make the journey back. You must rescue my great grandbabies."

Aaron was shocked. There was no way Mother Dear knew about Asher and Imani. They were born decades after her passing.

"Yes, you must save Asher and Imani," she said as if reading his mind.

"How do you know about Asher and Imani? And what do you mean I have to rescue them?"

"Don't worry about what I know. Like I said, we'll have to save that conversation for another time and place. Just know, you must save 'em."

"What are you talking about?"

"It is not 'what,' Scooter. It's 'who.' In the Book of Mark, chapter five, verse nine, Jesus travels to Gadarenes. While there, Jesus comes across a man who is possessed. When Jesus asks the man, 'What is your name?' the man states, 'My name is Legion, for we are many.'

"The demons you saw in Imani's room were the same forked-tongued serpents that Jesus met in Gadarenes. They possessed you. They do not want you to close the door."

"You're losing me."

"There is a portal between the world of the living and that of the dead. Through the ignorance of you and your friends, you have left the door joining our two worlds open."

"Wait a minute. What do you mean I've left the door open? I didn't even know such a door existed?"

"I tried telling you, but we had a bad connection. You can never depend on the phone company. What I was trying to tell you was that it is the tray."

"The tray?"

"Yes, the divination tray. The divination tray reaches across the planes that separate the living from the dead. If handled properly, it briefly unlocks the door between our worlds. I can't explain everything to you right now because there isn't enough time. The door is ajar. Spirits, both good and bad, can travel freely between our worlds. It is through this door that Asher and Imani were taken."

"What do you mean, 'taken?'"

"Those in Darkness would benefit the most from having Asher and Imani in their possession."

"Wait a minute! This is ludicrous! You're losing me. How could taking Asher and Imani benefit anyone?"

"With Asher and Imani trapped on the other side, the Shadows believe you will do their bidding. With that said, you must shut the door. In doing so, you must make a choice. Either you will sacrifice the lives of your children or your own. In either case, the consequences will be dire.

"As long as the divination tray exists, the possibility of Armageddon is very real. Darkness is preparing to unleash Hell on Earth as we speak. I do not have to tell you what that means. We're talking about the end times. Revelations." Mother Dear paused to let her words sink in.

"That is why you cannot stay here. You must go back," she said.

A burning sensation surged through Aaron's body. At first, Aaron feared it was indigestion. Then there was another rushing through his veins.

"What's happening?" Aaron asked.

"It's time, Scooter. You got to go."

"Clear!" someone in the distance yelled.

"Who is that?" Aaron asked.

"You have to go back," Mother Dear repeated.

Suddenly there was excruciating pain. The nauseating green walls melted away. The twin-sized bed transformed into a gurney.

"Mother Dear!" Aaron shouted. He reached for his grand-mother's hand, only to have a stranger grab a hold.

"Hang in there! He's responding," she yelled.

Snapshots of people moving frantically about cluttered his mind. "I got a pulse! We're going to need more blood!" someone else screamed.

"His vitals are growing weak. We're losing him again!" a man yelled.

"Hit him again!" someone ordered.

"Clear!"

PART II
INTO THE SHADOWS

"The boy followed out his instructions to the letter, and arrived safely in Deadland, where he saw his mother seated near a spring, around which many other dead people were walking slowly or sitting down.

"He approached his mother and called to her, whereupon she rose and came to him, saying, 'What brings thee here my son? Why hast thou come to the land of the dead?'"

—Excerpt from a Yoruba Fable

SECRETS

The spicy taste of the hotlink lingered on Aaron's tongue while a rhythmic ping danced in his ear. Fearful of where he might be, Aaron slowly opened his eyes. He immediately recognized Donna. He wasn't familiar with the portly gentleman standing next to her. Judging from the intravenous drip, and the gentleman's lab coat, Aaron gathered he was in a hospital.

Donna started to cry. "Hey, you."

"Hi," Aaron groaned.

"You gave us quite a scare."

"Sorry." Aaron looked up at the wall, curious if he would see a portrait of Jesus. "Am I dead?"

"Now, would I be here if you were dead?" Donna asked.

Aaron contemplated Donna's question before answering, "To be honest with you, I don't know."

The doctor interrupted. "Hello, Dr. Langford. My name is Dr. Trujillo."

Aaron reached out to shake his hand.

"No, need for that. I'm more interested in finding out how you feel."

Aaron let his hand fall back to his side. "Fine. I feel fine. I guess?"

"How is your wrist?"

Aaron looked down at the bandage wrapped around his left forearm. "I really can't feel anything."

"Your wound was pretty deep, particularly the laceration from your palm to the middle of your forearm. You severed some tendons. You are going to have some trouble with the movement of both your middle and ring fingers in your left hand for the time being. I'm hopeful the tendons will heal naturally. If there is no improvement in the mobility of those digits over the next few months, we may have to perform surgery for you to regain motion in those fingers.

"I must say, judging by the amount of blood you lost, it is a miracle you are even alive. You were pronounced clinically dead for close to five minutes before the paramedics were able to revive you. That is quite a feat. Your condition was very dire. I made the decision to induce you into a coma to stabilize you. Not until yesterday did we see promising signs that your condition was improving. That was when we decided to slowly bring you out.

"We've been giving you painkillers to deaden the pain. We will start to slowly wean you off the painkillers over the next few days. During that time, you will begin to feel discomfort and pain in your left arm. That is to be expected."

Aaron looked at the doctor's badge. The insignia was the university. The last thing Aaron wanted was to be on suicide watch in the same hospital he worked.

"The wound may itch," Dr. Trujillo said. "You know better than to scratch it. We need to let the liquid adhesive do its job and keep that cut closed. Like I said, the cut was deep, so it's going to take some time for it to properly heal. You'll have a pretty nasty scar. Do you have any questions for me?"

"No," Aaron said.

"Good. I will check in every so often to see how you're doing. Right now, I would like a word with your wife."

* * *

Roughly ten minutes passed before Donna returned. "The doctor says that you're going to have to stay here for a while."

That came as no surprise. Aaron knew the hospital was required to perform a comprehensive psychiatric examination to determine a patient's mental state.

"Right now, he is going to prescribe you a sedative. Hopefully, it will help you relax," Donna said.

"I'm not crazy."

"What?"

"I said, I'm not crazy."

"No one said you were crazy."

"I know you think I am."

"What makes you say that?"

"I heard someone in the house," Aaron said.

"Excuse me?"

"I heard people in the house, talking. I heard them upstairs in Imani's room. That is why I went upstairs. Didn't you see them and hear them?" he asked.

"No, I did not see anything."

"How could you not see them? They were everywhere."

"I'm sorry, Aaron, I did not see anybody."

"I can't believe you did not see the shadows."

"Shadows?"

"The shadows. They were alive?"

"I didn't see anything."

Aaron knew he had not imagined the entire episode. The shadows came to life. He heard their voices. "I can't believe you didn't see them?"

Donna sat there. "Baby, I'm going to call Otis. He wanted me to call him when you were awake. I'll be right back."

Before Aaron could say another word, Donna had left.

* * *

Aaron knew he had to meet with the hospital's psychiatrist if he wished to be discharged. Dr. Liu picked and prodded at every thought and word that came out of Aaron's mouth. At first, Aaron didn't say much, but eventually, shame would not allow him to remain silent. He admitted to being a murderer.

"I killed Jennifer Taylor," Aaron said.

"Did you? May I ask, who is Jennifer Taylor?"

"She is the young woman whose body was found in the woods near Granite Falls."

"How do you know you killed this woman?"

"I just know I did. I killed my parents, and I think I killed my kids."

The psychiatrist flipped through his notes before stopping and looking up at Aaron. "It states here your parents died in a car accident."

"They did. I was the one that made the car accident happen."

"Is that so?"

"Yes."

"And how did you manage that?"

"I threw a paper airplane that caused my father to take his eyes off the road."

"I don't think that means you killed them, Mr. Langford. You did not physically make one car crash into another."

"But I did. I killed them."

"Also, if I am correct, Ms. Taylor was murdered at least six months ago. It states here you moved to Seattle three months ago. With that being the case, I fail to see how you killed Ms. Taylor. You were in Washington, D.C. at the time of her death. Why would you travel to Seattle, murder Ms. Taylor, and then return to Washington, D.C.?"

"I don't know why, but I did it. I killed her. I hit her in the head with a shovel." Aaron started to cry.

"Have you been taking any medication? Possibly fluoxetine?

"No, I haven't taken fluoxetine in a while," Aaron sobbed.

The doctor handed Aaron some tissue. "I can assure you, you did not kill Ms. Taylor or your parents. And I'm quite certain you did not kill your kids. These are all compulsive thoughts of violence."

"No, they're real."

"That's because you've convinced yourself that they are real, but they are not. If you think about it long and hard, you'll determine that it would be virtually impossible for you to leave Washington, D.C. six months ago, come to Seattle, and murder a woman, only to get on a plane and fly back to D.C. without anyone knowing."

"I refuse to fly. I drive everywhere I go."

"That makes it even more unlikely that you killed Ms. Taylor. Driving three thousand miles to kill someone, only to turn around and drive back, would raise a ton of questions," the psychiatrist said.

"Maybe, but I know I did it."

"You know these obsessive thoughts regarding violence is a form of obsessive-compulsive disorder, OCD. Yours is called Pure OCD, characterized by compulsive, unwanted or uncontrollable thoughts."

"I know, that is what my previous therapist told me."

"Then you know that you must continue your therapy in order to understand these thoughts and develop coping mechanisms whenever these thoughts arise. How did you cope with these thoughts in the past?"

"Cognitive behavioral therapy, trying to challenge the thoughts, but it's really hard sometimes."

"Well, I suggest you continue your therapy. Otherwise, these thoughts can come back even stronger."

Aaron sat there quietly, listening.

"Let's try prescribing fluoxetine again and getting you back into therapy. Does that sound good?"

"Yeah, I guess so."

As Aaron had predicted, he was discharged into Donna's care and told to follow Dr. Trujillo's orders.

Cleared to go home, Aaron sat on the edge of the hospital bed struggling to tie his shoelaces. His inability to grip the laces with his ring and middle fingers on his left hand made a simple mundane task difficult. When the door opened, Aaron assumed it would be Donna.

"What took you so long? I'm ready to get out of -" Aaron said, before looking up to see Detectives Mourning and Smith.

"Well, if it isn't Tweedle Dee and Tweedle Dum."

Detective Mourning smirked. "Cute. We heard you had an accident. So, we thought we would drop by to see how you were doing."

"I'm fine, gentlemen. Thank you."

"I don't mean to sound like an ass, but you don't appear to be faring too well, if you ask me, doc." Detective Mourning looked down at Aaron's shoelaces.

"You seem to be having trouble tying your shoe. By the way, your doctor told us you're suffering from some type of,"

Detective Mourning snapped his fingers as if that would help him recall the term he was searching for.

"OCD," Detective Smith said.

Detective Mourning smiled. "Yeah. He said you suffer from unwanted, uncontrollable thoughts."

"I can assure you. I am fine."

"That's not what the doctor said," Detective Mourning stated.

"Believe me, I am fine."

"Well, we wanted to come to see for ourselves," said Detective Smith.

"I surely hope that you didn't cut your own wrist for a particular reason and then try to hide behind some mental health disorder," said Detective Mourning.

"And what reason would I attempt to commit suicide over, Detective Mourning? Please humor me."

"Who knows, possibly stress, grief, anxiety, or possibly guilt."

Aaron bristled. "What are you implying?"

"I don't know. You tell me? I find it very coincidental that after we tell you we're going to need for you and your wife to submit DNA samples, you go off the deep end and slice open your wrist.

"Add to that the fact that your home security provider informed us the alarm system was activated at nine o'clock the night your children allegedly disappeared and remained active until roughly six o'clock the following morning," said Detective Mourning.

"Fortunately for us," Detective Smith added, "our lab technicians were able to swab the lining of your wife's mouth, and we were granted a court order to allow the hospital to legally release a blood sample to us. So, we will be able to differentiate between you and your wife's DNA in case anyone else's DNA shows up in the evidence collected. By the way, lab tests proved the speck of blood found on the floor in your daughter's room is your daughter's."

"Our lab also found what appears to be strands of an African American male's hair on your daughter's bed. My gut tells me those strands of hair are yours. Am I right?" asked Detective Mourning.

"How would I know?"

"Your wife told us you occasionally slept in your daughter's bed," said Detective Smith.

"Yes. I sometimes lay in my daughter's bed to comfort her when she was scared."

"Why?" Detective Smith asked.

"Did you not hear what I said? Don't try to make this out to be some heinous act."

"No one said there was anything wrong with that," said Detective Mourning.

"Then why are you here?"

"For two reasons. The first being your story of your kids running away does not add up. The alarm was not disarmed at any time during the night. Your wife stated she turned off the alarm at six the following morning. That means your son and daughter never left the house."

"Rather than harassing me, Detective Mourning, don't you think the odds of the police department finding my children might go up exponentially if you and your partner were out on the streets searching for them? I truly hope my son is not out there in crisis somewhere because if he has to depend on you two, he's in trouble."

"I'm not harassing you. I'm stating the facts," said Detective Mourning.

"Is that what you call them?"

"For someone who has nothing to hide, you are very testy," stated Detective Smith.

"Are you sure there isn't something you might want to tell us? Like did someone bring something into the house that might harm your son or daughter?" Detective Mourning asked.

"What? No! No one has brought anything in my home that could harm my children. What does that have to do with finding Asher and Imani?"

"You wouldn't be lying to me would you, doc? Because I can get a search warrant."

At that moment, Donna walked into the room. She looked surprised to see the detectives. "Aaron? What is going on?"

"Nothing you need to worry about, Mrs. Langford. We were catching up with your husband."

"If you gentlemen don't have any more questions for me, I would like to go home," Aaron said.

"Sure thing, doc. We got to be going, ourselves. Do bother to give us a call if you happen to remember anything else you might have forgotten to tell us before. Like you suffering from violent, compulsive thoughts," said Detective Mourning.

"That is none of your business," said Donna.

"Until we find your son and daughter, Mrs. Langford, everything is our business," said Detective Mourning. He patted Detective Smith on the back. "Let's go. We'll leave the two of you alone. Get well soon, doc. And don't forget to tie your shoes."

VOICES

The smell of disinfectant smacked Aaron squarely in the face as soon as Donna opened the door. Clearly, she had tried to cleanse the house of Aaron's sin. The general premise behind suicide is that you wanted to end your life. Not live with the fact you failed miserably at something everyone presumed was easy to do.

At home, Donna didn't let Aaron out of her sight. Fearful he might harm himself, she kept a constant vigil on his whereabouts. She tolerated his alcoholic binges because they eventually resulted in him passing out. Aaron sensed his claim of seeing the shadows come to life in Imani's room was a bit much for her to handle. So, they barely spoke to one another. She'd known of Aaron's OCD, but his insistence on having seen the shadows in Imani's room was too much for her to grapple with. Trapped in a prison of his own design, Aaron discovered a peculiar way to pass the time. He listened for voices. They were not the intrusive thoughts of committing acts of violence. They were something else. Something more perverse.

One evening after settling in for the night, Aaron heard someone in the living room. Immediately, it reminded him of the voices he heard in Imani's room. At first, he assumed he was hearing things, a byproduct of the alcohol. Yet, when they persisted, he felt the need to investigate. Rather than barging into the living room, as he did in Imani's room, Aaron decided to creep close enough to listen.

The next time Aaron heard someone in his house talking, he was sitting in his recliner. Rather than interrupt the conversation, Aaron decided to record the dialogue with his audio recorder on his cellphone. If he was indeed imagining he heard people talking, the recording would simply be dead air. That night, when he replayed the recording, there were people talking. This was evidence that he did not fabricate what happened in Imani's room. Intent on proving he was not hallucinating that night in Imani's room. Aaron went about recording the random ramblings whenever he heard them in the house. Sometimes, the conversations lasted for hours. Other times, they were brief. One thing was certain, whoever was in his house was not alone and roamed the house.

After a while, Aaron had stockpiled a sufficient collection of the gibberish. Every night, after recording, he would replay that evening's recording back to make sure the voices were indeed audible. He probably would've continued to record if he had not run out of storage space on his memory card. Despite this fact, Aaron felt he had compiled enough evidence to prove to Donna that he did not imagine what he had seen that night in Imani's room. Only one thing perplexed Aaron: What were they saying? What he had been hearing was not a language Aaron had heard before. He needed to know if the dialogue was indeed a language at all. There was only one person Aaron knew of who could get him that answer, Otis.

Otis and Teri dropped by the house often to check on Donna. After slicing open his wrist, Aaron was too embarrassed to face his friend. How do you start a conversation with someone after you've tried killing yourself?

Hey, how have you been?

Okay, I guess?

What have you been up to lately?

Nothing much. I tried to kill myself.

How did that go?

Not so good.

To understand the recordings, Aaron had no choice but to see Otis. Otis associated with many of the professors in the college of anthropology. Aaron figured an anthropologist or a linguist would be best qualified to translate or at least determine the language being spoken. So, when Otis informed Donna that he and Teri were stopping by, Aaron instructed Donna to send Otis downstairs. In the basement, Aaron figured he would be able to talk to his friend in private.

Aaron sat in the dark, with a fifth of vodka, wiggling his middle and ring fingers as he wrapped them around the bottle. When the front door opened, thoughts of Asher and Imani ran through his head. He figured if he could figure out what the voices were saying he might be able to rescue his children, especially Asher. He feared for his son's health.

The stairwell light came to life, followed by Otis's heavy footsteps coming down the stairs. "Aaron, are you down here?" he asked.

"Yeah, over here."

Otis followed the general direction of Aaron's voice. His eyes had yet to adjust to the dark, so he stumbled about. It had been a while since the two had seen one another.

Otis was visibly taken aback by Aaron's haggard appearance. "What are you doing down here in the dark?"

"Thinking."

"Long time no see."

"Yeah, ain't that the truth."

"Are you alright?"

"Besides my kids having run away and me trying to kill myself? I think overall I'm doing great," Aaron said.

"Stupid question, huh?"

"Do you think?"

"Everybody at the university sends their regards. They want you to know their prayers go out to you and Donna."

"Fuck 'em and their prayers. Until my kids come back home to me, God can kiss my ass." Aaron took a sip of vodka. "That's not the reason why I told Donna to send you down here."

Aaron caught Otis staring at the scar on his wrist. "Pretty, isn't it?" Aaron held his wrist out for Otis to see. "l had limited mobility of my middle and ring fingers. Yet, I've noticed I'm getting some movement back in them. I should be able to flip people off again pretty soon."

Otis looked away and quickly tried to change the subject. "Aaron, I'm —"

"I didn't call you down here to give you a hard time. Or listen to your sympathetic dribble. I need you to do me a favor."

"Sure, anything."

"The night I slit my wrist—" It was difficult for Aaron to openly admit to such a deed. "I had seen and heard something in Imani's room."

"Donna told me about that."

Aaron glared at Otis. "Will you shut up and let me finish?"

"Sorry."

"Anyway, whoever they are, they're in my house. I hear them almost every night."

"What do you mean that they're 'in your house' and you 'hear them almost every night?'"

"What about that don't you understand? There are people in my house. I hear their voices almost every night. I don't know who they are or what they want, but they're in my house."

"You're kidding, right?"

"Do I sound like I'm joking? I know what I am hearing!" Aaron took a gulp of vodka. "I recorded them talking on my cell phone throughout the house. I did it to prove to you that I did not imagine those voices I heard in Imani's room. To prove to you and Donna that I am not crazy."

"Nobody thinks you're crazy," Otis said.

"Please, spare me. I'm going to give you my phone. I tried but couldn't seem to download the audio files. They were too large. I trust you with it. Besides, if anybody wants to talk to me, they can call me on the home phone. Take the phone to one of your anthropologist or linguist buddies for me. Maybe they can translate what it is I'm hearing. Maybe it has something to do with the kids." Aaron held the cell phone out for Otis to take. Otis stared at the phone before grabbing it.

"You know, this whole ordeal has gotten me thinking about what you said to me at the Thaiger Room," Aaron said.

"And what was that?"

"You talked about spirits or souls."

"I vaguely recall the conversation."

"That night in Imani's room, I heard voices and watched the shadows come to life. I saw them spiral down from the ceiling and peel away from the walls."

"Aaron, you know the shadows didn't really come to life. That was your mind trying to process the trauma from your wound."

"No, it was not! I know what I saw!"

"Okay, the shadows moved. Sorry."

"Don't patronize me! I know what I saw!"

Aaron pressed his lips against the bottle and drank. "Regardless," Aaron continued, "there are hours of these people talking in various parts of my house. If you listen to the recordings, it sounds like many voices on some occasions, and on others, it sounds like many voices talking as one. It's weird. I've marked each time I heard them by announcing the day, date, and time. The passcode to the phone is 1027."

"So, do you think it is one person or several people?"

"God damnit, Otis! I don't know!"

"What do you think it is?"

"Who knows? Ghosts."

"Ghosts?"

"I know how foolish it sounds."

"What you're saying makes no sense."

"Imani told me something before she disappeared. She said that a woman came to her and asked her how to get back home."

"I have no doubt in my mind that Imani said that to you. However, we're talking about a six-year-old. One with an overly active imagination."

"Look, as I see it, there is no other way Asher and Imani can vanish off the face of this earth without a trace unless those who took my son, and my daughter, were not of this world. So please, work with me on this."

"I'm trying."

"I mean, how else could Asher and Imani disappear without the alarm being tripped or a door or window being opened? It doesn't make any sense. It isn't like Asher and Imani's rooms are on the ground floor; their rooms are on the second floor. There is no way someone could get into their rooms without causing a commotion."

"I hear you. It simply boggles the mind to go from not

believing in ghosts to suddenly believing ghosts abducted your children. I mean, it's not like ghosts are running around kidnapping people's kids every day."

"I know. Logically, it makes no sense, but I have proof on that cell phone. I've recorded them." Aaron pointed at the cell phone. "Do you think you can get the phone to one of your linguist or anthropologist buddies?"

"Yeah. I think I can get Marc to listen."

"You're really going to take it to him?"

"Yeah. I'll take it to him."

"I appreciate it. I'll be able to pick up my phone in a couple of days."

"I'll do it first thing in the morning. Do you want me to leave the lights on?" Otis asked, making his way towards the staircase.

"No, turn 'em off."

Otis walked up the steps. When he reached the top, the basement went dark. It took Aaron a minute for his eyes to adjust. When they did, he was startled by the sight of Jennifer Taylor standing across from him.

"What do you want?" Aaron asked.

"You're in danger."

"I know. You've told me." Aaron took a gulp of vodka. "I'm just curious, how long are we going to do this?"

"Until they find my killer."

"I truly hope that does not take long," Aaron said, before taking another sip.

* * *

Aaron lay in bed restless. He couldn't sleep. His thoughts kept circling back to something Mother Dear had said to him. She'd told him, "It's the tray."

When Aaron really thought about it, things didn't start going haywire until Otis brought the divination tray into his home. Honestly, Aaron knew very little about the wooden tray other than Otis had bought it from a neighbor. If there was any truth to Mother Dear's claim, Aaron needed to learn more about the divination tray. The divination tray was the key.

A WAKE-UP CALL

The repetitive ringing of the doorbell did very little to rouse Otis from his slumber. Not until the doorbell chime turned into a persistent banging at the front door did Otis wake up. Startled, Otis searched desperately for the night-light. A tepid sense of relief passed over him as the small light reassured him that he was in his room.

"Are you going to get that?" Teri croaked.

Otis did not answer her at first. He was too busy trying to get his bearings.

"Are you going to answer the door?" she asked.

"Yeah."

Groggy, Otis stumbled out of the bedroom and into the living room. His contempt for the unannounced intruder quickly evaporated at the sight of Aaron standing at his door in the rain.

Shocked, Otis threw open the door. "What the hell are you doing here?"

"I need to talk to you."

"Sure, come on in. Get out of the rain." Otis ushered Aaron

inside. "Take a seat. Let me go get you a towel so you can dry off."

"That is alright. I'll be fine."

"So, what's up? Is Donna okay?"

"She's fine."

"Then what is so damn important that you drive over to my house at three in the morning?"

"I need to know where you got the divination tray."

"The divination tray?"

"Yes, the African Ouija board. The housewarming gift. I recall you telling me you bought it from a neighbor?"

"Why do you need to know about the divination tray at this time of night?"

"You would not believe me if I told you," Aaron said, taking a seat on the couch.

"Well, since you have come all this way in the middle of the night, I think you owe me an explanation."

"This might sound bizarre."

"Try me."

"The board has something to do with Asher and Imani's disappearance."

"What?"

"Let me explain."

"How in the world can you explain that?"

"Someone told me."

"Let me guess, it was one of the voices that told you that? Am I correct?"

"Sort of." Aaron appeared to hesitate before divulging his source. "It was Mother Dear."

"Mother Dear?"

"Yeah."

"You're sitting here and telling me your dead grandmother

told you the divination tray caused Asher and Imani to vanish?"

"It didn't go exactly like that."

Otis shook his head. Then, he got up and headed towards the bedroom.

"Where are you going?"

"Sit tight, I'll be right back."

When Otis returned, he held Aaron's cell phone in his hand. "I came home and listened to the recordings you gave me this evening. Do you know what I heard?"

"No."

"Here, listen."

Aaron's voice could be heard whispering the day and time into the phone: "Thursday, 1:36 a.m." Afterwards, there was nothing except Aaron announcing a new day and time: "Saturday, 3:25 a.m." Then dead air.

"Where are the voices?"

"I asked myself the same question!" Otis said. "Other than your voice, there is nothing. There are no voices. The recorder is filled with nothing more than you mentioning the day and time."

"That's not my cell phone," Aaron said.

Otis tossed Aaron the phone. "Looks like the same cell phone you gave me earlier today."

Aaron examined the phone. "I don't understand. There should be at least an hour and a half of voices on there."

Otis sighed. "Look, I know the disappearance of Asher and Imani has been tough. I can imagine. Nevertheless, you've got to figure out another way to channel your heartache and pain instead of through this outlandish idea about ghosts. If you don't, this fantasy is going to eat you up. The voices you are hearing are the ones in your head."

Aaron looked befuddled.

"Aaron, why don't you stay the night? I can make the bed in the spare bedroom, and you can sleep in there."

"No, I need to get home."

"I'm your friend, and you know I'm always going to give it to you straight. Right? I've known you for over thirty years. I've never been one to mince words."

"Spit it out."

"I don't think you're well. You're hearing voices, hallucinating, and wandering off in the dead of night. Such behavior is not normal. I feel Asher and Imani going missing has put an unduly large amount of stress and strain on you."

"You think I'm crazy, don't you?"

"I didn't say that."

"Like hell you didn't. What are you implying then?"

"Me saying that does not mean you're crazy. It means you need help. You and Donna have been through a lot. You guys need each other more than ever right now. Another thing. The police called me yesterday. A Detective Mourning. He asked me plenty of questions about you and Donna. From what I've heard, I am not the only person he's questioned. Several of your colleagues in the College of Medicine have been contacted as well. I know for fact they've spoken to Robert Klein."

"You're kidding me."

"I wish I was. He even asked me a weird question about the divination tray."

"Why would he ask you about the divination tray?"

"I don't know. The question seemed to come out of nowhere. Nevertheless, it sounds like this Detective Mourning and Smith have checked out everybody you stated had access to your house since you moved in and came up with nothing. If I were a betting man, I would say they have set their sights on you and Donna as the prime suspects in Asher and Imani's disappearance. Now, I know they're

155

wasting their time. Needless to say, I think you might consider getting an attorney."

"Why would I need an attorney? I've done nothing wrong."

"True. You never know what the police can cook up."

"You are right about that," Aaron said. "I better get out of here before Donna worries herself sick."

"Are you sure you do not want to stay the night? Like I said, you can sleep in the spare bedroom."

Aaron shook his head. "No. I don't want to inconvenience you or Teri."

"It would not be a problem."

"Nah. I'm fine."

Otis led Aaron to the door. "Drive safely. And if you need me, don't be afraid to call. You could've done that tonight."

Aaron smirked. "Yeah, I could've."

Before walking out the door, Aaron turned to his friend. "What?" Otis asked.

Aaron smiled. "I know we've been over this already. Hopefully, you wouldn't mind humoring me."

"Sure, what is it?"

"Where did you get the divination tray from, again?"

THE VOODOO PRINCESS

Urbi was running late. She did not have time to entertain the annoying knock at the door. It was 7:12. If she didn't hurry up and leave, she was going to miss the 7:30 #43 Metro into downtown. If she had to catch another bus, she would be late, which meant her boss would fire her. He never liked her. He would've already fired her if she hadn't requested a leave of absence to care for her ailing mother.

"Who visits someone's house at this time of the morning? Don't people have any manners?" Urbi mumbled.

Unable to ignore the nonstop knocking, Urbi ventured downstairs. Peering through the peephole, she was able to see a tall, slender black man standing on her porch. When she opened the door, the gentleman's body odor and scruffy beard told her he was in need of a bath and a shave.

"Sorry, no soliciting," Urbi said, promptly slamming the door shut.

Urbi was halfway up the stairs when the knocking began anew. She turned to see the vagrant still there. "You gotta be kidding me."

Heading back down, Urbi swung the door open again. "Please! There is no soliciting at this residence!"

The drifter appeared to be at a loss for words; this was a typical reaction when people laid eyes on Urbi for the first time. Her alabaster skin, fluorescent pink eyes, silver dreadlocks, coupled with her pronounced black features, confused people. Over time, she'd grown accustomed to it. She much preferred the unwanted stares and whispers over being hunted. In certain parts of the world, being an albino marked you for death.

Fearing the vagrant did not understand English, Urbi asked, "Comprenez-vous?" The stranger appeared even more confused.

"Do you understand?" she asked.

He said nothing.

"Great, a mute! Look, come back later, and I will give you a couple of dollars for your troubles, okay?"

A blank stare was his response.

"Look, I got to go to work. I'm late as it is, come back later."

Urbi tried closing the door. This time, the door did not shut. While she was talking, the vagrant had wedged his foot in the doorway. Fearing the man meant her harm, Urbi pressed her weight against the door to brace herself in case he tried to force his way in.

"Sir, if you do not remove your foot, I will be forced to call the police!" Urbi jammed the man's foot in between the door and the frame. Although in pain, he refused to move his foot.

Finally, he said, "Please, do not shut the door. My name is Aaron Langford. I live a couple of houses down the block. I'm a neighbor."

Urbi caught the unmistakable smell of alcohol on the man's breath when he spoke. He pointed towards a house down the street while enduring the pain of Urbi smashing his toes in the doorway.

"I'm looking for a gentleman by the name of Ousman. It's important I speak with him," he continued.

Urbi examined her supposed neighbor closely. She had never heard of Hunters going to such lengths. Of course, that did not mean they developed new tactics. She could not be careless. For all she knew, this was a ruse to get inside the house.

"My brother does not live here! Now, get your foot out of my doorway, or I'm going to call the police!"

"Please, hear me out! I need to talk to Ousman! Can you tell me how I can reach him?"

"Sir, I am going to ask you one last time to remove your foot!" To drive home her point, Urbi leaned even harder on the door.

"Okay! Okay! Promise me you're not going to shut the door. Please promise me you'll hear me out! Please!"

Urbi was certain she was on her way to missing the 7:30 a.m. Metro. If she listened to what her so-called neighbor had to say, it was a guarantee she would be late.

"I will not shut the door, but you must remove your foot."

Urbi eased her weight off the door just enough for Aaron to slide his foot out of the doorway. Apprehensive, she held the door slightly open. She wanted to be able to close it quickly if need be. Hunters were crafty. Who knew, this man could have gotten information on her and her brother from searching the internet or rummaging through her trash. Besides, she did not know what type of business this man had with Ousman.

"First of all, I'm sorry for disturbing you so early in the morning. As I stated, my name is Aaron Langford. And like I said, I need to speak with your brother. Is that possible?"

"As I told you, my brother does not live here. Why is it so important for you to speak to my brother?"

"A friend of mine bought something at an estate sale here several weeks ago and gave it to me as a housewarming gift."

"I'm sorry, Mr. Langford, but all sales are final." Urbi would not waste her time pacifying Ousman's disgruntled customers. "I hate to be abrupt, but I have to be heading off to work."

To prevent her from shutting the door, Aaron grabbed the doorknob. Terrified, Urbi panicked, "Sir, your behavior has crossed the line!"

"Please, don't shut me out. I need your help. There was an estate sale here a few weeks ago. A friend of mine bought something. I'm here to figure out exactly what it is he bought."

"What do you mean, you want 'to figure out exactly what it is your friend bought?' What did your friend buy?"

"He bought a divination tray."

"A divination tray?"

"Yes."

Urbi stared at Aaron long and hard, searching for some proof that his story was credible. Choosing to believe him, she invited him in. Urbi shut the door behind Aaron and instructed him to take a seat in the living room.

"Do you have the tray?" she asked.

"What?"

"The tray, do you have the divination tray?"

"Yes."

"Well, I am Ousman's sister, Urbi Houna. I am more than willing to pay you ten times the amount your friend paid for the divination tray."

"You can have the tray back for free. So long as I get back what I seek," said Aaron.

Urbi stared at Aaron. "And what might that be? You did not toy with the divination tray, did you?"

"Yes. We tried playing with it."

"Merde!"

"What?"

"Nothing. It is French. What happened when you used the divination tray?"

"I can't actually explain it. Things changed. My house is not my house anymore. My cat is gone. My children have disappeared. On top of that, I'm seeing and hearing things."

"Pour l'amour de Dieu! What type of things have you seen and heard?"

"I hear voices. People are talking in my house. Yet, nobody is there. I've seen the shadows peel off the walls and come to life. My dead grandmother has called me on the phone."

"Bordel de merde, Ousman! I told you to let me check Mama's belongings before you sold them! I had accounted for everything of importance except for the divination tray!"

"Can you please tell me what is going on? What is it with this divination tray?"

Urbi tried to contain herself. She would have to deal with her brother later. There were now more pressing matters that required her attention. "Mr. Langford, the divination tray is a way to converse with the dead."

"I know that."

"How do you know such a thing?"

"My friend told me."

Urbi eyed Aaron. How would his friend know of the uses for a divination tray unless he was African? Divination trays were not common knowledge amongst Americans. They were quite rare, except in African communities. The possibility that he or his friend could possibly be Hunters again crossed her mind. For all she knew, this gentleman's friend was waiting outside. Urbi cursed herself for being so gullible. She inched her way towards the kitchen. There were plenty of knives in the kitchen in case she needed to defend herself.

"Where are you from?" asked Urbi.

"What does that have to do with anything?"

Urbi listened intently to hear if Aaron was attempting to mask an accent. "Answer the question."

"I'm from Washington, D.C. I don't see what that has to do with the divination tray."

"Shut up! I'll ask the questions." Urbi backed closer to the kitchen. "What is your native tongue? What is your tribe?"

"Tribe? What?"

"You heard me; what is your tribe?" This was a trick question. Urbi knew that if her neighbor was black, he would not know how to answer such a question. If he were African, his pride and arrogance would compel him to state his tribal allegiance.

"What kind of question is that? I don't have a tribe. Hell, the tribe of Langford!"

Maybe she was being paranoid, though Urbi knew there was no such thing as being overly cautious. The demand in the black market for albino body parts by bush doctors was very lucrative. It would not surprise her if Hunters had begun to cast their net beyond the coasts of Africa.

"Are we done with the geography questions?" Aaron asked.

"There is no need for you to take that tone in my house."

"I'm sorry. I don't understand why you are asking me about my tribe. I'm here to learn about the divination tray."

The man sitting before her was no Hunter. Urbi eased her way back into the living room. "My mother used the divination tray to communicate with our ancestors and the spirits in the Land of Invisibles."

"Land of Invisibles? Was your mother some kind of witch doctor?"

"Witch doctor, no. My mother was a mambo, a Vodun priestess."

"Vodun?"

"Yes. You are probably more familiar with the more crude pronunciation of the word, Voodoo. The European translation of such a beautiful word is so repulsive. It sounds so much better when spoken in Fongbe, the principal language upon which it originated."

Urbi sat back down. "Vodun is ancient. It is older than the world itself. It has existed since the beginning of time. The word 'Vodun' means spirit. That is why Vodun exists in the air we breathe and the earth beneath our feet. It is all around us. For we all share in essence, a spirit. You might know of Vodun in its different variations such as Santería, Candomblé, Macumba, and Hoodoo."

"That is marvelous. What does that have to do with me and my children?" Aaron said.

"You are not listening. It has everything to do with you and your family. Vodun is everywhere. Vodun is life. It is the center of everything. It connects us all."

"That does not explain what it has to do with me."

"Il est difficile de donner la vue aux aveugles."

"English, please."

"It is difficult to make the blind see."

"See what? What you're saying to me is nonsense."

"Well, know this. In Vodun, you do not tempt fate and toy with the spirits without also risking feeling their wrath," said Urbi.

"What do you mean?"

"I'm speaking of you and your friend's dalliance with the divination tray."

"We didn't have any idea of what we were dealing with."

"And therein lies the problem. I understand your desire for the safe return of your children. However, at this juncture, they may be lost forever if you toyed with the divination tray. You have tampered with forces beyond your imagination and as ancient as time."

"Well, I think you need to educate me on this divination tray because I believe that tray has something to do with my kids turning up missing."

"You are probably right. Unfortunately, the possibility of ever seeing them again, or your children returning to you alive if they are in the Land of Invisibles, is virtually zero," said Urbi.

"You said *virtually*. That means that there is a chance."

"There is a chance. The problem is, it is the most minute of possibilities. You sealed your children's fate the moment you placed the horn of Eschu on the tray."

"The horn of who?"

"Eschu. The tapper."

"How is it that I sealed my children's fate when the tapper touched the tray?"

"Because you are not a diviner."

"A what?"

"A diviner, another term for oracle. A diviner reads the cowrie shells when they are tossed upon the tray. Do you have the cowrie shells?"

"Yes."

"All eighteen?"

"Yeah, I'm pretty certain," said Aaron.

"It is very important that you have all eighteen. The number eighteen is intentional. What about the tapper and the black stone?"

"I have everything."

"Good. My mother said that stone came directly from the

shores of the Sea of Agony. That stone is irreplaceable. The eggshell, on the other hand, is not. Any eggshell will do," said Urbi.

Dumbfounded, Aaron asked, "What the hell is the Sea of Agony and why do we need an eggshell?"

"The Sea of Agony is the sea of the damned. The stone and the eggshell are necessary for the diviner when reading the cowrie shells. These objects determine if the message being relayed from the spirit world is either good or bad."

"Why go through all the trouble?" asked Aaron.

Urbi smiled. "Because it is how it is done. I, too, used to ask such questions of my mother when she would leave our banlieue in Clichy-sous-Bois and go to Château Rouge in Paris for her fetishes. And she would say to me, 'C'est comme ça que ça se fait et ça se fera toujours.' It is the way it has been done and always will be done.

"You must understand that in France, and eventually America, my mother could not perform ceremonial rituals as she once did in Ouidah. So, she turned to the divination tray. She had been trained by her teacher and mine, Akosiwa. The divination tray allowed for her to continue to seek guidance from the spirits, inconspicuously.

"Though it appears unassuming, the divination tray does bring along with it many perils. Like in any ritual, a sacrifice must be made to appease Eshu, the gatekeeper between this world of the living and that of the dead. Eschu allows our ancestors and spirits from the Land of Invisibles to communicate with us."

"Sacrifice? What do you mean a sacrifice?" asked Aaron.

"A questioner's question is posed to the spirits when it is written on a piece of paper and bathed in the blood of a sacrifice to satisfy Eshu."

"Blood of what? A cat? A dog? What?"

"No. Usually a chicken, goat, or a pig. Once this has been done, the diviner can call upon the spirits for a response to the questioner's question. If this is not done, it brings dangerous consequences."

"What do you mean dangerous?"

"If the appropriate reverence is not shown to Eshu when seeking an audience with the spirits, then the questioner's question falls into the realms beyond the center, the dominion of the Invisibles that lacks balance and is ruled by Eshu's twin brother, Kalfu. As Eschu is the gatekeeper of our ancestors and beneficial divinities, Kalfu is the gatekeeper of the malevolent spirits, the bakas."

"So, since we didn't pay homage to Eschu, we've bothered this Kalfu?"

"Yes."

"What happens if we disturb Kalfu?"

"The divination tray will enter a plane where both our ancestors and bakas can gain access to the questioner's world. In your case, your inability to correctly operate the board left the door between the two worlds ajar. Your inability to properly shut the door has made it easy for spirits, both good and bad, to pass through."

"That probably explains Jennifer Taylor and my grandmother's visits."

"Yes, it may. My mother tried to mitigate Kalfu's influence on the board if used incorrectly, by making it out of the wood from a fallen baobab tree. The sacred powers of the baobab tree protect the diviner using the divination tray from bakas. Like Eshu, Kalfu can be placated. He is very temperamental. If the door between the world of the living and that of the dead remains open, then the results can be catastrophic. Christians often refer to such cataclysmic events as 'The End Times.' Revelations."

"How can you be so certain?"

"For I am a Vodun priestess. I have felt the fire of Canzo. I am positive bakas have found the doorway and abducted your children to ensure you do not close it."

"They know I will not close the door if I know Asher and Imani are on the other side?"

"Correct. And that is why you must close the door."

"What do you mean?"

"You must close the door," said Urbi.

"I can't shut the door if my kids are on the other side!"

"You must!"

"I will not sever the link I have to my children! There must be another way!"

"Either your children find their way out, or you must find your way in to guide them out."

"You're kidding me, right?"

"No. It is the only option you have."

"How would I get in?"

"There is a fable of a botono who attempted to test fate and journey to the other side."

"A botono? What is a botono?"

"A Vodun priest is referred to as a hougan. A Vodun priestess is referred to as a mambo. When a hougan or mambo dabbles in sorcery and calls upon evil spirits, we call them botonos. Up until today, I've always assumed this tale was told to children to discourage us from growing up to be mambos and hougans who would tempt the powers of the wicked. Regardless, the botono entered the land of the Invisibles."

"What happened to this botono?" asked Aaron.

"Legend has it that the sorcerer tried to outfox Kalfu and lost. Folklore states the botono's blunder almost unleashed Darkness upon the world."

"Did the Voodoo priest return?"

"He never returned. Kalfu exiled him into Darkness for eternity as punishment for thinking he could outwit him," said Urbi.

"Great. That's just great."

"Like I said, I believe this fable was intended to discourage mambos and hougans from testing the boundaries of Vodun. I doubt it to be true."

"Whether it is true or not, I have no choice. I cannot wait for Asher and Imani to find their way out. I must find my way in," said Aaron.

"If you journey to the other side, the chances of you finding your way out are slim."

"That is a chance I must take. I much rather die trying than to not try at all."

"If you choose to do this, a diviner must preside over the ritual. That divination tray has been tainted by evil. The evil that has passed through it must be contained."

"Where in the world am I going to find a diviner?"

"Did I mention to you I was a diviner, as well as a Vodun priestess?"

THE SCAVENGER HUNT

Heeding Urbi's warning, Aaron knew what had to be done. The thought of crossing over into the Land of the Invisibles seemed crazy. However, sitting by and waiting for the police to find Asher and Imani seemed equally ridiculous. This was the only way. With detectives Mourning and Smith appearing to be more intent on assessing blame than finding Asher and Imani there were no other options.

Urbi had devised a plan for Aaron to cross over into the Land of Invisibles. However, Aaron had to follow her instructions to the tee. The first phase required Aaron to secure the divination tray. So immediately upon arriving back home, Aaron went straight to the den closet. That was the last place he recalled seeing the divination tray.

Aaron rummaged through the games and junk cluttered in the closet, but could not find the tray.

"Where have you been?"

Aaron turned to find Donna standing behind him. "Don't do that!"

"Sorry. I wasn't trying to scare you. Where have you been?"

"I went for a walk," Aaron said, returning his attention to the closet.

"You were gone for a mighty long time for a walk."

"I went out, okay? Look, I don't have time to answer any of your questions! I got more important stuff on my mind!"

"I did not know my questions were so bothersome. What are you doing, anyway?" She peered into the closet.

"I'm doing nothing!"

"Aaron, I'm worried about you."

"Stand in line. It seems like everybody is worried about me. Hell, even I'm worried about me."

"What are you talking about?"

"You know damn well what I'm talking about."

"That's what I mean! Nothing you say anymore makes sense. You show up at Otis' house at three in the morning babbling on about your cell phone and hearing voices. Then you come back home and vanish."

Aaron turned on her. "Let's get this straight: I don't babble!"

"Who are you? I'm tired of this Jekyll and Hyde routine. Who the hell am I talking to right now? Is it Jekyll? Or is this Mr. Hyde? Why is it so hard to get a straight answer out of you?"

"Why do you choose every chance you get to question me? I don't have time for this."

"See what I'm talking about? Who are you right now? I want to know what is going on!"

"You wouldn't believe me if I told you."

"Who cares what I believe? I want answers! Try me, god damnit! I'm your wife!"

"As soon as I find the divination tray, I will explain everything to you."

"The divination tray?"

"Yeah, the wooden tray Otis brought over several weeks ago."

"What do you need that for? You're not going to find it in there. I threw it out days ago."

"You did what?"

"I threw it out! The thing gave me the creeps!"

"No! No, no, no!" Aaron slammed the closet door shut. "Why didn't you talk to me first?" he yelled, dashing into the kitchen and out the back door.

"Aaron, where are you going?"

"I need that divination tray!" he screamed.

When Donna caught up with him, Aaron was digging through the trash.

"Aaron, will you please talk to me? What the hell is going on!"

"We need that divination tray!"

"Well, you're not going to find it in there! The trash was collected yesterday! The garbage you're sifting through is what I threw out last night!"

"Shit! Shit! Shit!" Aaron shrieked, kicking over the garbage pail.

"You are really starting to scare me! Will you please tell me what is going on?"

Aaron needed to figure out his next move. He pushed past Donna and back into the house. He stood in the kitchen bewildered before sitting down at the kitchen table and crying.

Donna rubbed his back. "Baby, you need to tell me what the hell is going on."

"I need the divination tray to bring Asher and Imani back,"

"What did you say?"

"You heard me. I said I need the divination tray to bring Asher and Imani back."

"What do you mean bring Asher and Imani back?"

"I mean bring them back home!"

"What does the divination tray have to do with Asher and Imani?"

"They're trapped on the other side, in the spirit world."

"What?"

"Asher and Imani are trapped in the spirit world."

Donna sat down. She looked like she was trying to fight back the tears. "I think you need to see the therapist, Dr. Lui," she said.

"What good is that going to do?"

"Help you with these thoughts that keep interrupting your life. Telling you you're a bad person doing terrible things."

"What I'm telling you right now has nothing to do with my condition."

"I beg to differ. I think it has everything to do with what is going on with you. Can you please explain to me what the board has to do with Asher and Imani disappearing?"

"As it was explained to me, when we toyed with the divination tray, we opened a door, a door between our world and the spirit world. Unbeknownst to us, we did not shut this door when we were done fooling around with the divination tray. Thus, we left the door between our world and the spirit world open."

Aaron perceived the pure lunacy in his words. "Look, I know what I am saying sounds crazy. It sounds absurd, even to me. But, if you think about it, it makes complete sense.

"See, by opening the door between the living and the dead we allowed spirits access to our world. To prevent us from closing the door, evil spirits kidnapped Asher and Imani."

"Who told you this?"

"Huh?"

"You said, 'as it was explained to you.' I'm curious to know who told you this?"

"Urbi Houna. She lives down the street in the yellow Victorian house on the corner. Otis bought the divination tray from her brother."

Donna looked vexed. "Why would evil spirits want the door left open?"

"So they can unleash hell on Earth. Armageddon. The End Times."

A fresh stream of tears fell from her eyes.

"I know this sounds out there. You got to trust me on this. Believe me, if you allow me to do this, I'll start seeing the therapist tomorrow. It will not make any difference if I see the therapist today or tomorrow. A day is not going to make that big of a difference."

"It never hurts to try, right? So, what do we do now?" asked Donna.

"We've got to go!"

"Go where?"

"It dawned on me while we were sitting here that we've got to go to the city landfill. Hopefully, I will be able to find the divination tray there," Aaron said.

* * *

After making several phone calls and scouring the internet, Aaron learned that waste from King County went to the county's last operating landfill, Cedar Hills Regional, twenty miles south of Seattle in Maple Valley. The drive to Cedar Hills was close to an hour.

Pillows of clouds, heavy with rain, rolled in from over the Olympics. Trudging through trash during a downpour was not Aaron's idea of fun. Regardless, Aaron felt Asher's condition meant he didn't have a choice. During the drive to the landfill, Aaron explained everything he had learned about the divination tray to Donna. He conveniently omitted the part of how he intended to rescue Asher and Imani once he retrieved the divination tray. That was a detail best saved for later.

Crows and seagulls filled the ironclad sky, making themselves easy markers for the location of the landfill. The atrocious smell seeping into the car through the vents told them they were getting close. It wasn't long before rolling hills of trash began to crest on the horizon. The second they parked the car and got out, the vile odor slapped them in the face. Finding a solitary object amongst the heaps of trash would be daunting.

Cedar Hills was cut into sections. Gratefully, Aaron and Donna did not have to scour the entire nine hundred-twenty-acre landfill to find the tray. They only needed to search the section of the landfill currently in use. Following the sound of the bulldozers led them to the appropriate area. Wading through the muck was not something Aaron looked forward to. Donna's grousing made it clear she felt the same. Despite their misgivings, Aaron had no other choice. If he wanted to see Asher and Imani again, he had to plod through the mountains of trash.

"Can you do this?" Aaron asked.

"Oh, my God! Did you see that? That rat was the size of a Chihuahua!" Donna squealed.

Aaron looked over to see the rodent duck into a pile of debris. "Never mind the rats. We got to find the divination tray."

"Aaron, that was a rat! A very big rat!"

Aaron shook his head. "Do you want to see your children again?"

"Yes!"

"Then forget about the rat! We need to find the tray! If we split up, we'll be able to cover more ground and have a better chance of finding it. You head in that direction." Aaron pointed in the direction of the rat. "I'll go this way," he said, pointing in the opposite direction. "Can you do this?"

"I can do this."

"Okay, let me know if you find anything."

"Okay."

Aaron scanned the vast range of refuge, only to hear Donna scream. "Did you find something?" shouted Aaron.

"Yeah, another rat!"

The landfill was filled with a bounty of rubbish and debris. As he walked amongst the trash, Aaron happened upon a golf club buried in the midst of the garbage. He plucked the club from the waste to discover it was missing its head. The fact the head of the club was gone made the shaft of the club an excellent poker for shifting through the refuse.

The only question now for Aaron was where to start. He roamed through the trash aimlessly. The mounds of trash were all starting to look alike. Then, he heard Jennifer Taylor shout, "Focus! Don't be distracted. They want you to be confused! Focus!" she said.

Jennifer's appearance startled him, but he took a deep breath and tried to remain calm. Aaron tried to tell himself she wasn't real. Slowly, the anxiety subsided. Once regaining his composure, Aaron continued his search. As he traversed the landfill, Aaron came upon a repugnant smell. It was faint at first but grew stronger. He surveyed the trash for the smell's origin. The last thing he wanted was to stumble upon a corpse. As he inspected the landfill, his eyes fell upon what appeared to be the carcass of an animal. From the looks of it, it had once been a dog of some sort. Scavengers had already picked the animal's bones clean. Only the animal's intestines remained, thus, creating the putrid smell. How that animal came to be there did not concern Aaron. What did, was the carved piece of wood lying beneath the animal's remains.

Aaron held his breath and used his makeshift poker to move the carcass out of the way. When the remains were out of the way, Aaron grabbed the wooden tray and walked away. When he was far enough away to evade the smell, Aaron examined the piece of wood. It was the divination tray. Other than a few stains, the wooden plate was intact. Aaron could not believe he had found the tray so easily, but his delight was short-lived, for he had only managed to solve half of his problem. He needed to find the tapper and the cowrie shells.

The sound of Donna screaming echoed amongst the canyons of trash. He could not fret over what might've distressed her; he needed to find the tapper and cowrie shells. The sun broke through the clouds dispelling the various shades of gray that colored the landscape and exposed the statuette of Eschu at his feet. If he had taken another step, he would have missed it. Two feet away from the tapper was the satchel of cowrie shells. Aaron couldn't believe his stroke of good luck.

Reaching down, he grabbed the tapper and cowrie shells. With the divination tray in hand, Aaron stuffed the tapper and cowrie shells into his pocket and ran back to the car. Donna was already sitting inside, waiting.

"Did you find the tray?" she asked.

"Yeah."

"Now, what do we need to do?"

"We use the divination tray to bring Asher and Imani back."

Without warning, the heavens opened and rain fell from the sky in translucent sheets. With possession of the divination tray, tapper, and cowrie shells, Aaron had almost everything he needed to execute Urbi's plan. The other pieces of the puzzle were not as reliable and would require a significant amount of cajoling. Urbi insisted that Otis and Teri's participation were necessary for the plan to work. Since they were present when the door was opened, they must be in attendance when the door is shut, as Urbi stated:

"The divination tray does not know space or time. To the tray, the session where you opened the door between the worlds of the living and the dead, is still ongoing."

THE SÉANCE

Adorned in an exquisite white gown, the Voodoo priestess rapped softly upon the door precisely at eight o'clock. She was prompt. Urbi's dress blended flawlessly with her skin, making it difficult to determine where the dress began and ended. Her blanched dreadlocks cascaded down her back as her fluorescent pink eyes surveyed the room. She wore no shoes. Thus, her feet left dewy footprints on the hardwood floors. In her hands, she carried a tote bag and a caged rooster.

"Who is this?" Otis asked.

"This is my neighbor, Urbi Houna. She is a diviner. You bought the divination tray from her brother. It belonged to her mother."

"You got to be kidding me, right? Aaron, don't tell me this lady has conned you into believing she can bring Asher and Imani back?" Otis said.

"She conned no one."

"Aaron, I don't want to see you taken advantage of."

"I appreciate your concern. However, I've decided I'm going to do everything in my power to bring my children back.

Even if it means doing something a little unconventional," Aaron said.

"A little unconventional?"

"Otis, I'm the one that has to look at myself in the mirror every morning. As Asher and Imani's father, how can I say I did everything in my power to bring my children back home if I don't explore every possibility? What is the worst that can happen? Even if it is some cockamamie idea, I am willing to take that chance. At least then I can say I tried.

"If it makes any one of you feel any better, I swear to all of you if this is a con or charade of any sort, I will gladly check myself into a psychiatric ward tomorrow." Aaron looked around the room into everyone's faces.

Otis looked at Aaron, then Donna. "Aaron, this woman is nothing more than a swindler preying upon your grief. You must see this. How much is she charging you for this sham?"

"il ne me paie rien!" said Urbi. Up to this point, Urbi had kept silent. She placed her tote bag and rooster down and stared at Otis.

"What did she say?" Otis asked.

"I said he is not paying me a thing."

Urbi walked over towards Otis until she stood directly in front of him. "This is not a sham, dear sir. I am here to help this man. The question is, are you?" Urbi's pink eyes bore into him.

Otis was noticeably uncomfortable. "Donna, I would have expected you to be against this?"

"What do you want me to say, Otis?"

"Mr. Langford, we do not have time for this," said Urbi, never taking her gaze off Otis. "Do you wish to go through with this or not?"

"What are we going to do, Otis? Are you with me?" Aaron asked. "My plan cannot work without you."

"I'm with you?"

179

Urbi grinned. "Friendship is never easy, is it Mr. Otis?"

Feeling the impasse lift, Urbi took charge. "Everyone, please take off your shoes and socks.

"We need to move the dining room table off the rug," she said. "We will sit on the floor." As commanded, Aaron and Otis moved the dining room table to one side of the room. The area rug was not a traditional mat used when questioning the spirits, yet it would suffice.

"Aaron, please place the divination tray, tapper, and cowrie shells in the center of the rug. The feet of the divination tray must point east."

"The feet?" Aaron asked.

"The side with the serpent."

Doing as instructed, Aaron placed the divination tray with the tapper and satchel of cowrie shells in the middle of the rug.

"Who was the diviner at the time the gateway was opened?" Urbi asked.

"The what?" Otis asked.

"Who threw the cowrie shells after the first question was asked to the divination tray?" Urbi said.

"I was," Otis said.

"Then you must resume your place as the diviner for this to work. Everyone else except Aaron must gather around the divination tray."

Urbi went to her tote bag and grabbed a large jar of dirt mixed with cornmeal. She took the lid off and sniffed. She must have smelled the sweet smell of Benin. Then, she began sprinkling the dirt cornmeal mix in a circle around the rug.

"What the hell are you doing?" Donna asked.

"I am protecting us from evil spirits. This is dirt from the sacred forest in Benin," Urbi explained.

Donna glared at Aaron. "I don't give a damn where it is

from as long as you are going to clean it up afterwards," she said.

"Okay, now what? We've done what you've asked. We've sat our asses down on this rug and watched you pour dirt onto the floor," Otis said.

"Please, sit there and be quiet. I will tell you when I am ready," Urbi said. Urbi returned to her tote bag and produced several candles, which she placed in the dirt encircling the rug, lighting each one.

"At least tell me what's up with the chicken?" Otis asked.

When she was done lighting the candles, Urbi closed her eyes and tried to center herself.

* * *

Urbi listened to the rhythmic beating of the rain upon the house. The patter of the raindrops reminded her of hountors beating upon their ritual drums. The vibrations of the drums moving throughout her body always filled her with anticipation and energy. The tart smell of fear mixed with the sweet smell of the earth always compelled her to dance.

Sadly, those were not drums. Those were raindrops. That was not dirt beneath her feet; it was a hardwood floor. There were no serviteurs standing by to assist in translating the ramblings of someone who had been mounted. Gone was the reassuring hand of her mother. Ima now guided her in spirit. Urbi would be performing this ritual alone. A first. This filled Urbi with trepidation. She was still learning how to master her skills as a mambo. Bakas may sense this and test her.

Often, Urbi's mother had called upon the divination tray for spiritual advice. Unfortunately, Urbi had spent very little time familiarizing herself with the board's idiosyncrasies. Her naiveté would have to do for now. Of course, her lack of understanding of the divination tray made Urbi wish she could call upon the spirits through the customary tradition of sacrifice and dance. That was so much easier than the patience required to communicate to the dead via the divination tray. Ima had mastered the proper way to greet Eschu and steer clear of Kalfu over the years.

If there ever was a time when Urbi needed to draw upon her mother's strength and wisdom, it was now. When Urbi proclaimed she wished to become a mambo her mother told her, "I am happy. Understand, Vodun is everything and everywhere. Within its beauty, there is also the unsightly. Vodun is life and death. It is the need for balance. Balance is what matters in life."

Ima's words rang in Urbi's ears. Often, she relied upon her mother's words of wisdom. This time, her mother's words did very little to soothe the self-doubt that wrecked her body. The bad juju of the house manifested itself into a vile, evil smell. Such bad omens only added to her unease.

Urbi looked over at Otis, Donna, and Teri sitting around the divination tray and squeezed the small sack of pebbles given to her by her mother tied to rawhide around her neck. The cross of Damballah was inscribed onto the charm to ensure protection from bakas. Urbi had never parted ways with that necklace since the day her mother had given it to her. She hoped the spell cast upon the small sack of pebbles retained their sway, for the follies of Aaron and his friends had created an unholy link between the world of the living and that of the dead. Urbi would need strength to sever that link.

Urbi took a deep breath and assured herself everything that had taken place in her life up to that point had prepared her for this moment. She silently hoped everything Akosiwa and her mother had taught her would be enough to protect them. She made one last check of her tote bag, making sure she had brought everything. She mentally cataloged all the charms, as well as the pistol.

* * *

"What the hell is she doing, meditating?" Otis asked.

Urbi disregarded Otis. Instead, she re-examined the cornmeal dirt mix around the rug.

When she looked like she was satisfied that everything was in place, Urbi gazed over at Aaron. "Everything is in order. It is now up to you."

"Do we really have to do this?" Donna asked.

"There is no other way if we wish to see Asher and Imani alive again," Aaron said. He looked over at Urbi and said, "I'm ready."

Taking her cue from Aaron, Urbi pointed at Otis and stated, "Do not move unless I tell you to."

"I can't believe I am doing this."

Urbi pointed at Teri. "You. You must come inside the circle. Neither one of you make a move unless I tell you to."

With everything in place, Urbi said, "We must find the door."

Aaron knew where to look. "I'll go upstairs. Donna, you check the basement."

Aaron bound up the steps towards Imani's room. He was sure the door was in his daughter's room. That is where he had seen the shadows come to life and heard countless voices. It is also where a ghost tried to abduct his daughter.

Aaron stood there, agonizingly by the door. What if the doorway to the spirit world was on the other side? Aaron's heart raced. Would he be able to survive the journey? How would he even find Asher and Imani?

He opened the door. The smell of stale air greeted him. Aaron inched his way into the room, groping for the light. There was no scurrying of shadows. There were no voices. There was only Imani's sky-blue dress laid out on the bed, along with her white buckle shoes.

The door is here.

Aaron waited. There was nothing.

Then, he heard Donna call his name.

Sprinting out of Imani's room and down the steps into the kitchen, Aaron hit the door to the basement so hard the doorknob put a hole in the wall. He bounded down the steps to find Donna with Urbi. Before them, the very fabric of reality was peeling away. Layer by layer.

"That is the passage. That is the door," Urbi said.

"Are you sure?" Aaron asked.

"No, I am not. I have never seen the doorway to the afterlife. I suspect this is it. You must enter before it collapses. If you do not, there is no telling when or where the next portal will open."

Suddenly, Otis's voice came to them. "What the hell is going on down there?"

"Do not move!" Urbi yelled.

"Will I be able to come back?"

"I do not know. I assume what goes in can also come back out. You must decide if this is what you wish to do before the passageway closes. Like I said, we do not know when, or even, if another portal will open. I do know you must hurry! The door is already closing!"

Aaron embraced Donna and whispered, "I love you."

"I love you, too. I am so sorry I doubted you."

"That does not matter. I promise you; I'll be back with Asher and Imani."

"You're running out of time! The door is faltering!" shouted Urbi.

Aaron kissed Donna, then rushed toward the closing rift. He looked back at his wife one last time, before stepping inside. There was a sudden rush of light before a paper airplane went sailing by.

SHADOWLAND

Aaron did not know if he was in the basement or on the other side of the world. He was far too afraid to open his eyes and find out. One thing did strike him as odd: the utter stillness of it all. Aaron dug his fingers into the ground only to have the earth run effortlessly through them. Sand.

Then he heard her voice, "So, do you believe me now, Scooter?"

Mother Dear?

"Yes. You can open your eyes. You made it through."

Aaron opened his eyes and was immediately blinded by an iridescent light. Shielding his eyes from the glare, Aaron watched as the luminous glow took the shape of his late grandmother. A shimmering white gown draped her body down to her ankles; an elegant white headdress adorned her head.

Mother Dear looked at Aaron and smiled. "Get on up. It's okay."

In this strange new land, Mother Dear's coco brown skin glowed. She was healthy and full of life. "Come on now, you got to get up," she said. "You got work to do, and you're not going to be able to do it lying on your back."

Aaron rose to his feet and hugged his grandmother. The salty taste of his tears stained his lips. "I missed you!"

"I missed you too, Scooter. How I wish we were meeting on a more joyous occasion. Unfortunately, there is work to be done, and we have so very little time to do it."

Aaron did not want to let go for fear she would disappear. He reluctantly pulled away and surveyed the land. The world was a stark shade of gray. Gray sand dunes ran as far as the eye could see. They looked familiar, as if he had seen them before.

"Where am I? Is this heaven?"

Mother Dear smiled. "This place goes by many names. None of them is heaven. This place is commonly referred to here as Shadowland. The vast expanse between Light and Darkness. It is home to The Loathing."

"The Loathing?"

"The unwilling," Mother Dear said. "The souls that abhor the fact their prior lives have ended. Those who refuse to transition over."

"I don't see anyone here. This place looks deserted to me."

"Are you certain?"

"I see no one else."

Mother Dear smiled. "Your eyes have not adjusted to this world for they fail to pierce the veil."

"What am I supposed to see?"

"Oh, my dear child, you have come so far. But, you have so far to go. You truly believe the image you see before you are me, your precious Mother Dear? What you see are memories of me cobbled together to give meaning to an image your mind cannot comprehend. Your brain is transposing mental images upon your surroundings in a valiant attempt to make sense of it all, turning it into something your mind can vaguely understand. Believe me, I am very much Mother Dear, but I have become so much more.

"No longer is my essence confined by a physical vessel. I am untethered. My soul has been set free. I know that is hard to believe. I say that because I know how hard it is to let go of preconceived notions of life and death. Yet, here, you must, in order to see this world with brand-new eyes."

Aaron stared out onto the harsh landscape.

"Let go of what you think you see. See beyond what blinds you. Here there are no restrictions except one," Mother Dear said.

Aaron looked out onto the horizon. Without warning, wisps of smoke materialized around him. "What are they?" he asked.

"They are the spirits of those who refuse to let go, The Loathing. They yearn for their prior lives. They refuse to heed the summoning of the Light, so they wander out here, in this wasteland of shade. Out here, they congregate to wallow in self-pity."

Whimsical puffs of smoke darted back and forth around Aaron like gnats. "Why are they congregating around me?"

"You're proof that the rumors are true."

"What rumors?"

"The rumors that a door between the world of the living and that of the dead exists. There have been those who doubted this fact, even after your cat meandered through."

"Socrates?"

"If that is what you call the mangy thing, then yes," said Mother Dear.

"So, that is where he went."

"Your attendance has now turned innuendos into fact. There is indeed a door. Now, if you really want to see something magnificent, look behind you," Mother Dear said.

Aaron turned around to be blinded by a lustrous light. It was as if he was staring into the heart of the sun. "I can't see."

"You don't need to see. Feel. Close your eyes and let it wash over you."

A feeling of euphoria, a feeling of love and joy swelled in Aaron's heart. "Do you feel it?" she asked.

"Yes, I feel it!"

"Isn't it magnificent?"

"It's fantastic," Aaron gushed. He reached out to grab ahold of the warmth pouring into him.

"Light is the jubilation that fills your heart. It eases the fear that burdens your soul and relieves you of the stress that pulls your shoulder blades taut like a bow. It is the goodwill and peace that flows from one human being to another. It is what I have become."

"I don't understand?"

"When our physical form has perished, and our soul is unleashed, our spirit is nothing more than unbridled energy that reverts back to its primal form: light. Light is the building blocks of life. Light created the atoms and molecules that comprise flesh and bone, mountains, streams, and even stars. Light is life.

"In the beginning, it was light that gave birth to every particle in the universe. It also gave every particle and atom its individual characteristics. Did not God say, 'Let there be light?' Even nonbelievers believe the universe was created by a Big Bang, an explosion that emanated energy and light outward into the heavens."

Aaron turned to face his grandmother. He pinched his eyes shut long enough for the illuminating form to transform back into Mother Dear. "So, what are you saying? God is light?"

"I do not know. I cannot say. I do know the light is the one thing that can reach back into the past, exist in the present and pierce the future all at the same time. Light is the only thing that can be everything to everyone all at once. If God is not light, then light is the language of God. It is the way God speaks. For God speaks through all of us, the living and the dead."

Mother Dear's smile faded. "Regrettably, the Light is not where you must go. You must journey into Darkness."

"What is that?"

"For as light touches, everything so does darkness. It is as much a part of our eternal makeup as light. You cannot have light without darkness. The universe cannot exist without darkness. Neither can you. You do not need to concern yourself with that right now. I will explain everything to you along the way. We must walk." Without saying another word, Mother Dear started to glide over the dunes.

They walked for some time in silence. A wind sprung up out of nowhere, blowing grains of sand into frenzied corkscrews, spawning mini tornadoes. "We are getting close," Mother Dear said.

Aaron shielded his eyes from the swirling grains of sand in hopes of catching a glimpse of their destination. Mother Dear was not bothered by the whirling wind. Nor were The Loathing that followed. Plodding along through the sand, Aaron allowed his mind to race. There were so many questions he wanted to ask. One particular question beckoned for an answer. Broaching such a subject could be viewed as inappropriate, though, in the current situation, Aaron had nothing to lose.

Aaron garnered the courage to ask his grandmother. "Mother Dear, I have always wanted to ask you something."

"What might that be?"

Aaron hesitated. Although in a different form, this was still his grandmother and Aaron sought to be respectful. "What were you, Mrs. Yates, and Mrs. Miller doing to Mrs. Barksdale that afternoon in the basement?"

Mother Dear stopped. She looked over at Aaron and laughed. "Are you referring to the time you barged in on me taking that root off Thelma?"

"I guess?"

"On that occasion, Yolanda and Sherry, Mrs. Yates, and Mrs. Miller, to you, were helping me rid Thelma of a really bad hex. Thelma was always tiptoeing out with someone else's man. That time, Thelma had been sneaking around town with Ethel Walls' husband, Walter. Ethel suspected it. So, to teach Thelma a lesson, Ethel placed a horrible root on her. Before Thelma knew it, boils were popping up all over her body. The doctor would lance one, and several more would pop up, worse than the last. That day I had made flour, vinegar, and parsley paste to spread over her body. That is what you saw her covered in."

"Couldn't you have done that without being half-naked and dancing around her?"

Again, Mother Dear laughed. "We were calling on the spirits to help banish Ethel's curse."

Mother Dear started gliding over the dunes again, but her answer led to another question. "Were you some kind of witch doctor?"

"No, not at all. I used home remedies like chicken soup for the common cold, or the root of the purple coneflower to treat minor viral infections—and other remedies to ward off hexes, for example, vinegar and parsley to draw the pus out of a boil."

"Don't look dumbfounded," Mother Dear said. "You are not the sole healer in this family. You're merely the first to have gone to school for it. You come from a long line of healers. It's in our blood. It is our kismet. Our fate.

"My regret is that I did not recognize it in you sooner. I

should have seen it in you. I was too scared at the time to think straight. The accident had taken your mother and father's lives. I feared I was also losing you. I didn't know what to do. I was an elderly woman trying my best to raise a young man.

"Your gift is special. Our ancestral line is filled with spiritual practitioners who were gifted in the art of healing both the body and the soul. You possess a gift, Scooter. I would light a few candles and pray over someone whom I thought might have a root placed on them. I never fiddled around with the spirits. I never provoked or invoked their names. Some things are best left alone. I'm not like you. I cannot see them or hear them.

"That reminds me, speaking of your mother. She wanted me to tell you that she misses you. She wanted me to tell you to 'Lay your burden down and stop blaming yourself for what happened.'" Aaron stopped in his tracks.

Mother Dear gazed at Aaron and said, "Your mother is right, Scooter. It is time for you to lay your burden down."

"What are you talking about?" Aaron asked.

"Don't play dumb with me. You know exactly what I'm talking about. I am talking about the anchor you've hung around your heart. It has starved you of happiness for far too long. You must stop blaming yourself for what happened that afternoon. It was not your fault."

"I'm the one that threw the paper plane," Aaron said.

"Yes, you did. However, the events that followed were beyond your control. You must recognize this to free yourself from the prison you've encased yourself in. Within Darkness, you cannot carry this remorse with you. They will feast upon it."

"Who will feast upon it? And why are we going into Darkness?"

"Not 'we' Scooter, you."

"Wait. Why am I going into Darkness? Aren't you the one that told me evil lurks there?"

"Yup, treachery prowls in its midst. Sadly, this is where you will find Asher and Imani. The sooner you find my grandbabies, the sooner you can close the door. The evil that lurks in the dark is preparing to spread into the world of the living."

"What do you mean 'preparing to spread?'"

"As I told you before, the wicked are gathering for the final act, the fulfillment of the Prophecy, the Apocalypse."

"I don't understand. If you knew where Asher and Imani were all this time, why didn't you rescue them? Why must I?"

"Because of the one rule I spoke of earlier: there is a natural order that must be preserved. Balance. Everything must maintain balance. There cannot be positivity without negativity. Such opposites keep the scales from tipping too far in favor of one over another. For every action, there is a reaction. These forces create a balance, a harmony, a constant ebb and flow. As light lives in everyone, so does darkness. Light cannot dwell in the land of the dark, just as Darkness cannot survive amongst the light. It is like the ends of two magnets that are polar opposites and repel one another. The two cancel each other out. If I venture into the shade, my light will be swallowed up by the destitute. If Darkness attempts to enter the kingdom of Light, it will be scorched into oblivion. We can exist out here in between our lands; we cannot exist in each other's domain. It has been this way since the beginning."

"What does that got to do with Asher and Imani?"

Mother Dear did not answer Aaron's question. Rather, she came to a halt.

Aaron followed his grandmother's gaze to where the gray dunes abruptly ended, appearing to fall off into a void.

"Here we are," Mother Dear said.

Aaron marveled at the seeming oddity of her world. Out of the corner of his eye, he noticed something bolt into the gloom. "What was that?"

"More than likely a scout. Everyone, including those dwelling in obscurity, has been awaiting your arrival."

"A scout? Wait, they know I am coming?"

"Like I said, Aaron, light, and darkness can exist out here in the penumbra. The shades within that murkiness know it is in there where you must go. For it is within their realm where you will find Asher and Imani. I am certain plenty of lost souls seeking to curry favor for another chance at life have forewarned the wicked of your advent into Shadowland."

"I must wade into that? What is it?"

"I cannot answer that question, for I do not know. This is the closest I have ever gotten to such evil," Mother Dear said.

"I don't understand what Asher and Imani have to do with all of this?"

"Everything. They are the pawns. They are the insurance policy that you will not slam shut the door that separates our worlds. The evil that consumes all emptiness believes if Asher and Imani are in their possession, you will never close the door. The shadows believe you will sacrifice humankind to satisfy your own personal desires, believing your selfishness outweighs what is good for the whole."

"Why me?"

"Who knows why? Unfortunately, this is the burden you must bear."

"Where do I start to look for them?"

"That I do not know. I do know that you must first cross the Sea of Agony, the biblical Lake of Fire. Beyond the Sea of Agony, I do not know what awaits you. Within that desolate place, no one's fate is the same. I do know that your love for

Asher and Imani will lead you to them, for that is the one thing that is pure. You are the only one who can find them."

"That doesn't help me out a whole helluva lot."

"Bite your tongue when talking to me. I am still your grandmother."

"Sorry."

"You will have to put your faith in something other than science. Here, your logic will not win. Here, it will only confuse you. You will not find rational answers here. Here you'll have to let go and go on faith," said Mother Dear.

"Faith! That's the one piece of advice you give me. Is for me to have faith?"

"Scooter, it's all you got."

"You must restore the balance. If balance is not established, an epic battle will be waged to strike a new one. Remember, minutes or hours do not matter here. What may feel like seconds could be years or centuries coming from a place where time matters. The precept of time is nonexistent. It never existed. There is a chance the world you return to - if you make it out of the insanity beyond this wall - will be vastly different fromz the one you left behind. What may feel like years, here, may be nothing more than the passing of a minute, there. Stay focused. Do not deviate!"

Aaron stared into the void. It breathed. Aaron reached out to touch the darkness. It recoiled away from his touch. Then, it relented and allowed his hand to ease in, to flow freely within the murkiness. It felt gooey, like tar. Then something grabbed a hold.

Aaron looked over at Mother Dear as black tendrils extended out from the void and coiled themselves around Aaron's arm, tightening their grip like boa constrictors drawing in their prey.

Aaron panicked, trying to pull free.

As the void wrapped itself around him, Mother Dear looked at Aaron and said, "Remember, your love can lead you to them. Do not be fooled by what your eyes see. Trust your heart."

INTO THE ABYSS

Not until his feet were firmly planted upon a rocky shore of jet-black stones was Aaron able to fully gaze upon the gruesome, deformed bodies thrashing about in a sea of excrement. The fetid smell of sulfur, burning flesh, and excrement filled the air. Hands poking, prodding, tugging, and pulling him as he rode upon broiling waves of flesh.

The mere sight of the twisted, contorted flesh, caused Aaron's stomach to erupt, spewing forth its contents onto the rocks. Wiping the slobber from his mouth, Aaron examined this strange new land. A yellow hue cut a deep swath through a brooding sky of orange and fiery reds. A flotilla of clouds hung on the horizon. In them, the crackle of lightning could be seen winding its way across the sky, setting the heavens ablaze, to the deafening applause of thunder. Then he heard them. The voices. Faint at first, but growing ever louder, building to a crescendo.

Finally, giving way to an unmistakable sound.

WHERE THE VOICES GO

The alarm.

Aaron leaped out of bed, wondering where he was.

As if to answer his own question, Donna's drowsy voice came to him. "Can you please turn the alarm off or hit the snooze button?"

Aaron stood there motionless. How did he get home? How did he get in his bed? The alarm blasted the obnoxious drivel of a disc jockey. When the mindless blabber continued, Donna rolled over.

"Are you okay?" she asked.

No, I'm not.

"Are you okay?" Donna repeated.

Unsure on how to respond, Aaron said, "Yes."

"Are you sure?" Donna asked.

"I said yes."

Refusing to wait for Donna's next question, Aaron left the room, seeking out the sanctuary of the bathroom. At least there, he could collect his thoughts.

Was I dreaming?

Everything felt disjointed, out of place. As Aaron tried to understand what was happening, he noticed dirt on the doorknob and the floor. He looked at his hands to see them caked in grime. His feet were covered in mud.

Aaron opened the bathroom door to see muddy footprints from the bedroom to the bathroom. There was another set leading from the bedroom to the front door. Aaron examined the footprints closely. They were his. Rather than sort out how he had gotten mud on his hands and feet, Aaron decided it was best to clean up the mess before Donna noticed. The last thing he needed or wanted was Donna cross-examining him. Aaron shut the bathroom door and promptly washed the dirt from his hands and feet.

Clean, Aaron wiped the muddy footprints off the floor. He did not recall going outside, nor why he would've even gone outside. With the floor wiped clean, Aaron was leaving the bathroom, when he suddenly heard Donna calling out to him.

"What?" he asked, as he looked down the hall.

Donna pointed into the bedroom. "What is this?"

"What is what?" Aaron walked down the hall to see the bedspread covered in dirt.

"Silence. You got nothing to say?"

What could he say?

"I got muddy handprints on my bed and no reason as to how they got there, and you have nothing to say." Angry, Donna started removing the sheets.

"Aaron, what is going on?"

"I don't know. What do you want me to say?"

"Is everything okay? Are you okay?"

"I'm fine?"

"Then why is there dirt in the bed?"

"I don't know."

"You have no clue how you happened to get dirt in the bed?"

"If I knew, I would tell you."

A lengthy pause grew between them before Aaron finally asked, "Where are the kids?"

"What do you mean, where are the kids?"

"I mean exactly that: Where are Asher and Imani?"

"Aaron, I don't understand?"

"Don't patronize me, Donna! Just answer the question. Where are Asher and Imani?"

"They're gone. They've run away. Have you forgotten?" She stared at him. "Are you sure you're, okay?"

"I'm fine."

"Where is the divination tray?"

"The what?"

"The divination tray, the housewarming gift Otis had given us."

"I told you. I threw it out with the trash," Donna said.

"We went to the dump, and I found it," Aaron said.

"What?"

"We found the divination tray, tapper, and cowrie shells at the city dump."

"No, we didn't. We never went to the dump."

Confounded, Aaron walked out of the room. The red and pink hues of dawn were bleeding into the house, as he glanced up the staircase. On a typical day, he would've trudged upstairs to wake Asher and Imani for school.

Walking into the kitchen and sitting down at the table, he glared at the scar on his wrist. That was real.

* * *

Traffic into the U-District was stop and go. In a strange kind of way, he had missed it. His research provided him with the perfect outlet to occupy his time. Donna did not think returning to work was wise. Aaron didn't care. It was better than going stir-crazy in the house.

On campus, Aaron ventured to his office to collect his notes for his eight o'clock lecture in Bagley Hall. In his office, he grabbed his papers and prepared for the trek up Garfield Lane. Rushing out the door, he ran smack dab into another gentleman.

"I am so sorry," Aaron said.

"No, it was my fault." The man had a thick accent. It sounded African or Caribbean. The gentleman was neatly dressed in a three-piece suit, and his dreadlocks were pulled back into a well-kept ponytail.

"Can I help you find something?"

"No. Not at all. I've found what I was looking for. Allow me to help you with your papers," the gentleman said.

"No, need. I got 'em."

Aaron gathered his notes that were scattered throughout the hall. Although Aaron did not request his help, the gentleman began collecting his papers as well, before Aaron departed for class.

The morning lecture hall was a disaster. It was an incoherent, rambling mess. Aaron prided himself on being prepared, but because his notes were out of order, he felt disorganized. Seeking to put the morning behind him, he called Otis and proposed they meet up for lunch.

* * *

Delfino's was filled with the usual lunchtime crowd. Upon finding a place to sit, Aaron was surprised to see the gentleman in the three-piece suit sitting at a nearby table.

"So how are you holding up?" Otis asked, through a mouthful of deep-dish cheese and pepperoni pizza.

"It's tough. I'm taking it one day at a time."

"That's about all you can do. There is no sign of Asher and Imani turning up anywhere?"

"Nope."

"Hmmm. Do you think you may be rushing it? Particularly after Asher and Imani's disappearance? Not to mention you know what?" Otis looked at Aaron's wrist.

"You can say suicide, Otis." Otis quickly buried his face in his slice of pizza.

"To answer your question, I struggle with whether I should've come back at all. I do know I was going crazy cooped up in that house."

As Otis shoveled more pizza into his mouth, Aaron thought about the gentleman in the three-piece suit. He wondered exactly what the man had been looking for, which he claimed he had already found. He looked over at the gentleman's table to see he was gone. Aaron looked around the restaurant. He swore he had just seen him right there at the table.

"If that is how you feel, I can only imagine how Donna must feel. She doesn't have a job she can escape to."

"You got a point. Sometimes, I wonder if we would have been better off if we had stayed in D.C. rather than trekking out here. More and more, coming to Seattle is looking like a mistake. My kids are gone, my marriage is in shambles, and my research is going nowhere fast. It has been one setback after another, especially after you brought that divination tray into my house."

"Oh, it's my fault now?"

"No, I'm not saying that. Things were not right in my marriage before that. However, life got weird after that night."

"What is it with you and this divination tray? It's like you are fixated on it. You're lucky your neighbor didn't call the cops on you for barging into her house spewing all that mumbo jumbo about voodoo and ghosts."

"Are you talking about Urbi?"

"I guess? I don't know her name. The albino woman that lives down the street from you. Don't tell me you don't recall harassing that poor woman?"

Meeting Urbi wasn't a dream. He knew this for sure.

"I didn't harass her."

"Like hell, you didn't. Like I said, you better be glad that woman didn't call the police."

"I didn't harass her! I wanted to understand what it was you brought into my house. Since you brought that divination tray into my house my life has been a living hell. You said you bought it from her brother. So I went to her house to find her brother."

Otis grimaced and shook his head. "Enough with the divination tray; I should've never insisted we play with the damn thing. Honestly, you have a lot more important things to worry about than a divination tray."

Suddenly, Aaron spotted the gentleman in the three-piece suit standing by the door staring at him. Something about him was unnerving.

"What are you looking at?" Otis asked.

"Nothing, really. I bumped into that guy over by the door this morning on my way to class."

Otis followed Aaron's gaze.

"The guy in the three-piece suit..." Aaron realized his voice was trailing off when he noticed the man was gone.

"What guy? Are you okay?" Otis asked.

"I'm fine."

* * *

The sight of Donna in the garden struck Aaron as odd as he pulled into the driveway. He didn't understand her newfound infatuation with gardening.

"What is it you see in this garden?"

She looked up at him. "You've been drinking."

"How do you know?"

"Because you're swaying."

"In that case, yes, I've had a few drinks. What does it matter?"

Before walking inside, Aaron noticed Donna only tended to a very small patch of dirt, while she allowed the rest of the garden to be overrun by weeds.

LOOKING INTO THE MIRROR

Aaron gazed at his reflection in the mirror. A woman wrapped her arms around him. He could not see her face. He could feel her breath on the back of his neck and feel the warmth of her embrace.

She raked her fingernails over his skin as she spoke, "Why have you come?"

"What are you talking about?"

Dragging her fingernails over his chest she asked again, "Why have you come?"

"I don't know what you're talking about."

"You lie!" She buried her fingernails into his skin.

Aaron sprung awake. He looked over at Donna; she was fast asleep. Not sure if he was dreaming, Aaron pulled the covers back to see scratch marks across his chest.

SCRATCHING THE SURFACE

The next morning, Aaron examined the scratches on his chest. They were fine and deep. He more than likely scratched himself in his sleep. His subconscious was trying to find a means to help him cope. It was another way to deal with everything besides liquor or work. In the end, Aaron didn't care, as long as it blocked out the despair. Sometimes, Aaron took to venturing out of the house to neighborhood cafés to help him escape his living hell.

One of Aaron's favorite haunts was a café called Belle Epicurean, a European-style café that served pastries, soups, and artisan sandwiches. The place allowed him to pretend he was sitting in a café in Europe sipping a cup of coffee and people watching. More importantly, it allowed him to escape to someplace else. Often, Aaron would enjoy a pastry with his coffee until closing, which was five o'clock. Every once in a while, the café would host an event that allowed for it to stay open beyond its usual hours. This evening, such an event was taking place, the celebration of a particular red wine grape, Beaujolais Nouveau.

Aaron sat in the café eating and sampling the wine when he heard, "How are you enjoying your time, here?" over the music.

Aaron looked up to see the gentleman in the three-piece suit. "Excuse me," Aaron said.

"I said, 'How are you enjoying your time, here?'"

"I think it is nice. Pretty festive."

"You have no idea what I'm talking about, do you?"

"You're talking about the celebration of the grape."

The man smiled. "If you say so. May I sit down?"

Before Aaron could reply, he had already taken a seat.

"Surprised to see me?" he asked.

"Yeah, slightly caught off guard, but this is a restaurant. It isn't that you are not allowed to eat here. So, tell me, are you a doctor?"

The gentleman smiled. "Yeah. I just might not be the type of doctor you're accustomed to."

"And what type of doctor are you?"

The gentleman's dreads swayed from side to side as he shook his head in disbelief. "You truly have no clue as to where you are, do you?"

"Yeah, I'm enjoying good music and fine wine here in this café," Aaron said.

The man stared at Aaron. "No. You're not hearing me." He looked at Aaron and said, "My name is Nora."

"Nora is quite an unusual name," Aaron said, shaking his hand.

"Yeah, maybe. That is a matter of perspective. To be honest with you, it is all I could come up with on such short notice."

"So, Nora is not your real name?"

"Maybe it is. Maybe it's not."

"How did you hear about the Festival Beaujolais Nouveau?" Aaron asked.

"I didn't. I came here because I'm waiting."

"Are you meeting somebody?"

"Yeah, you."

"What do you mean by that? I've never seen you before the other day."

"True. However, that does not mean I have not met you before."

"Did I meet you at a conference? Do you follow my research?" Aaron asked.

"No, I don't. I simply heard of your arrival, and I figured it is my job to keep you safe. Sort of like a guardian angel."

"I fail to see what you have to keep me safe from at the hospital?"

"Oh, I'm not keeping you safe from anything at the hospital."

"Then what exactly are you keeping me safe from?"

Nora lowered his voice. "I think you know. You've seen them."

"I don't have a clue as to what you are talking about."

"I'm talking about all of this." Nora waved his arms around. "These people. This place. I'm talking about everything."

"You're not making any sense."

"I beg to differ. I'm making perfect sense, and you know it."

Nora reached across the table and grabbed Aaron by the wrist. Aaron tried to pull his hand free. "What are you doing?"

Nora examined Aaron's gruesome scar.

"What are you doing?"

"Keep your voice down. They'll hear us," Nora said. "The only way to get here is for you to die. With that said, my question to you is this: What brought you here?"

DEAD MAN WALKING

The sound of pots and pans brought Aaron back to the world of the living. He squinted over at the alarm clock. It was ten o'clock. A raging hangover caused the pots and pans to sound like drums. He knew better than to mix wine and vodka. His first lecture hall was not until one, so he had plenty of time to shake off the effects of the previous night. Aaron rolled over and stared at the ceiling. He recalled his conversation with Nora; something about that conversation gnawed at him. What did he mean by, "The only way for you to get here is for you to die?" Trying to make sense of the strange exchange was impossible. Rather than consume himself with thoughts of Nora, Aaron decided it was best to get ready for work.

At work, Aaron spent most of his day at his desk pouring over lab results. Trying to avoid going home, he worked late into the evening. It was Friday, so the campus was deserted. A few students milled about here and there, but overall, the campus was quiet. Even the parking garage was sparsely populated. Many of the professors and staff had already headed home for the weekend. Aaron entered the parking ramp and descended the staircase to the third level.

He was walking past the cars to his parking space when he heard, "Have you figured it out, yet?" Aaron looked around to see Nora appear from behind a parked car.

"So, what is your story?" he asked, wearing the same suit from the previous evening.

"What are you doing? Are you stalking me?" Aaron said.

"I'm checking in on you."

"I don't need you checking in on me."

"You still don't get it, do you? You're still wandering around in the dark. Or better yet wandering in Darkness."

"What did you just say?"

"Ah, that got your attention."

"Look, I'm on my way home. What do you want?"

"I want you to wake up. For you to realize where you are."

"Why don't you tell me where am I? Because all I see is a parking garage. And honestly, I would like to get in my car and go home."

"I don't have a lot of time to wait for you to figure it out."

"Look, I've had a long day. I don't have time to play games." Aaron walked over to his car. He had gotten as far as unlocking the door when he felt the cold steel from the barrel of a gun pressed against his cheek.

"You're going to listen to me whether you want to or not!" Nora said.

"What is your problem?"

"The cat was let out of the bag yesterday. So, we can no longer wait."

"Have you lost your mind?"

"That depends on whom you're asking." Nora dug the muzzle of the gun deeper into Aaron's cheek.

"You know you don't have to do this."

"Shut up! I can do as I wish. If I want to, we can start all over again. I'll find you again."

"What are you talking about?"

"I intend to show you what I'm talking about."

Aaron tried to stall. He searched for the nearest exit. He wouldn't be able to make it without Nora getting off a shot.

"You fail to see the truth even when it is staring you right in the face!"

"I really don't think shoving a gun in my face is going to help me see anything!"

"Believe me, it will!"

The sound of a door slamming shut echoed throughout the parking garage. Aaron prayed campus security had seen the incident unfolding on the security cameras.

"They followed me here. I knew they would!"

Seizing on his chance, Aaron screamed for help.

"Shut up!" Nora screamed.

The sound of hastening footsteps grew louder. "Get down on your knees!" Nora ordered.

"What?"

"Get down on your knees!"

Aaron resisted. He was quickly reminded he didn't have a choice when Nora jammed the barrel of the gun into his jaw.

"Aaron, what's going on?" Aaron looked up to see Robert Klein. "Are you okay? I heard someone screaming. Who is this guy?" Robert looked at Nora.

"He's a lunatic! A fucking lunatic! He's got a gun, Robert! Run!"

"No, don't you move!" Nora said, turning the pistol on Robert. "You move and I'll blow his brains out. You can't fool me! I know what you are. You're one of them!"

"Run, Robert! He's insane!" Robert gazed at the exit door as if contemplating making a break for it.

"Did you not hear what I said? Don't you fucking move!" Speaking to Aaron, Nora said, "My friend, I am going to show you what you've been needing to see. It's time for you to open your eyes."

Then, without saying another word, Nora pulled the trigger.

A high-pitched whine filled Aaron's ears as the sound of the gun reverberated off the concrete walls. His own panicked screams sounded distant. Aaron watched in slow motion as Robert's body fell back against a car before slumping to the ground. Mortified, Aaron yanked himself free and rushed to Robert's side. The bullet hit him squarely in the forehead. The exit wound blew a good portion of his brain out of the back of his head. Acting on instinct, Aaron immediately administered CPR.

When it was clear Robert was not responding to Aaron's attempts to revive him, Aaron screamed, "You sick bastard! You killed him!"

"I needed for you to see the truth. This is the only way I can show you!" Nora said.

"Show me? Show me what? You killing a man?"

"Just wait and see!"

"You are crazy! Certifiably crazy!"

"Stop being melodramatic. You act like you've never seen blood before. You're a doctor, right? He'll be fine. Watch."

"Watch? Watch what? Watch you murder someone else?"

"Watch, you'll see," Nora assured him. "Get away from him. Leave him alone." Nora dragged Aaron away from Robert's lifeless body.

"Help! Somebody, please help me!" Aaron yelled.

"Hey, none of that! You'll draw more attention to us! I'm quite sure the others are already swarming to our location."

"What the hell are you talking about? Help! Someone, please help!"

Nora cocked the hammer of the .38 and pointed it at Aaron. "Now that's enough! Be patient!"

"Or what? You're going to kill me too?"

"Look, I'm warning you!" Nora brought the gun an inch away from Aaron's head.

"Do it! DO IT! I have nothing to live for! My wife hates my guts, and my kids have left me!"

"That is where you are wrong, my friend," Nora said.

That's when Aaron heard Robert gasp. "See, I told you. All you had to do was be patient."

Aaron looked over to see Robert struggling to breathe.

"See!"

The blood splattering on the parked car began to disappear. Robert's entry and exit wounds began to magically heal, and the gaping hole in his head became a faint scar.

"What the hell?" Aaron said, backing away.

"I told you. You needed to see it for yourself."

This can't be real!

"Oh, it's real," Nora said.

As Robert struggled to sit up, Nora said, "Ta da! I give you life here in Darkness." Robert slowly rose to his feet. He was unsteady at first. Then, he found his footing. "See, he is one of them."

Nora trained his gun on Robert. "Be careful; he might go berserk."

Robert gazed at Aaron and smiled. He then walked over to his car and got in. As he pulled out, he rolled his window down and said, "See you tomorrow, Aaron." Then, he winked.

"What the fuck just happened?"

"Listen to me. We don't have much time. They're coming! Soon this place will be swarming with shades. They know I have contacted you. We must find your kids and travel back through the rift," Nora said.

"What are you talking about?" Aaron asked.

"I know this may be a lot for you to take in all at once; unfortunately, I don't have a lot of time to explain it to you. Both you and your children are in danger. Trust no one. They will be coming for you. So, be ready."

Then, without warning, Nora disappeared.

Aaron searched the garage, but he was gone.

"Is everything all right?"

Aaron turned around to see campus security. "Everything is fine," he said.

"Are you sure?"

"Yeah, why?" Aaron asked.

"Because you got blood on your shirt," the security guard said, pointing.

"Oh. That's nothing."

"Are you sure you're, okay?" the guard asked.

"I accidentally cut myself. I'm good."

"That looks like blood from more than a cut. There is blood all over your shirt." The officer grabbed his walkie-talkie.

"No need!" Aaron said.

"Are you sure? I think you might have been mugged or something. I could see you on the parking ramp security cameras for a second. Then the cameras went dark."

"You could see me on the security cameras?"

"Yeah, briefly, then everything went dark. I came up here to see why the cameras stopped working." The security guard pointed at the security camera domes strategically placed on the ceiling at both ends of the parking ramp.

"Was I alone, or was someone with me?" Aaron asked.

"I saw you. Is there someone else here with you?"

"So, you didn't see anybody else?"

"No, the cameras died. Are you sure you are okay?"

"I'm fine!"

"Are you sure?"

"God damnit, I said I was fine!"

"Sorry. I just wanted to make sure."

"Yeah, whatever," Aaron said as he walked over to his car.

"Sir, I think you should come with me to get looked at?"

"Thanks for your advice."

Once inside the car, Aaron sat there for a moment, befuddled. He couldn't believe what he had seen. He was even more baffled as to how Nora managed to vanish.

* * *

Aaron sat in his driveway for half an hour trying to understand what had transpired. Common sense told him he had witnessed a murder. His eyes told him he saw something far more peculiar. He gazed at his house. He didn't want to go in.

Aaron climbed out of the car. He removed his shirt before entering the house to negate any questions regarding the blood. Goosebumps dotted his chest as a brisk nighttime breeze kissed his skin. Inside, he went directly to the cupboard and grabbed the gallon of vodka. He twisted off the cap and guzzled, carrying the bottle with him back to the bedroom.

He could hear Donna's slow, rhythmic breathing cut through the darkness. Aaron put the vodka bottle down on the nightstand and contemplated what to do next. He noticed there was also blood on his trousers. He decided it was best to get rid of his clothes, toss them in the trash. That way Aaron could avoid any questions.

He took two huge gulps of vodka as he undressed. Gathering his shirt and trousers, he walked outside to the trash. He rushed back inside and went straight to the bathroom to wash away any trace of blood that might've gotten on him.

Feeling clean, Aaron made his way to the bedroom to retrieve his bottle of vodka. "When did you start parading around outside without any clothes on?"

Aaron failed to see Donna sitting there in the dark. "I thought you were asleep."

Donna turned on her lamp. "I was until you came in here making all that noise. That doesn't answer my question."

"I really didn't think about not having any clothes on until you said something about it."

"So, you go outside with no clothes on, and you think nothing of it?"

"I really didn't see it as a big deal."

"Are you alright?"

"I wish everyone would stop asking me that question. Why wouldn't I be alright?" Had she been awake long enough to have seen his clothes?

"You come in here, remove all your clothes, and go outside to the trashcan butt naked. That doesn't make sense."

"I was changing the toner in the copy machine at work, and it got all over my clothes. Totally ruined them."

Donna eyed her husband suspiciously.

"What?"

"You're acting really weird."

"I think you are making something out of nothing." Aaron crawled into bed. "I'm fine."

Donna watched him closely.

"I'm serious. Now, can you turn off the light so we can go to sleep?"

As Donna reached over to turn off the lamp, Aaron noticed there were remnants of blood under his fingernails.

SIFTING THROUGH THE CHAOS

The flare from the muzzle of Nora's gun flashed before Aaron's eyes, as he eased himself into the bathtub. Images of Robert on the concrete in a pool of blood, repeated over and over again. To witness Robert getting up and driving away as if nothing had happened was surreal. The way he nonchalantly said, "See you tomorrow, Aaron," and winked was frightening.

After making an extra effort to scrub under his nails, Aaron climbed out of the shower. He dried off, hoping to be out of the house by the time Donna awoke. Any plans of leaving undetected were dashed when he opened the door and saw Donna standing there with his bloody clothes from the night before.

"What is this? It does not look like toner to me," she said.

There was no explanation that would make sense. How could he tell her he witnessed a murder, but there was no cause for alarm because there was no body? The dead guy actually got up and drove away. Nobody in their right mind would believe that.

"I had assumed you were having an affair. I mean our

marriage hasn't been rock-solid lately. I know it sounds cliché, but I figured maybe you had gotten your lover's lipstick on your collar. Or you knew I might detect the scent of another woman's perfume on your clothes. What I didn't expect was to find bloody clothes," she said.

"I don't know what you want me to say."

"I want you to tell me the truth! How about we start there? I seriously doubt this is your blood since I don't see any scrapes or cuts on you. The question then becomes, whose blood, is it?"

"You would not believe me if I told you." Aaron walked past Donna into the bedroom.

"Try me!"

"Donna, I don't have time for this. I need to get ready for work."

"Work! It's Saturday! You're going to work on a Saturday?" Did you forget today was Saturday?"

"I know it is Saturday!"

"You're not going nowhere until you tell me whose blood this is on your clothes."

"What does it matter whose blood that is? I hit a deer last night, okay! How about that? Does that satisfy you?"

"You hit a deer driving home from work. If so, why isn't there any damage to the car?"

Donna grabbed Aaron by the arm. "Do you take me for a fool, Aaron? You are not going anywhere until you tell me whose blood this is on your clothes! What did you do?"

Aaron yanked free. "I don't have time for this! I gotta go!" Aaron got dressed and prepared to leave.

"No! You're not leaving!" Donna blocked his path to the door.

"Move out of my way, Donna! I do not have time for this."

"No! I will not!"

"Donna, I don't have time for this!" Donna refused to

budge. Sensing he had no other choice, Aaron pushed her aside.

Donna screamed after Aaron as he walked out the door, only to be greeted by Detectives Mourning and Smith climbing out of an unmarked patrol car. "Hey, doc, did we catch you at a bad time?" asked Detective Mourning.

"I can't talk to you guys right now. I am on my way to work,"

"On a Saturday?" asked Detective Smith. "You're really dedicated to your job."

"I am a busy man. There are issues at work that require my attention."

"Yeah, tell me about it." Detective Mourning looked at Donna and smiled. "It appears there are a few issues here at home that need your attention as well. Not to mention, the few issues we would like to discuss with you. We need to talk to you about a double homicide last night."

Detective Mourning waved to Donna. "Hello, Mrs. Langford." Donna remained silent. She kept Aaron's clothes hidden from view.

"Wow, that's rude. She didn't even wave back. She doesn't look too happy," said Detective Smith.

"Is everything okay? We didn't mean to interrupt your little family dispute," said Detective Mourning.

"Everything is fine."

Detective Smith eyed the garden. "Wow! The garden looks immaculate. Especially that little patch of dirt."

"Yeah, Donna has taken up gardening."

"I didn't notice it the last time we were here. Why is she gardening in that one particular spot?" Detective Smith said.

"All bullshit aside, we really do need to talk with you. You're going to need to fit us into your busy schedule, it being Saturday and all. Now, we can do this inconspicuously, or we can cuff you and make a scene," said Detective Mourning.

Detective Mourning looked over at his partner. "You like how I threw that fancy word in there? Inconspicuously. I thought the doctor might appreciate the touch."

"I'll be back!" Aaron said, looking at Donna.

Donna replied with a simple nod of her head.

"We want to talk to your husband for a little bit, Mrs. Langford. That's all," said Detective Smith.

"We'll have him back home before dinner," added Detective Mourning.

Donna stood there solemnly as Aaron was led to the police car and driven off. As the car drove away, Aaron noticed a small shovel planted in the garden, and he wondered why Donna only tended to that tiny patch of dirt.

THE INQUISITION

At the precinct, the detectives put Aaron in a room equipped with a table and a chair. A closed-circuit camera monitored his every move.

An hour passed before Detectives Mourning and Smith returned. Detective Smith was the first to speak. "Sorry for keeping you waiting, Dr. Langford. We needed to go over a few things before talking with you."

"Why did you drag me down here?"

"Why don't you let us ask the questions?" Detective Mourning asked.

"I think I have a right to know why I'm being detained."

"You are not being detained, Dr. Langford," said Detective Smith.

"Then what do you call it? You place me in a room, lock the door, and tell me to stay put until the two of you return. In the meantime, I can't leave. I don't have the key to the door. Do you have the key? Because I sure in hell don't. I would say that sounds like I'm being detained."

"We want to ask you a few questions about your where-abouts last night," said Detective Smith.

A nervous giggle escaped Aaron. The mere mention of the night before brought forth images of Robert's vacant eyes staring back at him.

"What's so funny?" Detective Mourning asked.

"You're kidding, right?"

"Does this man look familiar to you?" Detective Smith slid a picture across the table.

Aaron took a look at the photo. It was Robert. His lifeless eyes gazed into the camera. He had a bullet hole in his head. "Yeah, that is Robert Klein. He is a colleague of mine at the university."

"Well, a campus security guard found Mr. Klein, along with another campus security guard by the name of Enrique Jimenez, died last night in the university's South Campus parking garage. Both men had been shot in the head at point blank range with what we surmise to be a .38 caliber pistol from a shell casing we found," continued Detective Smith.

Detective Smith slid another photo across the table. It was a picture of the security guard. Like Robert, he too had a single shot to the head.

"This doesn't bother you, Dr. Langford? You looked at these photos and didn't even flinch. You don't seem too surprised to see your coworker dead," said Detective Mourning.

"I'm a doctor, detective. I've seen dead bodies before."

"Or you already knew he was dead," Detective Mourning replied.

"If you say so."

"We know you were in the parking garage last night. We have security camera footage showing your car leaving the parking garage at 10:27 last night. Why were you at work so late on a Friday night?" asked Detective Smith.

"I was examining lab results. I didn't know working late on a Friday was a crime."

Detective Mourning cleared his throat. "Let me guess, you've been putting in more hours since your two children disappeared?"

"Yeah, I have. Is there something wrong with that?" Aaron asked. "Tell me, detectives, how is the investigation into my children's disappearance going? Are you two the only detectives working the case? Because I'm starting to wonder if the two of you lack the capability to find my children, judging by the way you are constantly harassing me."

Detective Mourning glared at Aaron. "Among many other things, we've also taken an interest in this double homicide."

"I hope you are showing the same amount of interest in finding Asher and Imani."

"We'll brief you on our progress regarding that investigation after we're done here," said Detective Smith.

"I seriously doubt you were examining lab results last night," said Detective Mourning.

"How would you know? And if you're so certain you know what I was doing last night, detective, please tell me."

The furrows in Detective Mourning's forehead grew deeper. "What if I told you we have footage of you entering the parking garage and going to your car on the third level at 10:00? We also got footage of Robert Klein entering the parking ramp at roughly 10:09 and exiting the stairwell at level three, the same level you had exited earlier. At 10:18, we have tape of a campus security guard entering the building and, as you guessed, he, too, exits the stairwell at level three. The security officer, Mr. Jimenez, radioed into command that the security cameras had stopped working on the third level of the parking garage, and he was going to check 'em out.

"Now, like my partner, Detective Smith, here said, you

exited the building nine minutes after guard Jimenez arrived. Dr. Klein and the campus security officer are not seen leaving the parking ramp any time after that. Both men are last seen entering the parking ramp and exiting the stairwell on the third level. Only you are seen exiting the parking garage. No one else was seen entering or exiting the parking ramp for almost twenty minutes after that. Not until campus security comes to check on why the security guard, Jimenez, is not responding to their calls. It is then when the bodies of Dr. Robert Klein and Enrique Jimenez are discovered."

"That is not true. Robert Klein left the parking garage during that time."

"Did you hear me? Campus security found his body. How could he have left if he looked like this?" said Detective Mourning, pointing to the picture. "At least you're admitting he was there."

"I saw him, we exchanged pleasantries, then he left."

"The problem with your story is that the surveillance cameras on the third level of the parking garage were disabled at the time this supposedly took place, thus, making it impossible for anyone in the security command center, or the parking garage office to see what happened, or for us to corroborate your story. There is no footage or use of his key pass to exit the parking ramp," said Detective Smith.

Detective Smith continued. "It was like Dr. Klein and the security officer had stepped into a black hole. They disappeared for over half an hour."

"The killer crudely tried to conceal their bodies in between two parked cars," said Detective Mourning.

Did I kill Robert and the campus security guard?

"Honestly, I'm trying to understand what any of this has to do with me. You and I both know everything you said to me is circumstantial. Anybody could have been in that parking garage waiting for Robert. Like I said, Robert was a colleague of mine. We did not interact outside of work. There was someone else in the parking garage at that time as well."

"Who else was there?" asked Detective Smith.

"A gentleman by the name of Nora. A well-dressed gentleman who has befriended me."

"If this Nora was there, why doesn't he show up on security cameras? At least entering or exiting the building?" questioned Detective Mourning.

"I don't know. It's possible he didn't leave the parking ramp."

"We scoured that parking ramp and the surrounding area searching for the killer. We've checked the surveillance footage of all levels of the parking garage, and there is no sign of no one else besides you, Dr. Klein, and security guard Jimenez. As I said, you enter the parking garage at 10:00. Dr. Klein enters the parking ramp at 10:09. Jimenez enters the parking garage at 10:18. Then you are exiting the parking ramp at 10:27. No one else enters or leaves the garage," said Detective Mourning.

"My question is, why would somebody tamper with the security cameras unless they intended on committing a crime?" asked Detective Smith.

Should I tell them I witnessed Nora kill Robert? Yet, does that mean I killed the security guard?

No, I need to keep it together. That can't be it. It can't be.

"If you ask me, I think what happened was that the perpetrator intended to kill Dr. Klein, but it went south. The security guard must've walked in on the murder, and the perp, in his haste, panicked and put a bullet in the security guard's head as well. Is that how it went down, doc?" Detective Mourning asked.

"How am I supposed to know? Like I told you, I wasn't

there. Nor was I the only person in the parking ramp," said Aaron.

"Right, a guy named Nora was there. Doesn't it sound odd to you that a man named Nora does not show up anywhere on the security cameras?" asked Detective Mourning.

"I assure you he was there."

"I bet you do," said Detective Mourning. "It strikes me as odd that it is your co-worker, Robert Klein, who is murdered. Your friend, Mr. Otis Thomas, told us that he had mentioned to you that Mr. Klein had been questioned by us regarding our investigation into your missing children."

"Are you implying that I killed Robert because he had spoken to the police?"

Did I?

"I don't know, you tell us?" asked Detective Smith.

"I've told the two of you everything."

"I surely hope so because you can rest assured we will be looking into your story," Detective Mourning said.

"Go right ahead. I take it I am free to go?"

"Not so fast," said Detective Smith.

"And why not?"

"Because we still have some questions about your kids," said Detective Mourning.

"Why are we continually rehashing this? Instead of asking me the same questions repeatedly, the two of you should be out there trying to find my children."

Detective Mourning looked at Aaron and smirked. "We'll ask you the same damn question over and over again a thousand times, a thousand different ways, if necessary, until we get the right answer."

"Oh, is that how it's done here? You manufacture evidence?" Aaron said.

Detective Mourning stared at Aaron. "That would be against the law."

"That's enough," Detective Smith said. "If I recall, you told Detective Mourning, the night your children disappeared, that it was no different than any other night." Detective Smith reached over and grabbed the picture of Robert Klien on the table.

"Correct."

"The kids went upstairs to bed at their usual time. You did not hear anything unusual or see anything out of the ordinary?" Detective Smith said, folding the picture.

"Nope."

"Are you certain?"

"Yes. Why?"

"Well, when we questioned your wife, she told us that the two of you had reconciled sometime during that week. She said the two of you had an argument pertaining to her wanting to return to Washington, D.C. She said she had caught you drinking the night before. You are a recovering alcoholic, am I correct?" Detective Smith asked, carefully putting a crease in the photo.

"Yes, I am. I assume you already knew that. For your information, I did have a sip of wine. That was the night Imani scared us. I fail to see what this has to do with anything," Aaron said.

"What did your daughter do?" asked Detective Mourning.

"She claimed to have seen a ghost."

"Was this the first time she had seen a ghost?" asked Detective Smith, fumbling with the photo.

"Who knows? My daughter is six."

"Let me ask you something, Dr. Langford. Did you resent your wife for making you stop drinking?" Detective Mourning asked.

"What? No!"

Detective Mourning pressed. "Are you sure?"

"Yes. Why would you ask me such a stupid question? I wanted to stop drinking."

"We want to know if there would be a reason for you to lash out at her," Detective Smith said.

"Are you insinuating that I would kill my children to punish my wife?"

"People have killed for far less, believe me. Anyway, we didn't say you killed them. Honestly, why are you so certain they're dead?" asked Detective Mourning.

"Now you're trying to twist my words."

"Are we?" Detective Mourning asked. "You're the one who brought it up. You've readily admitted to being in the vicinity of the murder of Dr. Robert Klein and security guard Enrique Jimenez. Who is to say you wouldn't kill your kids?"

"People were on the Titanic when it sank. That does not mean they steered the boat into the iceberg. What happened to Robert and the security guard has nothing to do with me."

"Why doesn't it? Tell me, isn't it odd that Dr. Klein turns up dead after cooperating with us regarding the investigation into your children's disappearance?"

"Where are you going with this?"

"Let me make it easy for you. Your wife threatened to return to Washington, D.C. before Asher and Imani disappeared," Detective Mourning said.

"Yeah. What does that have to do with anything?"

Detective Smith made two more distinct folds in the picture of Robert Klein. "What he's saying is, you sought to hurt your wife for threatening to leave. She wanted to go back to Washington, D.C, and take the kids with her. She was going to return to D.C., with the kids and, most importantly, she was going to force you to make a choice between either your job or your family. What better way to stop her from leaving than for the kids to suddenly go missing? She wouldn't dare leave Seattle until they were found."

"Or maybe your kids had a secret they were hiding, and you had mentioned it to Mr. Klein in passing?" Detective Mourning asked.

"You guys are seriously reaching. Are you serious?"

"Very serious. Did you ever sleep with your daughter?" asked Detective Smith.

"I've told you, whenever Imani had nightmares, I would lay in bed with her to comfort her."

"When he says sleep with her, he doesn't mean did you *sleep* in her bed. Did you molest your daughter?" said Detective Mourning.

"You are way out of line, detective."

"We told you we found your hair in your daughter's bed. What we didn't tell you was that the hair was a pubic hair," said Detective Smith.

"What? That can't be. You've made a mistake!"

"That's what I thought. So, I had the guys in the lab recheck the sample. Guess what? They told me there was a 99% percent probability that the pubic hair was yours," said Detective Smith. He made one last fold in the picture.

"I don't know how that can be."

"We tried to approach this from every possible angle. After thinking it through, we came to two conclusions. The first one is that while you slept with your daughter, strands of your pubic hair got in the bed. Innocent enough. That led us to another conclusion. You either had to be wearing underwear or nothing at all when you slept with your daughter," said Detective Mourning.

"How can you jump to such a conclusion based on a sole pubic hair? I'm offended you would even suggest that I had any inappropriate behavior with my daughter! What is it? Are the two of you so incompetent at doing your job that you can't find a suspect, so you readily blame the parents?"

"We're not talking about your wife, doc. We're talking about you. She does not appear to be the problem," said Detective Mourning.

"Other than a pubic hair that you found in my daughter's bed in my house, what other evidence do the two of you have of this ludicrous idea that my daughter was being molested? And like I said, that is my house! I am quite sure you can find my pubic hairs in the most inappropriate places - even the kitchen! My wife and I christened the kitchen when we moved in. Plus, my wife washes everyone's clothes together. You guys got to do better than this."

If I did this, I would be a truly hideous person.

"If you ask me, this is the most obvious example of the two of you throwing shit against the wall and hoping something sticks. Wouldn't there have been traces of my daughter's blood, bodily fluids, or my semen on the sheets?"

Detective Smith looked at his folded piece of paper and smiled. "So, you're saying you don't know how a pubic hair showed up in your daughter's bed?"

Aaron shook his head in disgust. "I can't believe this is why you guys brought me down here!"

"Answer the fucking question!" demanded Detective Mourning.

"No! I don't know! There! Now, do you have any more questions?"

"Why didn't you tell us about the divination tray?" Detective Mourning asked.

"What?"

"The divination tray. When I spoke to you that afternoon, I asked you, has anyone brought anything into your home that may have been peculiar?" Detective Mourning continued.

"So."

"Why didn't you tell us about the divination tray?" Detective Smith asked.

"I didn't see how it had anything to do with my children being missing."

Detective Mourning glared at Aaron. "Do you know?"

"I don't understand why we are talking about a divination tray when my kids could be out there somewhere in danger."

Detective Mourning lunged across the table. "You're so full of shit!"

"Okay, why don't we collect ourselves before everybody gets carried away, here?" said Detective Smith, restraining his partner.

Detective Mourning slammed his fist on the table. "You really are a crazy son of a bitch if you think for one minute, we're going to buy your 'I'm clueless' alibi! Most likely, you washed the sheets! I bet you molested your daughter and killed your son because he found out! They were probably going to tell your wife! You probably slit your wrist because you could not live with the guilt! You sick fuck!"

"Keep right on pulling accusations out of your ass, detective! The two of you need to take this good cop/bad cop routine on the road. It's worthy of an Oscar."

Detective Mourning inched closer towards Aaron and smiled. "You don't have a clue what I am capable of."

"Don't worry; he'll not get away," said Detective Smith, scribbling something on the photo. "Why don't you go grab a cup of coffee or something? I can finish up here."

"Yeah, why don't you go get a cup of coffee and cool your jets," Aaron said.

Detective Mourning glared at Aaron. "All this can possibly

go away if you tell us where the divination tray is," he said, as he walked out of the room.

"What is he talking about?"

With Detective Mourning gone, Detective Smith took a seat next to Aaron. "Dr. Langford, do you have a clue what they do to individuals who molest children in prison? Let's just say they do the most heinous of things to them. In most cases, the guards look the other way. Hell, the guards might set the whole thing up. Why? Because there is nothing both convicts and COs can't stand more than a pedophile.

"In prison, there is one thing both correctional officers and convicts have in common: They have families. They have kids. Sadly, I don't think you're going to find your kids."

Detective Smith looked at Aaron and smiled. He picked up the photo and unfurled the wings of a paper airplane. Tossing the plane over towards Aaron, he said, "You're free to go, Dr. Langford." When Detective Smith left the room, Aaron looked over at the paper plane to see the words, "U killed them" written across Robert Klein's face.

THE COOKOUT

Aaron smelled the smoke as soon as he got out of the Uber. Plumes of smoke rose from behind the house. He wandered past the garden to the gate. As he rounded the corner, he found Donna sitting in a lawn chair next to the grill. Beside her sat a container of lighter fluid and a bottle of wine.

She sipped from her wine glass as Aaron walked towards her. She watched him closely as the flames leaped from the grill. When he was close enough, Aaron could see his bloody shirt and trousers in the fire.

A SECRET IN THE GARDEN

E ven after being named as a person of interest in the murders of Robert Klein and Enrique Jimenez, there was no mention of Aaron's bloody clothes. As expected, the university quickly distanced itself from him. He was immediately placed on leave pending investigation. It would be only a matter of time before the university terminated him. Aaron would lose access to all his data and research.

He was a pariah. Friends and colleagues no longer fielded his calls. Even calls to Otis automatically rolled over to voicemail. Seeking to avoid shame and public humiliation, Aaron became a recluse. Occasionally, he snuck out of the house to venture down to The Arboretum, but that was about it. At The Arboretum, Aaron was allowed to escape all the noise and enjoy a moment of peace. One evening, upon returning home from the park, he observed a commotion outside his house. The police had cordoned off the street. Officers moved expeditiously in and out of his home.

To avoid being recognized, Aaron pulled the hood of his

windbreaker down over his face. He weaved his way through the crowd, attempting to get a closer look at what was going on.

He overheard someone say, "They're looking for the bodies."

They found the bodies.

That's when Aaron saw police officers digging in the garden. He was curious to know what might be of interest to them. Aaron looked into the sea of faces hoping to find Donna. Not seeing her, Aaron assumed she must be inside the house, so he walked past the police barricade towards his home.

"Excuse me! Sir, can you please stay behind the yellow tape!" an officer shouted.

"That's my house!"

The officer examined Aaron closely, then smiled. "I thought this place looked familiar," he said. "I told you I'll be seeing you around."

Aaron recognized the officer. He was the patrol officer that followed him home from Mont's. "I just want to know if my wife is in the house," Aaron said.

"That is not my concern. My job is to make sure you stay behind that yellow line and do not interfere with the investigation."

"I just want to know if my wife is in there!"

"I don't know, nor do I care. My job is to make sure you stay behind the police line!"

Refusing to listen, Aaron tried to brush past the officer. The officer quickly restrained him. "Are you deaf? I said you gotta stay behind the yellow tape!"

"Get your hands off me! That's my house."

"Is there going to be a problem?" The officer placed his hand on the butt of his gun.

"That's my house!"

"I heard you the first time. Regardless of that being your house, I cannot let you pass."

"What are you doing?" someone in the crowd yelled.

Aaron turned around to see Donna. Snatching his arm away from the police officer, he hurried over to his wife. "Are you okay? I was worried about you."

"I'm fine. I see you came just in time to see them tear our house apart."

Immediately, they were blinded by the cameras and bright lights. A microphone was thrust in Aaron's face. "Doctor Langford, would you like to say something in regard to the allegations?" Aaron slapped the mic out of the way.

"Why won't you answer the question, doctor?" another reporter asked.

Aaron and Donna tried to walk away but were cornered. "What are they doing?" Aaron asked.

"They're asking questions," Donna said.

"Not them! The police?"

"They're collecting evidence."

"Collecting evidence? For what?"

"Well, I guess if you're a person of interest in a double homicide, the police would like to have proof on whether or not you committed the crime," Donna said.

"Why did you let them in?"

"What was I supposed to do? They have a warrant. They're the police. I basically had two choices. Either I could've stood by and watched them trash our house, or I could've endured additional embarrassment by being arrested and paraded out in front of our neighbors and news crews in handcuffs. Since I'm standing here with you, which choice do you think I made?"

"Didn't you at least ask someone on what grounds they had to invade our home?"

"Aaron, did you hear me? They have a warrant! What am I

supposed to do? Ask for the authenticity of the warrant? Besides, the officers barged into the house and escorted me out."

"Did you ask to see the warrant?"

"No, I did not."

"Well, I'm not going to stand here and take their word for it!" Aaron pushed beyond the barrier again.

"Aaron, no! Don't do this!" Donna screamed.

"I thought I told you that you cannot go beyond the police line!" the officer yelled.

"I want to talk to whoever is in charge! I want to see the search warrant!" said Aaron.

The officer stared at Aaron briefly before calling over another officer. "Trevor! Go tell him he wants to see the warrant."

Satisfied, Aaron moved back behind the yellow tape.

"Dr. Langford, did you kill your colleague, Dr. Robert Klein and security guard, Enrique Jimenez?" a reporter yelled.

Aaron ignored the reporter. Soon he saw Detective Mourning sauntering over. "Why are you in my house confiscating my belongings?"

"Because this says I can." The detective held up a search warrant.

Aaron snatched the warrant out of the detective's hand.

"If you can read there, my friend, it says the Seattle Police Department has the right to search the premises unencumbered. I like that legal mumble jumble bullshit. Who the fuck says 'unencumbered' other than a lawyer with a stick up his ass?"

Aaron skimmed the document. "This is bullshit!" He crumpled up the warrant and threw it at the detective's feet.

Detective Mourning looked at the wad of paper and smiled. "That was your copy."

"Kiss my ass!"

Detective Mourning chuckled. "You first."

"Come on, Aaron, let's go," Donna said.

Aaron looked over at the officers in the garden. "What is that all about? Why are they digging up my garden?" he asked.

"Well, after you mentioned your wife has suddenly taken an interest in gardening, Detective Smith was curious as to know why. I mean, it is a little odd for such a small part of the garden to be so well kept and the rest to be overgrown with weeds.

"Don't worry, we haven't found much other than a dead cat. Are you aware you are not allowed to bury pets in your yard within the city limits? Don't worry; I'll overlook it," Detective Mourning said.

"And my personal belongings?" Aaron asked.

"Concerning your personal belongings, those items are vital in the department's ongoing investigation into the disappearance of your children as well as anything that might tie you to Dr. Klein and Mr. Jimenez's murders."

"I fail to see how my laptop and personal computer are important?"

"We will keep the items we feel are relevant to the investigation. All other personal belongings will be returned to you once we've closed the case. However, we still haven't found the divination tray yet. Why don't you tell us where it is."

"What does the divination tray have to do with anything?" Detective Mourning appeared irritated.

"Where am I supposed to go while you ransack my house?"

"That's your business. If you continue to harass me or my fellow officers, I'm going to charge you with obstruction of justice, and you can sit in the back of a patrol car if you like."

"Come on, Donna let's go!" Aaron reached to grab Donna's hand only to have her pull away.

Detective Mourning laughed. "Seems like there is trouble in paradise. By the way, we haven't found your friend, Nora. You might want to call him and tell him to come into the precinct for questioning. In the meantime, don't wander off too far. I'll be watching you." With that said, Detective Mourning walked back toward the house.

Aaron turned to Donna. "What is your problem?"

"I don't want to talk about it right now. I want to get out of here." She forced her way past the reporters and the cameras.

"What is wrong with you?"

"Do you have the keys to the car?"

"Yeah."

"Give them to me!"

"Here."

Donna waded through the throng to the car. She unlocked the doors and quickly climbed inside.

"Will you tell me what is wrong with you?"

"You are what is wrong with me! You! You've brought this on us!"

"You're blaming me for this?"

"Yes!"

"I can't believe you," Aaron said.

"Believe it! What was the detective talking about when he said you told him I've been out in the garden? I haven't touched that garden! I hate gardening! You've been the one out there fiddling around! And where is the divination tray?"

Aaron paused. "I've been out in the garden?"

"Don't tell me you don't recall how eager you were to plant tulip bulbs for the spring?"

"What?"

Donna shook her head in disgust. "Judging by the expression on your face, I'm to assume not."

Donna started the car.

"Dr. Langford, did you kill Dr. Robert Klein and security guard Jimenez?" a reporter shouted.

"How about you, Mrs. Langford, would you like to say something?" another reporter yelled. "This is your chance to tell your side of the story."

Aaron opened the glove compartment to grab a tissue to wipe his runny nose. He immediately noticed Papa Joe's .38 caliber pistol. Shocked, Aaron slammed the glove compartment shut.

"What?" Donna asked.

"Nothing."

"Whatever." As Donna navigated the car out of the driveway, she looked over at Aaron and asked, "Did you kill my cat?"

CLEANING UP THE MESS

How did I kill Socrates?

I was covered in mud that one night. That's the night I must have buried him.

Did I use Papa Joe's .38?

How did Papa Joe's gun get in the glove compartment?

I think I killed Robert and the security guard. They were killed with a .38 caliber gun.

I must've used Papa Joe's gun.

Security cameras only catch me on the third floor of the parking garage. There is no sign of Nora.

Should I confess to killing Robert and the security guard?

Maybe I should get rid of the gun? If I get rid of the gun, then there is no proof that I killed anyone.

Yeah, I'll get rid of the gun!

THE ACCUSED

Clearly, breakfast was a trap to lure Aaron into a conversation he would've otherwise avoided. "Set the table," Donna told him. "I'm glad you're awake; we need to talk."

"What do we need to talk about?"

"Plenty."

Donna sat down. "I miss the old Aaron. I want to know what happened to him."

"What do you mean?"

"I mean the man I married. I see no resemblance of that man sitting here."

"I don't know what to make of that comment."

"Well, I feel like I'm living with a complete stranger." Aaron didn't disagree. He just felt more like the stranger was Donna.

"You are very much always on edge. Anything I say to you is met with anger. Or you appear out of it. You have trouble recalling where you've been. Or what you've said. You don't remember being out in the garden. I assume your sudden interest in gardening was to ensure I never found out you buried Socrates out there."

I don't recall killing Socrates. How did I kill him?

"It's frightening for me to imagine what you might've done during those times you don't recall. Have you thought about what Detectives Mourning and Smith said about you and Robert Klein being in the parking garage at the same time?"

"I told the detectives I saw Robert in the parking garage that night."

"Do you think you might have blacked out?"

"What are you trying to say? Are you sitting here calling me a murderer?"

"I'm not saying that."

"Oh, you're not? Then what are you saying?"

"I'm suggesting that maybe you blacked out and have no recollection of what happened."

"So, I'm crazy now?"

"Sometimes I don't know who you are. It's like you are not even here. Like you're in your own little world. Sometimes, you fly off the handle for no reason whatsoever."

"That is not true!"

"See! Look at you! You're in a rage right now. You act like I'm not concerned about Asher and Imani's wellbeing, too. What if they never come back? That is a reality we must face. What happens to us? What do we do?"

Mentioning Asher and Imani agitated Aaron even further. Thoughts of Asher's health and the fear of a crisis plagued him since their disappearance. "I don't have time for this! Asher and Imani are coming back! I don't want to have this discussion," Aaron said, getting up from the table.

"Where are you going? You don't have nowhere to be."

"I don't want to talk anymore! And for your information,

Asher and Imani are coming back!" Aaron marched out of the kitchen.

"Where are you going?"

"Out!"

"In your underwear?"

Aaron realized he had not put on any clothes. "Why do you care?"

"You are my husband. That's why I care. Aaron, I think you need help. You need to see someone."

"What do you want to hear, Donna? That I think I killed my kids! Not to mention a colleague and a security guard! That I think I am a monster, and I'm not sure if I killed them or not?"

"If you feel this way you need to check yourself in, so you can sort out these thoughts."

"You're kidding, right? We've already tried that before."

"I wish I was kidding. What can I say? I'm scared. I'm scared for you and of you. I'm scared of what is going on in your head. These thoughts. I'm scared you might've acted on these impulses and hurt someone.

"I mean, you can't tell me how you got blood on your clothes. You can't tell me how you managed to track mud into the house even though your feet and hands were covered in it. Do I have to go on for you to get the point? I cannot continue to ignore the obvious. I've reached my rope's end. I don't have it in me anymore, especially with this talk of a pubic hair being found in Imani's bed." Donna sobbed.

"Who told you that? I never mentioned anything to you about a pubic hair."

"Why does it even matter?"

"Have you been talking to Detectives Mourning and Smith? You can't possibly believe what they have cooked up?"

Donna fell silent.

"Do you?"

"What do you want me to say?"

"I want the truth!"

"Put yourself in my shoes."

"You believe them! You fucking believe I molested Imani!"

"I have a husband who thinks he is violent. Some days you spend hours on the internet researching serial killers or listening to murder podcasts trying to figure out if you share similar traits with killers rather than talking to me. You've told your best friend you've been having conversations with your late grandmother. My husband's colleague and a campus security guard are found murdered, and my husband was possibly the last person seen with them. You do the math."

Aaron had heard enough.

"Where are you going?"

"Away from here! Away from you!"

Aaron hit the front door and started running. His mind simply told his feet to run.

* * *

As if he was watching a rerun, Aaron saw patrol cars parked along the street in front of his house. He feared Donna might have done something rash in his absence, so he hurried into the house. Inside, he found Donna on the couch, distraught. He feared the detectives had found Asher and Imani, and the news was not good.

"It's okay. We got him right here," Detective Mourning said into his radio.

"What's going on?"

Both detectives were stunned to see Aaron standing there in his underwear. "Please tell me you didn't go outside in public dressed like that?" Detective Smith asked.

"You bastard! You fucking bastard! You killed them! I know that you killed them!" Donna screamed, lunging at him.

Aaron tried to fend off Donna's attack until the officers could restrain her. "What the hell are you talking about?"

"Oh, don't you play dumb with me, motherfucker! You probably killed them?" she screamed.

"What are you talking about?"

"I think she has made it clear as to what she is saying," said Detective Mourning.

"It's obvious you've told her something that's not true!"

Without warning, Aaron found himself being wrestled to the floor. "What are you doing? Let me go!"

Detective Smith planted his knee firmly into Aaron's back, pinning him to the ground. Upon cuffing him, Detective Smith lifted Aaron to his feet and whispered, "We're not going to let you close the door."

10

How did I get here? Aaron tried to retrace his steps. He wondered why he was gagged and bound to a gurney in a pink pastel room reeking of disinfectant. The soft pink coloration was intended to subdue him and make him docile. It had the direct opposite effect.

Missus Sophia Farmer, the head nurse, escorted by her enforcer, a bald, burly black orderly referred to as Mr. Wilkes, walked into the room.

"There you are," she said. She knew where he was. She had put him there.

For the short period of time, Aaron had come to stay in the psychiatric ward at Western State Hospital, he had come to know Missus Farmer quite well. Many of the patients in the ward referred to her as "Lucifer." Rather than be offended by the nickname, Missus Famer relished the title. She wore it like a badge of honor. For her, it struck the right amount of fear in the ward's patients, which in turn kept them in line. Although petite, the stringy blonde-haired woman with gray roots was quite the intimidating figure. Men twice her size cowered in her presence. All Missus Farmer had to do was glare at a person with those icy blue eyes. Those who tested her usually ended up like Aaron: gagged and bound to a hospital gurney or subjugated to more severe and sadistic punishment.

"So, have you decided to behave yourself, Dr. Langford?" Missus Farmer's voice came to Aaron in its usual coarse tone. "You're going to have to learn how we do things here at Western State." Missus Farmer's raspy voice and tar-stained teeth professed her love for cigarettes.

Aaron grunted and nodded in affirmation.

"Good. Because we don't want any more trouble out of you. Will we get any more trouble out of you?"

Aaron feverishly shook his head.

"Good. Mr. Wilkes here is going to strap you into this wheelchair so you won't do any harm to yourself or any of the other patients in the ward." Missus Farmer was so genteel it was hard to believe she was a sadist.

Of course, Aaron did not want to be confined to a wheelchair. However, it wasn't as if he had a choice. He could either be strapped to the wheelchair or pinned to the gurney. The wheelchair was definitely the lesser of the two evils. At least the wheelchair offered him some sense of mobility.

Missus Farmer motioned her lackey, Mr. Wilkes, over towards Aaron. The orderly typically meted out Missus Farmer's punishment to her specifications. Mr. Wilkes had done three tours in Iraq. He served time as a detention center guard. Judging from his physique, there was probably a time when he'd been in tiptop shape. Aaron could envision him with a washboard stomach, barrel chest, bulging arms, and thighs the size of oil drums. The washboard stomach had given way to a gut, and his chest was most notably in need of a bra. His arms tried to maintain some semblance to their glory days.

Depending on his mood, his punishment ranged from agonizing beatings to the macabre. Having spent time detaining the mujahideen in Iraq, Mr. Wilkes was skillful in the art of using sick, demented techniques to make people comply. He was a technician at his craft. He left very little evidence on the skin. Stories of sleep deprivation, starvation, electric shock and confinement to the gurney for days on end without food were folklore in the ward.

Mr. Wilkes placed the wheelchair next to the steel gurney and looked back at Missus Farmer. Like an obedient dog, he awaited her command before proceeding.

"Now, Mr. Wilkes is going to take your gag off. I trust we will no longer hear any foul obscenities from you?" Missus Farmer asked.

Aaron nodded.

"Good. I'm a decent Christian woman, and I will not have this place turned into some house of ill repute by you, or anyone else for that matter." She gave Mr. Wilkes a nod of the head. "Go ahead, Mr. Wilkes."

The orderly violently ripped the duct tape away from Aaron's mouth. Aaron opened and closed his mouth to stretch out his jaw. "Thank you," Aaron said.

"No need to talk. I'd much rather you be as quiet as a church mouse," said Missus Farmer.

"Yes, ma'am."

Missus Farmer shot Aaron a steely glare. "Did you hear what I said? No talking. I know you are here for a brief stay. However, what you fail to realize is that I determine whether your stay is short or extended. And believe me, I can make this place far worse than any prison. Do you understand?"

Aaron nodded.

"Good, now zip it!" The nurse brought her hand to her mouth and turned an imaginary key. Then, she tossed it over her shoulder. "Finish untying him," she ordered. Mr. Wilkes finished untying the restraints around Aaron's wrists and ankles.

Enjoying the brief moment of freedom, Aaron flexed and stretched his limbs. "That's enough. Get in the wheelchair," commanded the hag.

Aaron could have easily gotten into the wheelchair on his own. All the same, Mr. Wilkes wanted Aaron to know that, although he was Missus Farmer's flunky, he had the latitude to inflict pain when he saw fit. So, he slammed Aaron down into the chair. He smiled, obviously pleased with himself.

"Careful; we don't want to bruise him or leave any visible marks. He's not our property yet," Missus Farmer said.

"Yes, ma'am," replied Mr. Wilkes. He quickly tied Aaron's arms and legs to the chair.

"Not too tight. We don't want the restraints cutting into his skin." Mr. Wilkes made sure the straps didn't bruise the skin.

"Do we need to gag you?" Mrs. Farmer asked.

Aaron shook his head.

"Can you behave?"

Aaron nodded his head.

Missus Farmer smiled, exposing her grisly brown teeth. "You're a quick study, Dr. Langford." She turned to Mr. Wilkes. "Take him out to join the others."

Mr. Wilkes wheeled Aaron out of the room and down the hall into a much larger room where the residents of the ward were allowed to congregate. "Look who's back!" Ten shouted, as Aaron was wheeled in.

"Ten!" Mr. Wilkes yelled. Ten ran to the nearest corner.

Ten was the reason why Aaron had spent an entire day in the pink room in the first place. His maniacal badgering had become too much. His swollen lip and black eye were testament to how far he had pushed Aaron.

Ten's real name was Edward J. Lutz. To the naked eye, he appeared meek, obedient, almost docile. His scrawny frame and unruly, blonde mop gave off the aura of a passive, misunderstood young man. Beneath that exterior beat the heart of a monster. Ten suffered from so many things. His one habit that drove everyone absolutely crazy was a compulsive disorder centered around numbers called Arithmomania. He was particularly fascinated with the number ten. His love for the number earned him his nickname. He counted his fingers, his toes, a stranger's fingers and toes, anybody's fingers and toes! He was mesmerized that every time he counted anyone's fingers or toes it would always equal ten. Sometimes he would run from one side of the room to the other shouting numbers out loud.

The fact Ten brutally murdered his mother was the reason why he was a resident at Western State. The story goes that, after a day of enduring Ten's nonstop counting, Ten's mother, Ethel Lutz, couldn't take it anymore. Taking matters into her own hands, she snuck into her son's bedroom while he slept and taped his mouth shut and bound his hands and feet to the bedposts to prevent him from wandering away while she slept. She'd been hoping for a moment of respite. Rumor had it, Ms. Lutz poured herself a glass of wine, read a couple of chapters from her favorite novel, and fell asleep. When Ten awoke in the middle of the night to find himself gagged and bound to his bed, he went berserk. After hours of struggling to break free, he was finally able to loosen his restraints. Seeking revenge for his mother's misdeed, Ten went into the kitchen, grabbed a knife, and proceeded to his mother's bedroom where he murdered her in cold blood.

The next day, when Ethel Lutz did not return her daughter's phone calls, the Olympia police department conducted a welfare check. When one officer saw a bloody knife on the kitchen counter, the police kicked in the door. Inside, they found Ten sitting in his bedroom bathed in blood, counting Cheerios in lots of ten. When the police found Ethel Lutz, her body had been brutally mutilated. She was non-recognizable. Ten had stabbed his mother two hundred times. The coroner was only able to identify her through dental records. When the judge asked Ten why he stabbed his mother so many times, Ten stated that he had stabbed her ten times for every finger and every toe she had denied him from counting. Although Ten was able to avoid the death penalty, he was not able to elude Missus Farmer and Western State.

Mr. Wilkes wheeled Aaron over in front of the window overlooking the grounds. The TV played in the background: *Jeopardy*.

"Greek Mythology for four hundred. He is the son of Cronus and Rhea. He is also the brother to Zeus, Poseidon, Demeter, Hera, and Hestia," stated the moderator.

Aaron gazed out of the window, hoping to return to the King County jail soon after the state-mandated psychiatric evaluation. It was the psychiatrist's assessment of Aaron's mental state at University Hospital after his failed suicide attempt that convinced the judge to send him to Western State.

After placing Aaron by the window, Mr. Wilkes took his post by the door, as usual. Without fail, Ten's monotonous counting began, "One, two, three, four, five, six, seven, eight, nine, ten! Isn't it amazing! No matter how many times I count my fingers, they always equal ten! Every time! You know what will really blow your mind?" Ten asked, as if making a new discovery. "If I count my toes, they equal ten, too!"

"Hey, calm the fuck down!" barked Mr. Wilkes. Ten slinked away, cursing the orderly under his breath.

As soon as Mr. Wilkes's attention was diverted, Ten's repetitive counting blared throughout the room again. "One, two, three ..."

It went on like that all day. Every day. Even at night, Aaron could hear Ten's continuous counting through the vents. His mindless chatter dripping down on him. If Aaron was not crazy when he entered Western State, he would be certifiably insane upon leaving. As weird as it sounded, Aaron couldn't wait for the state's psychiatric evaluation to be done so he could leave that godforsaken place. Even if the psychiatrist's evaluation meant Aaron's next stop was Shelton or Monroe, he would much rather be in prison than Western State.

Aaron sat in the wheelchair staring out the window, trying his best to beat back boredom.

"What are you daydreaming about?" Ten whispered. Aaron could feel his breath on his earlobe.

"Get the fuck away from me!" Aaron warned.

Ten recoiled, fearing Aaron might be able to break free and strike him. When he saw the restraints holding, Ten seized upon the opportunity to exact revenge for Aaron laying his hands on him earlier. Ten looked over at Mr. Wilkes to make sure he was preoccupied before licking Aaron's ear.

"What the fuck are you doing, you fucking lunatic?" Aaron yelled. Spittle dripped from his ear onto his shoulder.

Ten cackled. "I see Missus Farmer has you on a short leash. Serves you right." Ten glanced over at Mr. Wilkes to make sure he wasn't looking. Certain the coast was clear, Ten slapped Aaron across the back of the neck. It was loud enough to catch the attention of everyone nearby.

"Ahhh! You motherfucker!" Aaron screamed.

"I got your motherfucker right here!" Ten said, grabbing his crotch. "And your fucker mother told me she likes it!"

Enraged, Aaron tried to break free.

Ten scurried behind another one of the ward's patients known as Mouse. He was a big muscular man built like a line-backer, but he had the IQ of a five-year-old. Ten peered at

Aaron from behind Mouse. Seeing the straps on the wheelchair had held, Ten continued with his torment. Again, Ten scanned the room for Mr. Wilkes. Seeing the burly orderly was preoccupied, Ten ran his tongue over his cracked lips and whispered, "You're never going to get out of here. You're Missus Farmer's now." He then slapped Aaron across the neck again. This time much harder.

"Motherfucker! You better hope I do not get free!" screamed Aaron.

"Ten, what are you doing?" Mr. Wilkes asked.

"He's hitting me!" Aaron screamed.

"Ten, will you sit your retarded ass down somewhere?"

"I'm not doing nothing, boss," Ten said.

"Sit your ass down somewhere! I don't want to have to tell your dumb ass again," Mr. Wilkes told him.

"I'm toughening him up. That was for punching me in the eye," Ten said.

Aaron squirmed in his chair. "You better hope I do not get free from this wheelchair, you fucking freak!"

Ten snickered. He drew close to strike Aaron again. He was prepared to slap Aaron when he saw Mr. Wilkes watching him. Seeking to avoid Mr. Wilkes's fury, Ten smiled and placed his hand in his pocket.

"We have to play nice. The boss is watching," Ten said under his breath. "You know why I call him boss? Because he is a stupid son of a bitch. That is what a boss is backwards."

Ten smiled at Mr. Wilkes while he talked. "I mean who else is best suited to understand someone who is crazy better than a crazy person?"

"What are you talking about? Get away from me!" Aaron seethed.

"Or what are you going to do? Huh? Bite me to death?"

"Please go away!"

"You can't make me."

"Get away from me, you idiot!" Aaron yelled.

"Now, that's not nice. I'm no more an idiot than you. You haven't figured it out. We're here forever, so we might as well get along. Has it ever dawned on you how warped of a place this shithole is? Haven't you wondered why they call this place a hospital? I mean where are the doctors? Have you asked yourself that?

"Think about it. Have you seen one doctor? Doesn't that seem odd to you? Have you not asked yourself: where are the doctors? There are no doctors here trying to cure us. Have you been to one therapy session? Here you are a professed murderer, and you have not spoken to one doctor. A doctor hasn't prescribed you any medication or nothing. What the hell is that all about? Right now, you should be in a prison cell with some dude named Bubba. Even I know that."

"How many times do I have to tell you that I am not a murderer?" Aaron said.

Ten rested his elbow on Aaron's head. "Now, if that is true, then what are you doing in this place? And if you didn't kill people, then doesn't it blow your mind that someone else is out there masquerading around as you? This person looks like you, talks like you, acts like you, and kills people just like you. Weird, isn't it?" A sinister laugh leaped forth from the deranged man's mouth.

Aaron bristled. "I am not a killer."

Are you sure?

"That's not what Missus Farmer told us. She said you were sicker than all of us combined. She said you will be staying here a long time because you need her help. If there is one thing I know, what Missus Farmer says comes true. Aren't your kids missing?" Ten asked.

"That's none of your business!"

"They are, aren't they? Who do you think killed them?"

"What? They're not dead. They've run away."

"Is that what you tell yourself? What if I told you they were dead? I probably also can tell you who killed them!" Ten started clapping his hands jubilantly.

Looking over at Mr. Wilkes, he smiled. Trying his best to appear innocent, Ten whispered in Aaron's ear, "The stupid son of bitch backwards is watching us. We got to act like we're playing nicely. We don't want to be put in time out again," he teased.

Aaron looked over to see Mr. Wilkes eyeballing them. "Help me," Aaron said. Mr. Wilkes ignored him.

"See, no one cares about you here. You're one of us, now."

Suddenly, with the dexterity of a psychotic mind cluttered with incoherent thoughts, Ten catapulted into a monologue about the number ten. "Did you ever think about it? What makes something what it is? Like, why is it when I count my fingers and toes, I always get ten? Who determined that the sum of each digit on our hands and feet was going to equal the number ten? Who made up the word ten? Who determined ten was the magical number? Do you understand what I'm saying? Why isn't it eleven? Or magenta? I've always liked the color magenta."

Aaron looked at Ten in disbelief. Ten winked. "What is wrong with you?" Aaron asked.

Ten slithered up next to Aaron and said, "Nothing. Absolutely nothing is wrong with me. That's what I've been trying to tell you. What is wrong with you?"

"Ten, leave that man alone!" Mr. Wilkes screamed.

Ten scampered away. "I wasn't doing nothing, boss."

From across the room, Aaron could hear Ten counting and regurgitating mindless mathematical facts about the number ten. Aaron tried to tune him out. He tried to envision life beyond those walls, away from people like Ten.

"Dr. Langford, it appears that you have visitors," Missus Farmer said, coming into the room.

A small commotion broke out amongst the other patients at hearing the news of visitors. "Shut up!" snarled Missus Farmer.

Mr. Wilkes wheeled Aaron around to face Missus Farmer. "Now, let me remind you, Dr. Langford, it is wise that you be on your p's and q's, and it is in your best interest to be on your best behavior. Do you understand me?"

"Yes, ma'am."

"Good. Take him downstairs," she ordered.

Aaron was wheeled out of the room and down the hall to an old, decrepit elevator that jerked violently when it stopped and started. It was much faster to take the stairs than ride that old rickety lift. Since Aaron was strapped to a wheelchair, he decided the stairs were not an option. The elevator jerked downward to the visitor's lounge on the first floor. Aaron hoped Donna had come to take him home. He had not seen or heard from her since coming to Western. He could assume that she was trying her best to get him out of there. Aaron had tried calling her several times to no avail.

The elevator jerked to a halt, and the doors squeaked open. Mr. Wilkes pushed Aaron out of the elevator and down a long, narrow corridor towards a door at the end of a hall. Unfortunately, when Mr. Wilkes opened the door, Donna was not there. Instead, it was Detective Mourning and Detective Smith.

"What's up, doc? ¿Qué pasa? What's wrong? You don't look too happy to see us," said Detective Mourning.

Detective Smith chimed in. "It looks like life on the funny farm is becoming of you," he said, referring to Aaron's leg and arm restraints.

"Serves him right since he's pretending to be crazy. If you ask me, strapping his ass to a wheelchair is fitting. All we're missing is the straitjacket. What they really should do is strap some electrodes to his balls and run a thousand volts of electricity through them until they shrivel up like raisins," said Detective Smith.

"Some straight Abu Ghraib shit," laughed Detective Mourning.

"Yeah, we need to do the same shit to him we did to those A-rabs over in Iraq. Fry their peckers right off," said Detective Smith.

Hearing of Iraq, Mr. Wilkes perked up. "Where did you fight in Iraq?"

"Who fucking knows?" said Detective Smith. "I was in Fallujah. Karbala. Ashura. Infantry. Mujahideen. You name it, I was one. I jumped around a lot. It was fun causing chaos, bringing out the worst in men. Watch them destroy themselves. Why?" Smith asked.

"I spent a little time at Camp Nama," Wilkes answered.

"Army. I jumped into a soldier there. I waterboarded a terrorist an inch from his life while there. It was hilarious to see their eyes damn near pop out of their heads. Those Black Rooms were notorious. Worse than what those fucks were doing at Abu Ghraib. I would jump into a soldier and do some medieval shit to those bedouins. I hadn't had that much fun since The Crusades," smiled Detective Smith.

"I haven't been out of the Dark since The Crusades. I missed out on both Iraq wars as well as Afghanistan. I will say you never know how much you miss the raping, pillaging, and murder until you're not around it," sighed Detective Mourning.

"Yeah, it can be such a joy," Detective Smith said. "All those attempts to open the flood gates. This time we're not going to let the opportunity slip through our fingers," said Detective Smith.

Aaron interrupted them. "What are you guys talking about?"

Detective Mourning looked at Aaron and started laughing. "He still does not have a clue where he is?"

"What do you want me to do with him?" Mr. Wilkes asked, laughing.

Detective Mourning motioned towards Aaron's hands. "Untie him."

Mr. Wilkes looked at Detective Mourning. "Don't worry, I'll take it up with the boss. Untie him," repeated Detective Mourning.

"Don't worry," Detective Smith said. "We can handle it from here."

Reluctantly, Mr. Wilkes loosened the straps restraining Aaron's arms and legs. With his legs and arms free, Aaron flexed his wrists and ankles in hopes of reviving the circulation to his extremities.

Detective Mourning then excused Mr. Wilkes. Begrudgingly, the orderly took leave.

Detective Mourning looked over at Aaron and laughed. "Well, I'm glad to see you're getting treated properly here. I used to think this place was getting soft, becoming more like an amusement park."

"What do you want?" asked Aaron.

"Well, we decided to stop by to see if you need anything. You know, maybe some bonbons or Milk Duds," Detective Smith said.

"Very funny. I fail to believe the two of you drove all the way here to crack jokes."

"Oh, the reason we are here isn't going to leave you in stitches, buddy boy," said Detective Smith.

"Oh, I agree. I admit you were pretty clever with that

friend of yours. What was his name again?" Detective Mourning asked.

"Nora," Detective Smith said.

"Yeah, Nora, that was it. It took me a while to figure it out. I mean, it was so god damn simple it was downright ingenious," exclaimed Detective Mourning.

"All of us know you're not that bright," said Aaron.

Detective Mourning chuckled. "Touché. There really is no need to continue to play dumb."

"How can I play dumb if I don't know what the hell you are talking about?"

"Well, if you wish to continue to play games, then I'll play right along. See, when we questioned you about the murders at the parking garage, you told us your friend Nora was there. Well, it took me a minute to figure it out. According to you, I'm not the sharpest tool in the shed. Until it hit me that Nora is your name spelled backwards. So, I assume when you spoke of your friend, Nora, you were actually talking about yourself," said Detective Mourning.

"What?"

"You heard me. Nora *is* you. You are Nora. What I'm curious to know is, who are you today? Nora or Aaron? Or do the two of you switch off? Is Nora the murderer? And Aaron is the mild-mannered doctor?" Detective Mourning asked.

"All bullshit aside, you've fucked up. We found your kids. That's the reason why we're here," Detective Smith said.

"Where are they? I want to see them! Are they okay?"

"Cut the crap. Even if they were alive, you wouldn't get to see them. Besides, you know they're dead. You killed them. We found their bodies buried in the clearing. You know? The one in the Arboretum?"

Aaron was in disbelief.

"Yeah, we had you followed. When your wife told us you

were always taking trips to the park, we decided to have someone tail you," said Detective Mourning.

"What are you talking about?"

"Denial will get you nowhere," said Detective Smith.

Tears swelled in Aaron's eyes. "You're lying to me! They're alive!"

"Are you truly delusional? Did you not hear what I said? They're dead! We found their bodies! From what the coroner said, they died of asphyxiation. You suffocated them," added Detective Mourning.

Aaron sobbed. "No, they're alive!"

"Here we go with the theatrics. Maybe you are a basket case," said Detective Mourning looking over at his partner. "You've created this elaborate story to cover your ass, and like all criminals, you slipped up."

"That's not true!"

"Then tell us, what is true?" said Detective Smith.

"The truth is I did not kill my kids! At least I think I didn't!" Aaron shouted.

"Well, doc or Nora, whatever your name is today, you're going to be charged with the murders of your children along with the murders of Dr. Robert Klein and Enrique Jimenez. That's four counts of premeditated murder. That is four life sentences and then some. You're lucky the state has gotten rid of the death penalty. You're pretty much guaranteed to spend the rest of your life in prison," said Detective Mourning.

Aaron leapt from his chair. "I DIDN'T KILL THEM!"

Detective Smith immediately forced Aaron back down into the wheelchair. "Sit down. Don't do that again. I might have to shoot you."

Mr. Wilkes peeked in. "Everything is fine. No need to worry, big guy," Detective Mourning said to the orderly.

Mr. Wilkes shut the door.

Detective Mourning turned his attention back to Aaron. "Doc, we can make a deal with you right now."

"What kind of deal?"

"Just tell us where the divination tray is, and we'll let you and your kids go back."

"What? You just told me my kids were dead?"

Detective Mourning grabbed Aaron and stared him in the eyes. "Just tell us where the fucking divination tray is. Otherwise, this might become your permanent home."

Detective Mourning got up and went over to the door. He gingerly rapped on the door and waited for Mr. Wilkes to open it. "See ya," Detective Mourning said.

"Catch you later," Detective Smith added.

Once the detectives had left the room, Mr. Wilkes came in and wheeled Aaron down the hall to the elevator. As they rode the elevator back up to the ward, Aaron tried his best to keep his emotions under control. If there was any truth to what Detectives Mourning and Smith had said, then Aaron needed to be able to think clearly. He needed to get out of there so he could figure out what was really taking place. First, he tells him he killed his kids. Then he turns around and tells him that Asher and Imani can go back if he reveals where the divination tray is.

When the elevator jerked to a stop, Aaron was a ball of confusion. He did not know if he should grieve or be angry at the detective's manipulation of the truth. As the elevator arrived at the floor, he heard Ten counting. He tried to compose himself as Mr. Wilkes wheeled him into the room, back in front of the window.

Am I Nora?

Aaron looked down at the twisted scar that ran the length of his forearm. He didn't recall cutting his wrist, nor how his feet and hands had become covered in mud.

Was that Nora?

Aaron looked around the room.

"Out of all languages, mathematics is the most universal. It is the language of God. Why? Because it is a language spoken by everyone." Ten attempted to sound magnanimous. "An angel told me that God's love and infinite wisdom is hidden within the numbers and his most prolific number is the number ten. She said, 'The number ten is the answer to all of life's questions.'" Ten looked over at Aaron. "That even goes for you. I'll prove it to you. Tell me, what is the passcode to your cell phone?"

"Does it look like I have a cell phone in here?"

"Okay, what was the passcode to your cell phone?" Ten asked.

So Ten would leave him alone, Aaron rattled off his passcode, "1-0-2-7."

Ten smiled. "See, he's proven me right! His passcode is 1-0-2-7. First of all, not only does a phone number have ten digits, but his code includes the number ten. Now, here is what is going to really blow your mind. If I was to add up one plus zero plus two plus seven, the total of those numbers equals ten."

Aaron thought about it for a second. Whether he wanted to admit it or not, Ten was right.

"See, the number ten is magical," Ten said.

Ten was in his element. Aaron had given him fodder, and he'd used it as a springboard to profess his divine gifts when, in reality, he had gotten lucky. Ten stood there amongst his gathering brood vaingloriously. He pointed at Aaron like a TV evangelist. "I kid you not! The number ten will solve all of your problems and answer all of your questions. The number ten holds the keys to your salvation.

"If you don't believe me, watch this; I'll show you again," Ten said to his captive audience.

Ten gazed into the eyes of the patients huddled around him and started to count. "One ... two ... three ... four ... five ... six .... seven ... eight ..." When his eyes fixated on the last person, he appeared flummoxed before saying, "Nine."

Roy Hibbing laughed. "Nine! Ha! That's nine. Not ten, you stupid sons of bitches!"

"See, he doesn't know what he's talking about. The only thing the number ten answers is this dipshit's IQ!" Roy said.

"That's not true! You take that back!" Ten yelled.

"I will not! I do not apologize to clowns in the circus who drive around picking up elephant shit!"

Ten looked prepared to hurl an insult back when his eyes lit up. "There are ten people standing here, right now!" he said.

"No there ain't!" Roy argued. "You counted nine."

Ten smiled. "Yes, there is! There are ten!" Ten then pointed at himself and declared, "I make ten!"

"You can't count yourself! That's cheating!" Roy screamed.

"Yes, I can because I am here. See, it's true. Ten is mystical. It is the number of God," Ten said.

"No, it isn't!"

"Yes, it is! You're a non-believer! Since you are a non-believer, you are banished to the other side of the room," Ten decreed, waving his hand.

"You asshole fuck! Get your hand out of my face! Who does he think he is?" Roy said.

"Did you hear me? I banish you to the other side of the room! Now go!"

Mr. Wilkes and Ernie, the other orderly on duty, chuckled. Ernie was a pudgy man. His face resembled that of a pig's, jowls and all. His head was crowned with a military-style crew cut. A portly gut and bad case of acne were caused by his copious consumption of soda pop. Like everyone else, Mr. Wilkes and Ernie enjoyed a little excitement to break up the tediousness of the day. They laughed as Ten and Roy squared off.

"I got ten dollars on Roy," Ernie said.

"I'll take that bet," Mr. Wilkes replied.

Roy slapped Ten's hand away. "Get your hand out of my face!"

"Make me!"

Ten waved his hand in Roy's face again. This time, Roy caught Ten's hand and shoved his fingers into his mouth. Screams of agony echoed throughout the ward when Roy bit down. With his fingers trapped in Roy's mouth, Ten desperately tried to free his fingers. He frantically punched Roy in the face. Roy bit down even harder. Not until blood seeped from the corners of Roy's mouth and nose did Mr. Wilkes and Ernie decide to break it up. As Mr. Wilkes and Ernie tried to pry Ten's fingers out of Roy's mouth, Aaron realized no one was guarding the door.

Aaron eased his way out of the wheelchair, slowly inching towards the door. The fact Mr. Wilkes had forgotten to strap Aaron back into the wheelchair after meeting with Detectives Mourning and Smith was a blessing. As long as Ten and Roy created a distraction, Aaron had a chance.

"Where are you going?" Mr. Wilkes yelled. Aaron turned to see the orderly looking at him.

"I'm going to the bathroom."

"Like hell you are!" Mr. Wilkes said, trying his best to keep Ten and Roy from killing one another.

"I got to go!"

"Don't you fucking dare! Sit your ass back down!" Dejected, Aaron walked back over to the wheelchair.

He watched as Mr. Wilkes and Ernie struggled to free Ten's fingers. Unable to withstand Ten's pummeling, Roy let go. Ten gingerly cradled his fingers, cursing. Roy came dangerously close to severing Ten's index and middle fingers.

"My fingers! You fuck face! How am I supposed to count? I'm going to kill you!" Ten charged Roy but was quickly restrained by Mr. Wilkes.

With blood profusely running from his nose, Roy snickered. "That's what you get, you little prick! I'd like to see you try killing me! I'll mop your little scrawny ass up and down this place!"

"Shut the fuck up! Both of you!" Mr. Wilkes screamed.

Mr. Wilkes looked over at Ernie. "Do you think you can take this one to the infirmary and get his fingers checked out?"

"Yeah. No problem. Are you going to be all right in here by yourself?"

"I'll be fine. Hurry back, so I can take this one down there and get his nose looked at," said Wilkes.

"Will do," Ernie said, dragging Ten towards the door.

It was when Ernie swiped his card and the door unlocked that Aaron saw his chance. When Ernie swung open the door and led Ten out into the hall, Aaron made a dash for it.

"Where the fuck are you going!" Mr. Wilkes screamed, alerting his partner.

Ernie turned around just in time to block Aaron's path. "Where do you think you're going?"

Without thinking, Aaron instinctively kneed Ernie in the groin. Ernie's knees buckled. "Ahhh! You son of a bitch!"

Wishing for Ernie to stay down, Aaron hit him squarely in the nose; he stepped over the orderly, and ran for the exit.

"Go! Go! Go!" Ten yelled.

Aaron made it a few yards before he was tackled by Mr. Wilkes. "Uh huh. I got your ass now," the orderly said.

"No, you don't understand! I must find my kids! They're alive!" Aaron cried, as Mr. Wilkes pinned his face to the floor.

Bedlam had broken out. Patients wandered the hall, screaming, shouting, and some were dancing, spinning around in circles. Others banged their heads against the wall, while some simply stared off into space.

A pair of white tennis shoes limped up to where Mr. Wilkes had Aaron pinned to the floor. "You little shit! You think you can knee me in the balls then break my fucking nose and get away with it? Do you have him?"

"Yeah, I got him. This bastard ain't going nowhere."

"Stand him up!"

Mr. Wilkes brought Aaron to his feet. Ernie's face was bloody and swollen, with blood oozing from a nose that pointed distinctly to the right.

"You don't understand! I don't belong here!"

"Hold him up! Straight! Oh, you don't belong here, huh? To tell you the truth, I don't give two shits if you leave here or not. I will tell you this, you can best believe you are not going to leave here without me getting a little payback. You're going to wish you never laid your hands on me." Ernie then reared back and delivered a crushing blow to Aaron's jaw. Aaron's legs went limp.

"How does that feel, ass wipe!" Ernie said. "Hold him up. I owe him a kick to the balls."

Mr. Wilkes gleefully smiled. "I got him."

Ernie reared his leg back and was about to deliver a devastating kick when Aaron heard Missus Farmer. "That's enough! Is that him?"

"Yes, ma'am," Mr. Wilkes said. That was the first and last time Aaron was ever glad to see the head nurse.

"Why wasn't he strapped into his chair?"

"I, I forgot," Mr. Wilkes said.

"You forgot? You forgot!" Disgust dripped from her lips.

"You're about as stupid as the patients! Do I have to continually remind you on how to do your job?"

"No, ma'am."

"Do I have to do everything?"

"No, ma'am."

"I will deal with you later. Right now, we need to show the doctor how we do things here at Western. It seems the pink room didn't give us the desired result. He needs to understand how we handle troublemakers! Take him to the medical procedures room!

"You're going to learn the hard way, Dr. Langford, on what is appropriate and inappropriate behavior in my ward!"

Woozy, Aaron mumbled. "No, please. I need to find my children."

"That you will not do. See, you have been placed in my care and I'm going to make sure you are cared for properly," she said. "Take him. You, help the other orderlies get this place cleaned up and back in order. Then go to the infirmary to get looked at," she said to Ernie.

"She's going to zap him!" Ten shouted, cradling his fingers. "He's going to get zapped! You're going to get zapped!"

Ten laughed and jumped around in circles like a little kid. "Zapped!" he shouted.

Missus Farmer glowered at Ten. "That is enough, Ten. Unless you wish to join him!"

Ten quickly suppressed his enthusiasm. "I told him not to do it."

"No, I can't. I got to find my children," Aaron mumbled.

Missus Farmer made her way down the hall. "Bring him in here. Put him on the table and strap him down."

Aaron could feel his body being dragged into a room and laid down on a steel table. Another orderly held Aaron still while Mr. Wilkes tied him down. Once firmly strapped in place, Missus Farmer leaned over Aaron and smiled.

"Do you know what this is, Dr. Langford?" She held up what looked like an ice pick. "It's called an orbitoclast. Long ago, if a patient was being difficult, unruly, or 'unresponsive to conventional treatment,' we would use this instrument, along with a small hammer, and drive it into the corner of a patient's eye into their brain.

"The doctor would then move the orbitoclast in a circular motion within the skull until we were certain we had severed the frontal lobe of the brain from the thalamus. We called it a transorbital lobotomy. It was dubbed the 'ice pick' procedure."

She looked Aaron in the eyes. "After a while, they made us give up this practice," she said, sounding disappointed. "The medical community stated the side effects from such a procedure were disastrous. I, on the other hand, found the method to be rather successful. It always achieved the desired result of ridding the patient of the unwanted behavior.

"As you can see, I long for the good ole days. Although the old techniques were quite macabre, they were effective." Missus Farmer drew the point of the orbitoclast closer to Aaron's eye. Aaron tried to move his face away.

"You can't do this," Aaron said.

"Oh yes, I can. And don't you forget it." The steel rod drew even closer.

"No!"

"Calm down!" she said, pulling the instrument away. "We won't be using this today. I thought I would show it to you in case you tried to pull another stunt like the one you just did. What I have in store for you is a little less permanent. It's what we call electroconvulsive therapy. I'm quite sure you've heard of it. It is generally known as electroshock or shock therapy.

This used to be the main way we treated people who had bad thoughts. Like I said, I miss the good ole days."

Missus Farmer's sinister grin stretched across her weathered face. "Besides, who's to say that new always means better? Believe me, that if this doesn't work, this will be next." Missus Farmer held up the orbitoclast.

Missus Farmer then leaned over and whispered in Aaron's ear. "If you continue to test me, you will learn why they call me Lucifer.

"Get on with it," she said, looking over at Mr. Wilkes.

"Should we sedate him?"

"What for? There's a lesson to be learned here."

"No! You can't do this!" Aaron yelled.

Missus Farmer brought her face an inch away from Aaron's. The stale smell of cigarettes filled his nose. "What you fail to realize, Dr. Langford, is that here, I am God. I can do whatever I want.

"Put the mouthguard in," Missus Farmer ordered. "We wouldn't want him swallowing or biting his tongue in half, now, would we?"

Mr. Wilkes pulled Aaron's jaws apart and jammed the mouthguard in. He then applied gel to the electrical paddles, which were then placed on his temples.

"I promise you; I won't try to leave again! Please, don't do this!" he mumbled.

She smiled as he begged. "There is no mercy here, Dr. Langford. There is only me. Then, looking over at Mr. Wilkes, she said, "Turn it on."

FORSAKEN

A single thread of consciousness pierced through the void. Aaron had an excruciating headache. The glare from a sole light blinded him. He could make out the grainy silhouette of a woman.

"Hello, Aaron," the woman said.

The voice was familiar.

Missus Farmer?

"Mother Dear?" Aaron asked.

"No, I'm not Mother Dear, although it is nice to see you are awake. I was starting to wonder if you would ever wake up," she said. "How do you feel?"

She knew him.

"I don't feel too hot," he said. Aaron tried to sit up, wincing in pain from the tug of the restraints that kept him pinned to the bed.

"They thought it was best if you were confined to your bed for your safety and the safety of the other patients," she said.

As she came into focus, glimpses of this woman flashed throughout his memory. "How long have I been asleep?"

"They've kept you sedated for close to seventy-two hours."

Suddenly, scenes of Ernie on his knees replayed in his head. "Am I at Western?"

"Yep."

Aaron stared at the woman closely. Images poured in. Images of her younger, happy, and sad dotted the landscape of his mind. What she meant to him was beyond reach. One thing was clear, judging by her attire, she was not a nurse.

"You have not figured out who I am, have you?"

"No, I can't say I have."

"They told me this might happen. They said some memory loss is a common side effect of shock therapy. Nurse Farmer told me that it would be temporary. She said it will get better over time."

As if it wasn't bad enough that he was trapped at that hospital, Missus Farmer was now robbing him of his memories.

"You speak as if it's okay to play around in my head?" Aaron felt the tears in his eyes at the thought of Missus Farmer wiping away his life.

"There is no need to get emotional. Everything will gradually come back. By the way, Otis says, 'Hello.'"

Aaron's eyes lit up.

"Ah, I see now you know who I am. It took you long enough."

"Donna? Where have you been?"

"Away. I had to get myself together."

"Why did you let them do this to me?"

"Let them do what?"

"This!" Aaron screamed. "I'm a doctor. I know you gave them authorization to electrocute me!"

"Please. You did this to yourself."

"And how did I manage to get strapped to a bed?" Donna did not answer him. Instead, she stood there in silence.

"I told you I wanted to go home," she finally said.

"What does that got to do with anything?"

Donna walked over to the window. "They take such immaculate care of the grounds here. The manicured lawn and the gardens are so well cultivated. I wish I could've done that in our garden. Do you honestly think you killed Asher and Imani without me knowing?"

"What are you talking about?"

"I don't know what it was about that night. Maybe it was the nonstop rain? Whatever it was, it felt like an itch just below the surface that I couldn't scratch. It might have been the kids and their bickering or the brooding tension between you and me. I really can't put my finger on it. Whatever it was, it had a hold of me, and I couldn't shake it. I needed to get out. I needed to get away. I needed to be back home in D.C., where I could be me again."

"What are you talking about?"

"I don't even recall walking up the stairs to Asher's room that night or picking up the pillow. Something inside of me had snapped, broken beyond repair. Asher didn't put up much of a fight. It was almost as if he welcomed it. You were so hard on him."

Aaron realized what she was telling him. "No! NO!"

Donna went on. "Of course, I didn't stop there. I couldn't stop there. I had to finish the job. We couldn't have one without the other. I had to make it complete. It had to be all or nothing."

Aaron started crying. He wanted Donna to stop. "No! No more! Please, I don't want to hear no more!"

"In a fit of rage, I killed the cat. I thought taking a life would be hard. Weirdly, killing wasn't like I had imagined. It's kind of like riding a bike. It's difficult at first, but with practice it gets easier."

Donna appeared to take pleasure in torturing him. "Imani

was different. I stood over her and watched her sleep for at least a minute before placing the pillow over her face. She looked so angelic. I didn't want to interrupt her serenity. I remember stroking her hair and kissing her forehead before smothering her.

"You favored Imani. I knew if Imani were gone, you would be devastated. You would finally be forced to feel what I felt every day you forced me to live in this God-forsaken city."

"You're crazy!"

"You might be right. I might be," Donna said. She walked slowly back over to Aaron. "I wanted you to suffer for bringing me here. I wanted you to feel as miserable as I did. So, I took from you the one thing in life I knew you cherished the most: your children."

"Why didn't you tell me you wanted to go home?"

"I DID! Don't you remember? I thought after I killed Socrates, I thought the guilt of bringing me here would be too much, and we would go back home. You told me six months. Six more freaking months! The problem was, I didn't have six more months in me to give. I wanted to get back home to where I had a life, where I had family and friends. You took me away from all of that. You brought me here to where I was alone and had to start over. I couldn't breathe. You were so deep into your research you failed to see how desperate I was. I had no one to turn to.

"I was left to count raindrops all day. Can you imagine that? Do you know how mind-numbing that is? Counting raindrops?"

Donna continued to rip Aaron's heart apart. "Imani put up such a fight that it woke you. I scratched her while I was trying to keep her hands and feet from flailing. That's where the blood came from. I heard you rushing upstairs. But the deed was done.

You barged into her room to find me standing over our daughter's lifeless body. It was weird because I could see your mind trying to register what you were seeing. Then the doctor in you took over, and you tried to resuscitate her, to no avail. I had taken her away from you the same way you had taken everything away from me."

"Shut up!"

"Like I said, it was weird. I watched you detach from reality right there before my eyes. It was a chore for me to get the children's bodies downstairs into the garage. There, I wrapped their bodies in plastic. After that, I put them in the trunk of the car. If the police had been wise enough to go out into the garage and pop the trunk of the car, they would have found Asher and Imani. However, what was amazing was how you played everything. I mean you were magnificent. I suspect the trauma forced you to block everything out. You withdrew into this make-believe world. Marvelous touch, I must add. If you hadn't, I would've had no other choice but to kill you. Yet, your diagnosis of OCD came in handy.

"After the police had left, and you were asleep, I drove Asher and Imani down to the Arboretum. I dragged their bodies up to the small clearing I had followed you to one evening and buried their bodies."

"You're a liar!"

"Am I? Think about it, Aaron. Think about it really hard. Of course, you killing your coworkers was an added bonus."

"I didn't kill Robert or the security guard."

"Whatever. Whether you did it or not, I don't care. It shifted the focus on you. To totally implicate you I put your grandfather's gun in the glove compartment."

"Why?"

"Because I knew when you found it, you'd start to doubt yourself. Your thoughts would cause you to question whether you actually did kill your colleagues or not. Plus, more importantly, I wanted to go home."

Tears fell from Donna's eyes as she knelt down and whispered in Aaron's ear. "Simply tell them where the divination tray is. Then this will all be over. You can be reunited with Asher and Imani."

"What is it with the divination tray? Why is everyone talking about the divination tray?"

Donna shook her head. "Then you leave me no choice. Just know I killed Asher and Imani because of you. The medical examiner will be releasing Asher and Imani's bodies to me this afternoon. I am having them shipped home. I will not be coming back. I love you."

Donna kissed Aaron on the cheek. "Good-bye."

ESCAPE

"Aaron, wake up!" someone whispered.

"Mother Dear?" Aaron asked.

"Rise and shine, sunshine. Time to raise the dead. We don't have a lot of time. Unfortunately, you're going to feel a little loopy for a while until the drugs wear off."

"Who's there?" Aaron asked.

"Right now, this might be hard for you to comprehend. Sadly, we don't have a lot of time to talk. I'll have to explain everything to you on the way there. The sooner we can get out of here the better. Security will be doing a bed check soon, and we need to be long gone by then. This will probably be the only chance I will get at rescuing you. If you don't help me help you, then you will never see your kids again."

Suddenly, Aaron recognized the voice. "Nora?"

The restraints that held Aaron firmly in place loosened. The intravenous drip that fed into his arm was disconnected. "Nora?" he repeated, in disbelief.

"That's me," Nora said, coming into view.

Aaron looked up at the illusion. "You're not real! You're a figment of my imagination."

"I'm very real, my friend."

"You lie. You're not real. Go away. Leave me alone!"

Nora placed his hand over Aaron's mouth. "You got to be quiet. You're going to alert everyone. Look, who cares if I am real or made out of pixie dust? That is irrelevant. What's important is that I'm here to rescue you. That is what is important. We can discuss how real I am later. Right now, we need to be getting out of here."

Nora hoisted Aaron up off the bed. As he was lifted into the air, Aaron caught a glimpse of his legs. They were twigs. "How long have I been strapped to that bed?"

"I don't know. They've kept you restrained for a while."

Nora dragged him towards the door. "I've been meaning to ask you, how do you manage to keep your suit so clean and neat?" Aaron asked.

"I'll tell you about it when we get out of here. Right now, I got to get you out of here."

"Speaking of that, where have you been?

"I've been around."

"Obviously not, if I've been lying on that mattress long enough for my legs to turn into wet noodles."

"Things had gotten too dangerous. They took you, so that totally changed everything," Nora said. "Since you would not tell them about the tray, they felt the best thing to do is keep you here, making it impossible for you to find your kids. I warned you in the parking garage they would be coming for you."

"Obviously."

Nora swung Aaron's arm over his neck to keep him upright. "We got to hurry," he said.

Nora peeked through the door's small glass window into

the hallway. "Let's go." He opened the door and dragged Aaron out into the hall.

"How did you get a key?" Aaron asked.

"I have my ways."

In the hallway, Nora leaned Aaron up against the door. He immediately began examining the wall. "What are you doing?" Aaron asked.

"I'm trying to find the marker."

"A what?"

"I'll explain in a minute."

Suddenly, Aaron heard, "Pssst! Pssst!"

Nora looked like he feared they had been discovered. "What is that?"

"Pssst! Over here!" Aaron looked across the hall to see Ten glaring at him through his window.

"Over here!" Ten said.

Aaron stumbled towards Ten's door, but Nora protested. "What are you doing? We don't have time for this!"

Aaron shrugged off Nora's complaint. "Ten, I don't have time for your nonsense." Aaron propped himself up against the door. "My imaginary friend is here to take me home, so I got to go."

Ten pressed his face against the small glass pane and stared at Nora. "Who's he?" he asked.

"Nobody. He doesn't even exist."

Ten gave Nora a weird grin. "Whatever, man. I need your help."

"What is wrong, Ten?" Aaron asked.

"I got a bad case of gas. Add to that, the ventilation sucks in here."

"I don't have time for your games, Ten."

"I'm serious."

"How about laying off the fiber," Aaron said.

"Don't go! I got something I have to tell you," Ten said.

"I don't have time."

"No, I'm serious. I told her I would tell you when I got the chance."

"You told who, you will tell me what?" asked Aaron.

"My angel. She made me promise to deliver this message to you."

"What message?"

"Aaron, we got to go!" Nora said.

Ten pressed his face against the glass pane. "She told me to remind you that you should, 'Remember your love can lead you to them. Do not be fooled by what your eyes see. Trust your heart.'"

Aaron had heard that before. Was it a famous quote, or something he had read someplace? "Who told you to tell me that?"

"My angel."

"For real, Ten. Who told you to tell me that?"

"My angel! I swear. She made me promise to tell you. She can be a nuisance at times. She just interrupts my thoughts and confuses me. Plus, she comes and goes when she pleases. She is always whispering in my ear."

"Found it!" Nora exclaimed.

"Is there anything else you want me to know before I go?" Aaron asked.

Ten smiled. "Don't forget ten is the magic number."

"Got it."

"Aaron! We got to go!" Nora said.

"How are we getting out of here?"

"This way."

Nora reached down to a point where the paint had started to peel away from the wall. It was exactly where the floorboard and the wall met the door. If Nora had never brought it to

Aaron's attention, he would've never noticed it. Nora grabbed the little fold in the paint and began to peel it away from the wall. Rather than seeing a bare wall beneath the paint, Aaron found himself staring out onto a deserted road. Amazed, Aaron looked over at Nora in disbelief.

"Having been here long enough searching for a way out, you find out the bakas can get sloppy. It's not often, but every once in a while you can get lucky. That's why it took me so long to get to you. I had to find a way to rescue you undetected. Hang on to me," Nora said.

Then as if the wall did not exist, Nora and Aaron stepped through and out onto the abandoned road. Nora then turned and pulled the fabric of reality back as if he was pulling a curtain closed. Aaron watched as Ten's face disappeared, as if being covered by a veil. He reached out to touch the void created by Nora only to feel nothing but nighttime air.

"How did you do that?"

"Like I said, if you've been here long enough, sooner or later you find out the bakas are not always good at masking one reality from another. It's rare, but sometimes there are fissures that you can pull back and step into an alternate reality. I've learned you've got to be patient and wait for one reality to start to warp and crack."

Aaron stared out into the night in shock. "You're serious?"

"Come on, we got to go."

THE GAUNTLET

Nora hustled Aaron towards a beat-up Honda Civic stationed on a frontage road near some shrubs. Aaron floundered to keep up. Once they reached the car, Nora opened the door and placed him on the backseat. Aaron searched for a comfortable position that didn't allow for every pothole or bump in the road to rattle throughout his body.

"How do you feel?" Nora asked.

"I'm starting to feel more like myself. I think I am losing my sea legs."

"Good."

The shroud of night was starting to slip from the shoulders of the world, and the faint, distant glow of the sun cast vibrant shades of purple, orange, and red on the horizon. Aaron was certain Missus Farmer was fully aware of his absence by now. He envisioned her polishing up the orbitoclast in anticipation of his return. Soon, every trooper in the state would be fanning out along the I-5 corridor in search of him.

"Now do you believe me?" Nora said, peering at Aaron through the rearview mirror.

"Huh?"

"Where are you? Are you sure you're, okay?" Nora watched Aaron closely.

"I'm sorry. I wasn't paying attention."

"I said, 'Now, do you believe me?'" Nora repeated.

"I don't know what to believe, right now." Rather than trek along I-5, Nora decided to take the streets.

"Look, if you wish to see your children again, you're going to have to listen to me and do as I say. Before, we got sloppy; we made it too easy for them to track us and figure everything out. We can't do that again.

"That is why they isolated you. They knew if they could isolate you, they would have a better chance of keeping you away from your kids. They did not think I would brazenly defy them and resurface. I guess they should never underestimate the determination of a desperate man."

Nora appeared to keep his eyes on the street signs. "We're almost there."

"Where are we going?"

"Where they are keeping your son and your daughter."

"What do you mean by, 'Where they are keeping my son and my daughter?'"

"I mean where they are keeping your son and your daughter." Nora looked at Aaron again. "Are you sure you are feeling better?"

"Yeah."

"I hope so, because when we get there, we will need to act fast. Get in and get out, undetected."

"How do you know where my children are?"

"I have my sources."

"You kidnapped them, didn't you?"

"No, not at all."

"You have them, don't you? You kidnapped my son and

daughter, didn't you? There is no other way you can know where they are unless you are the one who abducted them."

"I do not have time to explain how I know. Believe me, I know they got them," Nora said.

"Who is 'they?' You keep saying they."

"The bakas."

"The bakas? Yeah, right. You've got them! You've been stringing me along this whole time!"

"I can assure you I had nothing to do with the abduction of your children."

"You're a liar!"

"I know it might be hard for you, but ask yourself, what do I have to gain from stealing your kids?"

"I don't have a clue who you are! So how would I know?"

"Rest assured, my friend, I had nothing to do with this. Now, we can waste time arguing, or we can save your children."

"Take me to my children."

"I plan to."

Honestly, Aaron had no choice. He couldn't tell Nora to pull over and let him out. He was a fugitive. Besides, he needed to see Asher and Imani alive, especially after hearing Donna speak of murdering them.

"So, tell me, what brought you here?"

"Darkness is the appropriate name for 'here,'" Nora said.

"And what is that?"

"This is eternal damnation."

"Are you saying this is Hell? If so, I find that hard to believe."

"Hell? If that is the term that suits you, then that is what it is. And why is it so hard to believe this place is Hell, as you call it? If I were to tell you a father is accused of murdering his children and is sentenced to spend possibly the rest of his life suffering for a crime he did not commit, what does that sound like to you? Heavenly bliss?"

"I guess you're right."

"Here, each person's torment is custom-made."

"Sounds like life."

"What if life really was not life at all?"

"What are you saying? Are you saying that what I think is reality is not?"

"You tell me. You are the one persistently questioning if I am real. Take the scars on your wrist. From the looks of it, you tried to kill yourself. In your mind, you believe you were unsuccessful. What if you were successful?"

"Wait a minute, are you saying I am dead?"

"I'm not saying anything. I'm saying, what if? It makes complete sense if you think about it."

"If that is the case, then what do you want from a dead man?"

"I have my reasons. It does not matter to me if you are dead or alive. What matters is how you got here."

"What?"

"I've heard whispers of your arrival from those lurking in The Dark. They seem surprised that you would venture into Darkness to save your children. They gambled that you would leave the door open. I hoped, and it appears wagered correctly, that you were foolish enough to try and rescue your kids. What is important to me is that you came voluntarily. I figure if you know the way in, you must also know the way out."

"So, you are not doing this out of the kindness of your heart? You want something out of this. You want out," said Aaron.

"Wouldn't you? I was not brought here by choice."

"It sounds like both of us is insane."

"I have been a captive here for far too long."

"Is that so? How did you get trapped here?"

Again, Nora eyed Aaron cautiously through the rearview mirror. "My name is Kwami. I am a hougan. How I got here is complicated."

"Your name is Kwami? Then why do you call yourself Nora?"

"When I approached you, I thought you would feel more at ease if my name didn't sound foreign. When I approached you before, and told you my real name, you did not trust me."

"Before?"

"No need to worry about that right now. When I told you that evening in the coffee shop that my name was Nora, it was all I could think of at the time. I took your name and turned it around. Thus, the result was Nora."

Apparently, Detective Mourning was right in that summation. "You thought a man named Nora didn't attract attention?"

"It was all I could think of at the time."

"That does not tell me how you got here."

"That's a long story."

"Well, right now all I have is time."

"My tribe feared the advancement of the Kingdom of Dahomey from the northern city of Abomey. The Fon warriors are legendary for their military skill and fierceness, especially their women. My tribe's king feared the advancement of King Akada's army.

"I knew the advancement of King Akada's warriors from the north was inescapable. His warriors were advancing quickly and were swiftly consolidating their power across the land. Akada's army was encircling us. The Fon had already marched on other coastal kingdoms to consolidate the kingdom's control over the slave trade. Soon, our kingdom of Whydah would fall. Their warriors were feared throughout the land. Warriors captured in battle, along with their women and children, were sent off to the slave ships in exchange for trinkets and guns. Akada believed that, by dispelling competing tribes, he would have access to all the land's riches, including its people.

"Desperate, I called upon the spirits to assist me in defeating Akada's advancement on Whydah. Eshu, the keeper of the crossroads between the worlds of the living and that of the dead, refused my offering to let the spirits pass. Akada's hougan had somehow swayed the gatekeeper of souls to not act on my behalf. Since I was unable to call upon our ancestors, my king, King Haffon, took it as an omen. He saw it as a sign that the spirits favored Akada over him. Refusing to give up, I decided to call upon Eshu's twin brother, Kalfu. I knew calling upon Kalfu was dangerous. Kalfu is very volatile. He is the keeper of malevolent spirits. I was desperate. I did not want my tribe to suffer the same fate of those who came under the Fon's rule. So, I used an ancient incantation that summoned Kalfu. My inability to appease the temperamental spirit is why I was banished here as punishment."

"And people say I'm crazy," Aaron said.

But before Aaron could accuse Nora of spinning a tall tale, Nora stopped the car. "We're here," he said.

Aaron looked out the window to see his neighborhood. Gone was the Seattle skyline. Fir trees and manicured lawns were replaced with row houses and concrete. Aaron was back in Columbia Heights. Unsure of how they had found their way back to his childhood neighborhood, Aaron assumed he must've been hallucinating.

"They're keeping your children nearby. We must park here, so we do not alert them to our presence," Nora said.

"Where are we?"

"Here."

"You got to be kidding me," said Aaron.

"No, this is it. You need to come. We do not have much time."

The neighborhood was exactly the way Aaron remembered it. He looked up at the street sign: 10th Ave. NW. He was not far from Mother Dear's house. Aaron was no stranger to the rowhouse Nora had parked in front of; that house had belonged to his childhood friend, Tommy Jackson, and his grandmother, Isabella Jenkins. Aaron had spent many days sitting on that stoop. Getting out of the car, he stared at the rowhouse.

"Come on! We must hurry!" Nora shouted, disappearing into the house.

Aaron trailed Nora inside. He still was somewhat weak. The moment he passed over the threshold into Isabella Jenkins' house, he was swallowed up by the dark. Only tiny shards of light managed to snake their way into the house through the blinds.

"What are we doing here?"

"Rescuing your son and daughter."

"I don't see my children anywhere here."

"As I told you in the car, they are not here."

"Then what are we doing here?"

That's when Aaron heard her. "Don't you be eyeballing me, boy?"

Aaron assumed he was hearing things. There was no way that could be Isabella Jenkins. Aaron looked over into the living room. "Boy, you best stop eyeballing me! If you know what's good for you!" Aaron couldn't believe it. Sitting there in her favorite recliner was Isabella Jenkins.

"If you keep eyeballing me, I'm going to take this extension cord and put it to your backside! I don't care who your grand-mamma is!"

Aaron wandered into the living room to see Miss Jenkins sitting in front of a vintage TV, staring at a fuzzy screen. She used to sit in that recliner in front of the television all day watching her soap operas. She rarely left that chair. In fact, she died in that chair.

"What are you doing?" Nora asked.

Aaron pointed towards Miss Jenkins. "Miss Jenkins," Aaron said, "She's sitting right there."

"Who?"

"Miss Jenkins. Don't you see her?"

Nora looked into the darkness. "I don't see nothing."

"How is it you do not see her sitting there? She's as clear as day."

"Whatever it is you see, it is specifically meant for you. Like I told you, this place has a way of tailor-making one's own misery. I do not always see nor hear what you see or hear. Whatever it is you see or hear, it is meant specifically for you. Ignore it. It will only derail you. We got more pressing matters. Come on." Nora tugged on Aaron's smock, forcing him to follow him into the kitchen.

Nora walked into the kitchen and looked out the window. "What are you looking at?" Aaron asked.

"I'm waiting for the signal."

"What signal?"

Nora peered back out into the alleyway. "You did not answer my question. What exactly are you looking for?"

"I'm waiting for someone to show up over there," Nora said, pointing down the alley towards a dilapidated old house. Aaron followed Nora's gaze to see he was pointing at Mother Dear's old home.

"Judging from the expression on your face, you're familiar with that place."

"That's my grandmother's old house."

"You used to live there?"

"Yeah."

"Well, that is where they are keeping your son and daughter."

"Asher and Imani are in that house?"

"Yes."

"You're joking, right?"

"Not at all."

Aaron looked at Mother Dear's old home. "If my children are in there, why are we standing here?"

"Because we are waiting."

"Waiting for what? If what you say is true, my son and daughter are in that house! What the hell are we waiting for? There is no telling what is happening to them!"

Aaron headed towards the back door. "No! We need to wait for the signal!" Nora said.

"Signal! What signal?"

Nora pulled Aaron back to the kitchen window and pointed. "That signal." A skinny blonde-haired man stepped out of Mother Dear's house and lit a cigarette.

"Who is he? He looks like a meth head!"

"He is. Lucky for you, he's a meth head who is desperate and wants to get out of here. We have very little time to get in and get out of that place without being detected. Once inside, we got to move fast. We must retrieve your children and get out!"

Nora headed to the back door and out into the alley. He spoke rapidly as they walked. "Let me remind you, if we're discovered, the shadows will wipe your memory of this, of me, and I will have to find you all over again."

"What do you mean 'all over again?'"

"We've been here before. Not here per se, but through this exercise of trying to rescue your kids, twice. Each time, the Shadows wiped your memory of me clean and made it even harder for me to find you."

"What are you saying?"

"I'm saying, this is the farthest we have come. Let's not mess it up. The previous two instances I could not get you to trust me. I need you to trust me. You need to listen to me and do everything I say. Otherwise, you will get wiped again, and the Shadows will make it even harder for us to find your kids."

Aaron looked over at the junkie. "If he's really a meth head, then why are we trusting him?"

"See, that's what I'm talking about. That's what doomed us the last two times. We're trusting him because we have no other choice," Nora said. "Before we go any further, I need to know if you can do this?"

"If my son and daughter are in that house, then yes. If not, then you will have hell to pay."

"Fair enough."

"Are you coming or not?" yelled the meth head. "We don't got all day!"

"Come on. We're wasting time!" said Nora.

The gaunt man fidgeted uncontrollably. A shirt proclaiming, "God Bless America," hung loosely over his bony frame. There were abscesses on his face, accompanied by track marks that laced his arms and webbing of his hands.

"What's wrong with him?" the junkie asked, looking over at Aaron.

"He's fine," Nora said. "He's just a little weak."

"He's no good to us. What the fuck can he do?"

"Don't you worry about him? He's my concern. Besides, you wouldn't be standing here if it weren't for him."

The junkie looked Aaron over. "Don't worry. I can hold my own," Aaron said.

"Come on," the junkie said.

As Nora followed their guide inside, Aaron stood there aghast at the condition of his grandmother's home. Graffiti adorned the exterior. The windows were boarded up and painted black. The address, 2017, was painted in bright red on the side of the house. Aaron looked at the spray-painted numbers and immediately recognized his cell phone's passcode. He was shocked. All these years he had subconsciously been using a variation of Mother Dear's address as the code to his cell phone. Again, he heard Ten say, two, zero, one, and seven: Added together, they equal ten.

"An angel told me that God's wisdom is hidden in the numbers and that His most prolific of numbers is ten. The number ten answers all questions. Remember your love can lead you to them."

Mother Dear had said that to me!

"Are you coming or what?" Nora said, holding the door open.

Aaron hustled towards the door. Inside, the repugnant smell of urine greeted him. The flicker of lighters danced in the dark like fireflies on a summer's eve. Eyes, empty and devoid of life, stared back at him. Mother Dear's house had become a junkie's paradise.

A frail elderly man approached Aaron. He did not say a word. He simply walked up to him and placed his brittle hand over Aaron's heart. He then smiled. "I can feel your heartbeat."

Before the old man could say another word, their gangly guide pushed him aside. "This is my ticket out of here, Gramps! Go find your own! This way!" the junkie yelled.

"What are all these people doing here?" Aaron asked.

"They are awaiting you," Nora said.

"Why are they waiting for me?"

"They heard you were here. They knew you would be coming. They too want to be delivered from Darkness. You've provided the destitute with hope. If you had a chance to escape your worst nightmare, wouldn't you try?"

The junkie hurried Aaron and Nora through the crowd to a staircase, the same set of stairs Aaron used to climb as a child. "Come on! We must hurry!" he said.

Time and decay had made the staircase unstable. The junkie pointed up the stairs. "They're up there," he said.

"Are you certain?" Aaron asked.

"The children are up there, I tell you!" he said.

"We've come this far; I see no reason to doubt the man," said Nora.

Nora climbed the rickety steps, making sure his feet were planted firmly on solid footing. Aaron followed, making sure to step in Nora's footsteps. Their guide waited at the bottom.

"They're in the room at the end of the hall," the junkie yelled. The room at the end of the hall used to be Aaron's.

Nora began to walk towards the door, but Aaron stopped him. "They are my kids," Aaron said.

"Well, you need to get them. We don't have much time."

"Hurry up! They will be here soon!" the junkie yelled.

Aaron cautiously eyed the bedroom door. The addict was right; there was no telling if someone had warned his children's captors. A sense of urgency did nothing to allay his fear of what might lie behind that door.

"We must hurry!" Nora said.

Frantic, the junkie yelled, "Is he in the room yet? We're taking too long!"

"Shut up!" Aaron screamed.

"Aaron, what is wrong?" Nora asked.

"Nothing." Aaron lied.

"Then open the door."

Anxiety swelled in Aaron's chest. He wanted to believe Asher and Imani were in that room. He reached for the doorknob, praying this was real. Praying Donna was wrong. He did not know if he could take not finding Asher and Imani in that room alive. In spite of his doubts, Aaron took a deep breath and pushed the door open.

The first thing Aaron noticed was the ugly green paint peeling from the walls. Then he heard the mumbling. He followed the murmurs over to a lone woman slumped in the corner. She had a belt wrapped around her bicep with a hypodermic needle dangling from her arm.

"I'm supposed to watch them. I'm supposed to watch them," she repeated.

Aaron followed the woman's eyes over to the silhouettes of two bodies lying on a mattress. As Aaron drew closer, he began to see they were Asher and Imani. The sight of them caused him to cry.

"We've got to go! They're coming!" the addict screamed.

"Is that them?" Nora asked.

Tears trickled from Aaron's eyes. He was so overcome with emotion that it was hard for him to speak. "Yes, it's them."

"We must gather them and leave. It is too dangerous for us here."

Aaron bent down to grab his son. "What are you doing?" Nora asked.

"I'm trying to get my kids and get the hell out of here."

"There is no way you can carry both of them."

Nora was right. There was no way he could carry both Asher and Imani. "I'll take my daughter."

"Why not let our guide take her? You're weak," Nora said.

"There's no way I'm going to let that junkie handle my children."

Drawing in closer, Aaron was able to see his worst fears had come to fruition. Asher was in crisis. Perspiration dripped from his forehead. He was struggling to breathe. Aaron placed his hand against his son's forehead; he was burning up.

"What's wrong?" Nora asked.

"We got to go now!" the junkie screamed.

"Aaron, what is wrong?"

"Nothing. Grab my son!" Aaron did not have time to explain. The junkie was right; they needed to go. The sooner they got Asher to a hospital the better. It was critical if they were going to prevent Asher from slipping into a coma and possibly dying.

Nora picked Asher up and hurried out of the room. Aaron grabbed Imani and cradled her to his chest. "Hold on, baby, Daddy's got you."

Abruptly, the room grew dark. The woman's incoherent ramblings ceased. Aaron looked over to see if she was still conscious. When he did, he found her staring back at him with jet-black eyes.

"We got to go! They're coming!" the junkie yelled.

The young woman smiled and said in a childlike voice, "We're here." Elongated fingers sprouted from her mouth as the demons crawled out preparing to confront Aaron.

"Go!" Aaron screamed, running out of the room.

"We got to go now!" Nora said, from somewhere up ahead.

Aaron sprinted down the hall towards the stairs. Nora had already scaled the staircase and was on his way out into the alley. The stairs crumbled beneath Aaron's weight as he hurried down. The ensuing panic amongst those inside caused Aaron to lose sight of Nora. Not until he was out in the alley, did he spot Nora climbing the stairs into Tommy's house. Desperate not to lose track of his son, Aaron tried to quicken his pace.

Inside Miss Jenkins' house, Nora awaited. "We need to get out of here!"

That was when they heard the horrific scream. Aaron turned to see grotesque limbs, reaching from the shadows on the wall to grab their guide. Spiraling arms and heads descended from the ceiling to ensnare the junkie. Aaron was not aware the junkie was even behind him. He had assumed he had made it out of the house with Nora. The shadows engulfed him, stifling his screams until they were no longer.

"RUN!" Nora said.

Aaron stumbled out the door and down the stoop towards the car. He wasted no time placing Imani on the backseat next to her brother. Nora jumped into the driver's seat and revved the engine. Then, he heard it.

Aaron stood there, unable to move. "What are you doing? Get in the car!" Nora yelled.

A low-pitched drone emanated from inside Isabella Jenkins' home. It grew louder. "Get in the car!" Nora screamed.

The sound grew to a deafening pitch. Fearful of what was to come, Aaron jumped in the car. "GO! GO!"

Just as the car peeled away from the curb, the thunderous roar of locusts erupted from the rowhouse. Aaron looked out the rear window to see a cloud of them spread across the sky.

"Hang on, son. We're going to get you help. I did not come all this way to lose you," Aaron said.

"What is wrong with your son?"

"I fear he is in crisis. We need to get him to a hospital."

"Your son will not receive the type of treatment he deserves here!"

"What do you mean? We need to get him to a hospital right away!"

Nora violently swerved into oncoming traffic. "Do you see that behind us? We must get to the Sea of Agony! That is our only hope." Nora swerved back into traffic before colliding head on into another car.

"What are you trying to do, kill us?"

"No! I am trying to get us to The Sea of Agony!" Nora

pointed out the window towards a raging ocean. "We must cross that ocean in order to be safe!"

The row houses had disappeared. In their place were windswept bluffs and a rocky coastline. Aaron looked out of the rear windshield to see the swarm blotting out the sun.

"Drive faster!" Aaron said, but Nora was gone. Instead, Aaron was driving the car. His cell phone was ringing incessantly. In the backseat, two kids cried and screamed hysterically. They were not Asher and Imani. Gone was the swarm of locusts. In their place was a convoy of patrol cars.

Aaron looked over at the phone. Confused, he did not know if he should answer it. "What!" Aaron yelled into the phone.

It was Donna. She was frantic. "Aaron, what are you doing? You need to stop this! You need to give yourself up! They will kill you! Kidnapping someone else's kids is not going to bring Asher and Imani back!"

"What are you talking about?" Aaron peeked into the backseat.

"Aaron, Asher and Imani are dead! This will not bring them back! Taking someone else's kids will not bring them back!" Donna yelled.

"Turn yourself in! You need help! I promise you; I will not leave! We can work on getting you help! Please, give yourself up! If you don't, they're going to kill you! Give up before someone gets hurt!" she pleaded.

Disconcerted, Aaron tossed the phone onto the passenger seat. He could hear Donna still pleading with him.

"Aaron! Aaron! Do you hear me?" Nora shouted. Aaron looked over to see Nora behind the steering wheel.

"No. I didn't hear what you said."

"We don't have time for this! Let's go!" Nora climbed out of the vehicle.

Aaron looked out the window to see the police cars were gone. There were the locusts, and Asher and Imani lay on the backseat.

"Come on! What are you waiting for?" Nora grabbed Asher and hurried towards the raging waters.

"Where are you going?" Aaron yelled. Nora had already taken off running, so he did not hear him over the crashing waves. Aaron grabbed Imani and desperately tried to keep up.

"Come on!" Nora yelled.

The ocean spray made navigating the rocks tricky, especially with Imani in his arms. "Stop! I've got to stop!" Aaron screamed.

Disgusted, Nora marched back to him. "We are not close enough."

"I can't go any further! It is too much. Why do we have to be close to the water anyway?"

"So, we can cross."

"And how are we going to do that?"

"I do not know. That is why I needed you."

Nora measured the distance from where they stood to the waterline. "We might be close enough," he said.

"Close enough for what?"

"For you to do whatever it is you need to do for us to cross the sea."

"What you are saying makes no sense!"

Nora pointed towards the rolling waves. "I know you know how to get us beyond the Sea of Agony! You had to have crossed it to get here! There is no way in or out of Darkness without crossing the sea! It is the moat that separates Darkness from the Light! The tide always rolls in. It never rolls out! If you had journeyed here willingly, then you surely had planned for your escape."

"I don't have a clue as to what you are talking about!"

"You may want to act swiftly; we are running out of time!" Nora pointed towards the advancing cloud of locusts. The splatter of the grasshoppers hitting the rocks began to fill the air. Upon hitting the rocks, the locusts evaporated and extended the darkness' reach.

"We are running out of time!" Nora screamed.

"I don't know what you want me to do! I do not know how to get us across!"

"Wrong answer!"

"What do you want me to say? That is the truth!"

"You said you knew how to get us beyond the Sea of Agony!"

"I never said such a thing!" Aaron said.

Nora's face contorted into a gruesome scowl. "I've waited too long for my chance to be free of this place! I will not let you cheat me of my freedom! If I must be cursed to dwell in this place forever, then I shall not be alone!" Nora eased his hand around Asher's throat. "We can reset, and I'll have to find you again!"

"I swear to you, I do not know how to get us beyond these waters!"

Nora's anger had distracted him from the growing tendrils extending out from the cracks and crevices in the rocks, the shadows' elongated fingers entwining themselves around his ankles. Like in Imani's room, Aaron began to hear the voices. "Nora, you must listen to me. I'm telling you the truth. I do not know how to get us beyond the ocean."

"You're lying!"

Rage had consumed him, and Aaron could see that he was oblivious to the pending danger. The demons acted quickly to engulf him; Nora screamed for Aaron's help. Realizing it was too late, Aaron knew he could only save the life of his son, so he reached out and pried Asher free from

Nora's grasp before Nora was completely enveloped by the darkness.

Aaron watched in fear as the shadows swallowed Nora whole. Knowing he had no way of escaping, Aaron resolved himself to his fate. He sat down upon the rocks and cradled his children. He marveled at the setting sun as the darkness grew around him.

As the voices grew louder, a fleeting thought crossed his mind, *Are these really my kids?*

Just as fast as the thought had materialized, it was gone. The edges of reality started to become opaque and frayed. Memories started to be swept away into a river of oblivion one by one. Then the sun exploded into a thousand shards of light that danced upon the back of his eyelids.

This must be what death feels like?

He then heard her voice, Mother Dear. "Aaron, you must run! Run!" she demanded.

Aaron opened his eyes to see the ocean cleaved in half. The raging waves had been transformed into the rhythmic flow of contorted flesh. A path had been cut through the souls of the damned to the dying sun.

"Hurry, I grow weak!" Mother Dear warned.

Aaron looked back to see the shadows had recoiled from the sun's luminous glow. However, her energy was waning. Aaron grabbed Imani and Asher and did his best to run while carrying both of them.

"Hurry, Aaron!" The weight of Asher and Imani slowed him down.

"Stop! Don't move!" Aaron looked back to see Detective Mourning.

"Run!" Mother Dear urged.

"Stop, I said!" Detective Mourning shouted.

Fearful of what might come, Aaron hurried towards

Mother Dear's dwindling light. Then, he heard a pop, followed by another, and then another. Then, he felt a searing pain ripping through his flesh.

Suddenly, he was falling.

Summoning what little bit of strength he had left, Aaron lunged towards Mother Dear's dying light.

PART III
THE OTHER SIDE

"...the door-keeper of Deadland would allow him to enter, and he warned him not to touch any of the dead.

"Or else he would not be able to return to earth."

—From a Yoruba Fable

THE RETURN

The moment Aaron stepped into the void, Urbi had started counting down the minutes. Thirty minutes was all she was going to give him. After that, she would take matters into her own hands. The first thing she needed to do was destroy the divination tray and dispose of the cowrie shells. Although that would lock Aaron on the other side, she could not jeopardize life as she knew it for one man and his family. As with all things, sacrifices had to be made. Besides, she had warned Aaron about the risks if he crossed over into the Land of the Invisibles.

With Aaron on the other side, Urbi ushered Donna upstairs into the ring of candles. "Everyone must stay within the ring until Aaron returns!"

"Where is he?" asked Otis.

"He has crossed over," Urbi said.

"What do you mean 'He has crossed over?'"

"I mean exactly that. He has crossed over into the Land of Invisibles."

"Okay, I've heard enough. This has gone way too far! I

know we're not buying this mumbo jumbo. Are we? Aaron, you can come out now!" Urbi watched Otis stand up and look around as if expecting Aaron to magically appear.

"Otis! It's real. She's telling the truth. I would not believe it if I hadn't seen it with my own eyes," Donna said.

"I am not falling for it. Aaron, you can come out now, this is not funny!"

Urbi was furious. "Please, stay stationed by the board!"

"Where the hell is Aaron?"

"Otis, please listen to her! She is telling the truth!" pleaded Donna. Otis looked over at Teri, who also appeared uncertain.

"Okay, I'll play along for now," Otis said.

Donna sighed. "Thank you."

Urbi was thankful Donna was able to coax Otis into cooperating. The last thing she needed was dissention amongst them. Any lack of cohesion amongst the group made them easy pickings for a cunning baka.

The minutes piled on. Twenty minutes elapsed. No sign of Aaron. Urbi's hope for a safe return for him, and his children, began to wane. She remained vigilant. The door between the living and the dead remained open. Spirits, both good and bad, could pass through. Regardless of her feelings, she possibly had to abandon the idea of Aaron returning. Closing the door was priority. This would lead her into direct conflict with the others, particularly Donna, especially, if she understood what destroying the divination tray meant for Aaron and her children. When Urbi resigned herself to this fact, a door began to open.

Otis gasped. "What the hell is that?" as the rift developed in the living room.

"A passageway is opening," Urbi said.

Urbi prayed it was Aaron and not something more sinister.

She was not sure if she was prepared to confront the unexpected. "Everyone, stay where you are."

"What is going on?" Teri asked.

Urbi held her breath, fearful of what might emerge. She had seen Aaron disappear inside one of these "doors;" she had yet to see what came out. The air in the room grew heavy.

Then, without warning, Aaron, Asher, and Imani were belched out.

BAKULU

B eyond the silver mane of hair that graced his head, Aaron appeared to have aged a decade within the span of a half hour.

"Oh my God!" exclaimed Donna, bounding out the ring.

"No! Everyone must stay within the circle!" Urbi warned.

Evil was afoot. Urbi smelled it. Aaron had not returned home alone. He had brought along guests. Urbi sensed he had been mounted. She was not sure how many spirits had hitched a ride. The precipitous drop in temperature, along with the faint hint of sulfur in the air, told her that at least one of the hitchhikers was a baka. Donna did not heed her warning. Instead, she went to her husband's side. Aaron laid there with one arm around Imani and the other firmly around Asher's wrist. Urbi had to forcefully pull Donna away from Aaron and the children. There was no telling if the man lying there on the floor was indeed her husband. Or if those children were truly hers. Sure, they may look like Aaron, Asher, and Imani, but there was no way to know for sure if he was indeed her husband and those her kids. What the Land of Invisibles had sent back could be anything.

"Ne les touche pas! Don't touch them!" Urbi screamed.

"What is wrong with you? Can't you see they need help?" Donna screamed.

"He is not well," Urbi said.

"No shit," Otis said. He walked past Urbi towards Aaron.

"Stay inside the circle!" Urbi urged.

Aaron's eyes rolled around aimlessly in his head. "Aaron! Aaron, can you hear me, baby?" Donna screamed.

Aaron tried to talk but was unable to speak.

"Get away from him!" Urbi yelled.

Finally, Aaron mumbled, "Asher." Donna looked over at her son. He was sweating and having difficulty breathing.

"Oh my God! Otis, help me!" Donna cried. "Take Asher; he's in crisis." Otis immediately took Asher into his arms.

Urbi needed to regain order, and fast. They could not be disorganized with evil in the room. Bakas fed on chaos. Also, Urbi needed to work quickly to close the gateway between the two worlds.

Otis moved Asher and Imani into the dining room. Urbi did not detect the scent of evil on them, although she could not be certain. While Donna, Teri, and Otis examined the children, Aaron tried to stand, but collapsed back onto the floor.

"Oh my God!" Donna said, running to her husband.

"Do not touch him! Tend to your children!" Urbi said.

"He needs me!"

"What he needs, you cannot provide."

"We can't leave him there on the floor!" Otis said.

"Yes, we can. And we will."

If the baka was a jumper, all it would take was the slightest touch, a whisper, or for the demon to breathe in someone's direction. Jumpers needed to mount in order to survive in the land of the living.

Aaron babbled.

"What is he saying?" Donna asked.

"Right now, that is the least of our concerns. We must finish what we've started. We must close the door," Urbi said.

"God damnit, woman, what is wrong with you? Can't you see we need to call the paramedics? My best friend could be dying!" Otis said.

"Not to mention, my son is in the midst of a crisis!" Donna added.

"As soon as we close the door between the living and the dead, then we will call the paramedics! Regular medication is not the remedy that will relieve your husband of what is ailing him! Only I can free him from the demon dwelling within! However, we must close the door to the Land of Invisibles permanently!" Urbi ordered.

"This is nonsense!" Otis pulled out his cell phone. He looked prepared to dial 9-1-1, until Urbi aimed her gun at his head.

"Hang up the phone," Urbi warned.

"Are you insane?"

Urbi's hand shook. It was not as if she had never killed a man before. However, that was out of fear, not intentional. Besides, a gun was not like wielding a machete. Her uncle taught her how to shoot a gun on Ukerewe. Yet, holding a gun to someone's head and shooting at a tree were two different things. "Simply do what I ask. You will be able to call the paramedics shortly. If not, you will be paying a visit to the emergency ward, yourself."

"Lady, have you completely lost your mind?" Otis said.

Urbi tightened her grip and steadied her aim. She was

going to see this through one way or another. "It's your choice, Mr. Otis. We must close the door, period. If we don't, then Darkness will be set free here on Earth. With that in mind, I figure if I need to spill a little blood to keep that from happening, then so be it. The question is, what are you prepared to do? We don't have a lot of time for you to make up your mind," she said.

Otis eased his cell phone back into his pocket. "No! Give it to me! In fact, I want everyone's cell phone!"

Reluctantly, Otis and Teri handed over their cell phones.

"Good. Now, sit back down in the circle in front of the divination tray. I need you to place the cowrie shells back in the bag and lay the tapper flat on the tray," Urbi said. "I will inform you of the appropriate time to call the paramedics."

"Couldn't someone else have done this? Why does it have to be me?" Otis asked.

"Because you were the first one to command the tray. Since you were the first one to command the divination tray, you must be the one to signal the end of the session to Eshu."

Otis sat down within the ring of candles and did as instructed.

"Make sure you gather all eighteen shells. That is important. Leave not one shell behind," Urbi said.

Urbi quickly swung the gun over towards Donna. "Now, you-"

"Was this your intention the whole time? To rob us while my husband died?"

Urbi shook her head. "Rob you? I am not here to rob you. I am here to save you. What I am asking all of you to do is best for all of us. I brought this gun to ensure that I save everyone's life. Now, if you wish for your son to live, you will let me help."

Urbi went into her tote bag, then walked over to Asher. "I

have something that will bring down the fever. It will help." Urbi produced a small vial and presented it to Donna.

"Take a small pinch of this and place it on your son's tongue," Urbi said. Donna opened the vial and sprinkled the dry, pink substance onto Asher's tongue.

"That's enough," Urbi said, taking the vial back.

"What was that?"

"It is crushed Cassava leaves, dried beets, and cayenne pepper. The cayenne pepper and beets will deaden the pain while the Cassava leaves will temporarily oxygenate his blood."

"My son needs a doctor, not some home remedy," Donna said.

"Believe me, the small dose you have given him will cause the crisis to subside long enough for us to get him help."

"I've done what you asked!" said Otis. Otis neatly placed the tapper on the divination tray and bagged the cowrie shells as Urbi had demanded.

Urbi pointed the gun at Otis. "Break it!"

"What?"

"Break the divination tray."

Otis grabbed the divination tray and shattered it over his knee.

Splinters of wood littered the floor. Urbi did not have time to dispose of the shattered pieces. That would have to wait. With the divination tray out of the way, Urbi now needed to focus her attention on Aaron.

"Can we call the paramedics now?" Otis asked.

"Not yet."

"Why?"

"Because I am not done; we must deal with him." Urbi pointed the gun at Aaron. "I must rid him of the baka that dwells within him."

"The what?"

With everyone back inside the circle, Urbi stepped out to confront the demon. Although everyone was cooperating, Urbi held on to the gun. She did not trust Otis. With gun in hand, Urbi pushed the furniture aside. When she had created sufficient space, Urbi placed the pistol on the coffee table and retrieved the jar filled with the earthen cornmeal mix. Out of the corner of her eye, she could see Otis easing his way towards her.

"Don't think about it!" she shouted, brandishing the pistol again.

Otis eased back.

Once Otis was back inside the ring of candles, Urbi blessed the cornmeal soil mix and sprinkled it in a circle around Aaron. With the baka confined to the small area dictated by the earthen cipher, Urbi drew in closer to examine the demon. Foam had gathered at the corners of Aaron's mouth as he spouted what sounded like gibberish.

"What is he saying?" asked Donna.

Although it sounded like nonsense, Urbi had heard it before. "He is speaking a combination of several ancient dialects, the first languages of man. I hear Sumerian, Aramaic, and primordial African dialects. Languages that have not been spoken since antiquity, since the days the heavens and the stars came into existence," Urbi said.

"It all sounds like mindless drivel to me," said Otis.

"One must have a trained ear to hear the dead languages."

Urbi had heard such a speech before in the village of Aziza-coue outside of Ouidah. There she witnessed the banishment of several bakas from the body of a little girl.

Urbi turned to Donna. "I need you to gather the candles and place them in the dirt around your husband. We must keep the baka confined to this area." Urbi held on tightly to the gun, to discourage anyone from trying anything.

"How long do you intend to hold us, hostage, while my husband suffers?" Donna asked, gathering the candles and placing them around Aaron.

"This will all be over soon."

The sound of Imani waking caught Donna's attention. "Mama."

Donna rushed to her daughter's side. "Oh, baby! I am so glad to see you!"

"You. Help Mr. Otis finish placing the candles around the doctor," Urbi said to Teri.

Urbi could not allow her mind to deviate from the task at hand. To see the doctor's daughter conscious was a good sign. Unfortunately, Urbi could not get caught up in the euphoria. There was a baka in their midst, and she did not know what type of baka. Customarily, bakas took the shape of infants or nocturnal animals. Thus, the manner this demon chose to mount Aaron was rare. When a baka did mount, it was almost impossible to eradicate the demon without losing the life of the host. Urbi had to release the baka's hold on Aaron as soon as possible without jeopardizing Aaron's life and the lives of everyone in the room. If she did exorcize the demon out of him, there wouldn't be any time to properly banish the spirit or spirits back into the shadows.

With the candles strategically in place, Urbi reached into her tote bag. She produced a vial of elephant bone powder. The white powder would give Aaron's soul the strength and fortitude it needed to endure the exorcism. She sprinkled a smidgen into her hands and blew it out over Aaron. A thin film gathered on his skin. The demon growled.

Aaron's eyes trained themselves on Urbi. What originally sounded like gibberish turned into a chant: a simple phrase repeated over and over again. Urbi had heard the incantation before.

"Cover your ears," she told the others.

What they were hearing was an ancient curse intended to drive the listeners mad. Urbi had seen the incantation's effects firsthand. The hougan who had come to liberate the little girl in Azizacoue succumbed to the curse. He went mad. Ultimately, he dug a blade so deep into his throat that he almost completely decapitated himself. Because of the hougan's failure, Akosiwa, Urbi's mentor, had to finish ridding the little girl of the bakas.

Urbi moved quickly about the room, paying Aaron no mind. Time was slipping away. The longer she allowed the baka to remain in Aaron, the stronger its anchor to his soul would become. More than likely, Urbi would have to perform a crude extraction of the demon to force it to dismount. If she freed Aaron of the baka, Urbi would have to find another vessel in which to house the baka before properly exiling it back into Darkness. Unfortunately, there was only one person that could survive being mounted by a baka ... her.

"You," Urbi said pointing at Teri, "grab the bird cage and bring it to me."

Teri fetched the birdcage with the rooster and rested it at Urbi's feet.

Urbi reached into her bag and began to meticulously lay out the tools necessary to draw the baka out. There was the ritual blade, the elephant bone powder, a monkey's paw to counteract bad juju, and the ason that had been given to her by Akosiwa following her Canzo. For good measure, Urbi rubbed the small sack of pebbles that hung loosely around her neck and prayed to her guardian spirit, Damballah, for protection.

"Don't come near me," Urbi said, after praying.

"What are you doing?" Donna asked.

"Preparing to bring forth evil. So, stay clear of both me and your husband!"

Urbi placed another smidgen of elephant bone dust into her quivering hands. How she wished the steady hand of her mother, Ima, was there to guide her. Urbi had watched mambos and houngans far more experienced than her take on a baka and lose. This was Urbi's first exorcism alone. Typically, the task was performed with another hougan or mambo present. Normally, she confronted demons while under the watchful eye of her mother or mentor, Akosiwa. In the art of performing an extraction, Urbi was not a novice, nor was she a master. All Urbi could do was pray her mother and Akosiwa had taught her well. Urbi blew another dose of elephant bone dust onto Aaron, this time causing his body to convulse.

"What are you doing to him?" Donna cried.

"He's fighting!" Urbi said. "That is a good sign." The baka had not fully anchored itself to Aaron's soul. The elephant bone dust was giving Aaron's spirit the will to resist the demon.

Urbi picked up the ason and began to shake it. The snake bones and small stones rattled in unison while she danced and chanted around the earthen circle of dirt and candles. She chanted in her native tongue.

"What in the world is she doing?" Otis asked.

"I don't have a clue," Donna said.

Urbi did not hear them. She had slipped into a hypnotic trance. Physically, she was there. Spiritually, her soul walked upon the sacred ground of her homeland, Benin. Displeased with Urbi's act of aggression, the baka issued a warning: a deep, guttural, growl.

"You're hurting him!" Donna said.

Urbi paid Donna no mind. Rather, she grabbed her sacred dagger and blessed the blade with her spit.

"Oh my God, she is going to kill him," Donna said. She motioned to intervene but was restrained by Otis.

"Wait, let's see what she intends to do," he said.

Ignorant to the events around her, Urbi watched her spittle dribble down the length of the blade. She retrieved the rooster from the cage. Then, in one, fluid motion pinned the fowl to the coffee table and beheaded it with a clean swipe of the dagger. Blood spurted onto the table and floor: blood for the ancestors. Sacrificing the rooster supplicated the Land of Invisibles and curried favor with her ancestors. She raised the flaying carcass above her head, allowing the fowl's blood to spray out onto herself and Aaron. With her white gown a speckled red, Urbi drained the last remaining droplets of the rooster's blood onto Aaron. The blood cooked as it came into contact with his skin.

"What the hell?" Otis muttered.

"Dear Lord," Teri gasped.

Donna stumbled back away from Urbi as Aaron's body began to twist and contort from the droplets of blood. Unfazed, Urbi produced a jug of hooch from her bag. When she uncorked the bottle, the potent corn whiskey filtered throughout the room. Urbi took a sip, salutation to the ancestors. The potency of the moonshine brought beads of sweat to her brow. Urbi took a second swig, causing her mouth to burn. Rather than swallow, she swished the alcohol around in her mouth and then sprayed it out over Aaron's body. Again, the demon within voiced its disapproval. Disregarding the baka's displeasure, Urbi stood at the edge of the dirt circle shaking her ason and chanting. The pounding of the rain outside kept the beat.

Aaron rose to his feet. He glowered at her and, in a thunderous voice roared, "Bakulu!"

Urbi stopped in her tracks. The invocation of such a name chilled the blood in her veins. Bakulu was one of the most ancient of bakas. He was so vile not even botonos dared to invoke his name.

Sensing the fear at the mere mention of its name, the demon laughed. "You know not what you play with, little girl," the demon said.

Urbi ignored the baka and resumed dancing and chanting.

"Urbi! Stop! What are you doing?" Ima's voice spewed forth from Aaron's mouth.

Urbi stopped. "Yes, Esi, it is I. You must stop this nonsense at once!"

Urbi could not resist finding comfort in hearing her mother's voice. "Mama?" she whispered.

"Yes, Esi." Urbi's mother never called her by her short name, Urbi. She always called her by her given name.

As a child, Urbi used to wonder why her mother refused to call her by her nickname. "Mama, why do you not call me by my short name?"

Ima would smile and say, "You embody the majesty of a princess as Urbi entails. Your father was right in giving you such an appropriate short name. But you are my princess who was born on a Sunday. That is why we named you Esi."

"Mama is that you?" Urbi asked.

"Yes." The baka reached out to stroke Urbi's cheek.

Although she yearned to feel her mother's caress. Urbi knew that was not her mother. She recoiled, leaving Aaron's hand to linger there. She had to divorce herself from her feelings. She could not let Bakulu's bond with Aaron become permanent. Urbi needed to sever the link, or Aaron would be lost forever.

Realizing his first attempt to lure Urbi in did not work, Bakulu sought to influence a feebler mind. "Otis, I know you're not going to stand there and let this woman do this to me. Don't tell me you believe in this mumbo jumbo. Make her stop! She's hurting me!"

"Aaron, is that you?"

"Who else would it be?"

"I don't know."

Not able to resist the urge to toy with Otis, Bakulu asked, "So tell me, Otis, are you still afraid of the dark? Do you still sleep with the light on? You know that night light?" Aaron smirked.

"Judging from the look on your face, I assume that you do. What's wrong? You thought I did not know about that? I know of the horrid nights when your babysitter, Tammy Tucker, would lock you in the closet and tell you the closet monsters were going to eat you if you made a peep while she and her boyfriend fucked like rabbits on your bed."

"How do you know that?"

"How old were you?" Aaron continued, "Four. Or was it five?"

"There is no way you could know that."

"Who do you think sat in that closet next to you while your babysitter and her boyfriend fucked? Me! I know how scared you were when she told you how she would lock you in the closet and never let you out. How she would let the closet monsters eat you if you ever told your parents about how she sneaked her boyfriend in the house once they had left. Remember how you could hear them giggling as you cried? Don't you remember?"

"Who are you?"

Bakulu cackled. "I'm Aaron."

The baka was only getting started. Toying with Otis piqued his interest for more. It had been way too long for the demon. Centuries had passed since the baka had played amongst humans and wreaked havoc. The baka missed the pleasure of twisting their frail minds into knots.

Filled with arrogance, Bakulu turned its attention to Teri. "Don't think I forgot about you, bitch. I know you didn't think I was going to let you slide, did you?"

Teri looked at Aaron in disbelief.

Bakulu bellowed a hearty laugh. "Don't try to play innocent. Tell me, Teri, have you stopped turning tricks for hits?" the baka asked. "You remember those days, don't you? When you hid cocks where your thighs split. Remember quickies in urine-filled alleyways and stairwells so you didn't have to go too far from the dopeman for your next fix? Those were the days! Weren't they?

"I must say the weight looks good on you. A much-needed improvement over the leaner days," Bakulu teased.

"Oh, don't be surprised, ho. I was there when you cursed God and played Russian roulette with random cocks by letting them squirm inside your withered snatch. Oh, and how you swore to never turn another trick again when your body was wracked with a horrible cold. You feared you had caught the big one. HIV. Remember how you swore you wouldn't shoot up anymore? How you were going to quit? When the cold subsided, you were back at it again, fucking and sucking for a hit."

Bakulu smiled. "You were nothing more than a strawberry. Give a round of applause, everyone, for the original strawberry." Bakulu clapped emphatically. "If there ever was a strawberry, you were it. You know, if you had vanished off the face of the earth, no one would've cared. Girls like you vanish every day. Some people pray women like you disappear. I hear their prayers.

"Remember how you waited in anticipation for the smack to hit your veins and give you that feeling? It was heavenly.

Euphoric. True moments of bliss when you slid that needle into your vein and the world melted away. Pure fucking ecstasy." Aaron titled his head back and sighed.

Teri turned to Otis.

"Oops, did I say too much?" Bakulu crowed. "Don't tell me, I've ruined your surprise. I guess I don't know when to keep my big mouth shut. Judging from the look on Otis' face, he doesn't know too much about your past.

"Unfortunately, Otis, your girlfriend was a strawberry, who fucked for smack, blow, or whatever else she could get her pretty little fingers on."

"Make him stop!" Teri screamed.

Bakulu sneered with delight. "Oh, she's clean now, my friend. Aren't you, Teri? At least, we think so. Though you still have the cravings, don't you? You have dreams about having one more taste. A taste for old-time's sake, huh? Otis, my friend, if I was you, I would pay close attention to the shit in your house. If it starts coming up missing, you know who stole it. I would also go down to the doctor and get your wick checked. You might have Hep C or hit the jackpot and get HIV."

"Make him stop!" Teri shouted.

"I'll stop when she stops! Make her stop!" Bakulu said, pointing at Urbi. The demon eased closer to the edge of the circle. "Kill her, Teri! Kill this witch! Slaughter her like the pig she is! She is nothing more than a pig, a devil worshiper! Take the dagger she wields and drive it into her heart! Make her stop and I guarantee you you'll never have to be ashamed of your past again! I promise you!" Bakulu hissed.

Teri looked at Urbi.

"Yeah, do it, Teri. Kill her!"

Teri inched closer.

"That is enough!" Urbi screamed.

"Oh, back to you now, my little Voodoo Princess. Don't

worry, I didn't forget about your ass," Bakulu said. "Look at you, all grown up and looking like your mama. That bitch gave us fits."

The time for playing games with Bakulu was over. The demon was stalling. Urbi had to get the baka out of Aaron. There was no way she could match the demon's power. The best chance to free Aaron would be by outwitting the baka, turning the demon's vanity against it.

Urbi wiped the rooster's blood from the dagger and handed it to Teri. "Do not let him or me have that dagger, do you understand?" Urbi said.

"Yes."

Urbi brought her attention back to Bakulu. She smiled as she smeared the rooster's blood across her forehead. Then, without saying a word, she stepped inside the cipher.

"Otis, your cell phone is sitting on the coffee table. You may now call the paramedics," Urbi said, locking eyes with the demon.

Otis appeared to break his gaze from the spectacle at hand and retrieve his cell phone.

The demon laughed. "You must be joking."

Urbi taunted the demon. "Are you afraid, baka?"

Bakulu smiled. "Your mama is not here to save you, little girl. You are ill-equipped for me. I am ancient. I am older than time. I watched as the planets and the stars took their place in the heavens."

"That may be true, baka. What I do know is you sure do a lot of talking. I wonder why? Are you scared to find out how powerful I may be?" The time for subtleties had passed. She needed to draw the demon out.

Aaron's eyes burned a fiery red. Bakulu scanned the smudged tracks of blood across Urbi's forehead. "Do you know what you've done?" the demon said.

"I am well aware of my actions. Are you? What do you plan to do about it?"

Urbi knew the desire to possess a mambo was far too tempting for a baka to pass up. The demon's vanity would not allow for him to pass up such a savory opportunity. So, before Urbi could change her mind, the baka grabbed her by the wrist and jumped. Upon completion of Bakulu's transfer into Urbi, Aaron's body fell listlessly to the floor.

Right away, a battle was waged within Urbi. Bakulu feverishly tried to tether himself to her soul. At first, she was successful at thwarting the baka's attempts. Urbi knew she could not fend Bakulu off forever. He was too strong. Urbi glanced around the room. She needed to separate herself from the others before the demon fully took hold.

Otis tried to help her, but Urbi pushed him away. "The aid car is on the way," he said.

Urbi staggered towards the door. She needed to get out. She threw open the front door and tumbled down the steps. She crawled out onto the lawn. Not able to move any further, she lay there. Bakulu was merciless. Urbi needed to bide her time and wait for the right moment before revealing her true intentions in luring the demon to possess her. With Bakulu close to full possession, Urbi began to invoke an ancient binding incantation, binding the demon within her. She had seen this done once before by Akosiwa to keep a baka from jumping. The downfall was that Urbi did not possess Akosiwa's strength. She had no other options to prevent Bakulu from jumping any further. The young mambo's craftiness enraged the demon. He tried to wreak insurmountable damage on her body to make her stop. It was too late.

So, there she lay on the lawn in the rain. She did not know when would be the next time she would feel the rain upon her face or look up into the heavens and be mesmerized by the stars. Bakulu was pulling her down into the abyss. She was not strong enough to resist. She could feel herself slipping away. Urbi fingered the small sack of charmed pebbles around her neck and prayed. She would need Damballah to watch over her. As the world faded from view, Urbi relished the glow of the stars. They looked like a million tiny pin pricks on the floor of heaven.

THE IN-BETWEEN

A sweltering heat broiled Urbi's skin. The air was heavy and thick, making it hard to breathe. The humidity sat on her shoulders, like a weight. She could hear it; Bakulu was out there. Death or an eternity spent in limbo were real possibilities for her gamble. She was not sure if she was in-between life and death or dead.

The haze began to slowly wipe away, revealing Lake Nokoué expanding out in front of her. She was back in Benin. Lake Nokoué was a known tourist attraction thanks to Ganvié, the famous stilt city that rested out on the lagoon. Ganvié was revered for the ingenuity of its people, the Tofinou. The Tofinou evaded enslavement by the Fon by relocating their village upon the lake. The wisdom of the village's elders to relocate the village over the water was an ingenious maneuver to avoid enslavement during the expansion of the Dahomey empire. The elders were aware the Fon's religion forbade them from waging war over water. Besides its unique history, Ganvié was very near and dear to Urbi's heart for another reason. It was where Urbi partook in the Canzo, the ceremony of fire. It was the initiation taken by all individuals entering the inner sanctum of Vodun. It was during her Canzo that Damballah, the wisest and most revered spirit in the Land of Invisibles, had chosen to be Urbi's protector.

As a young woman, Urbi had stood on the banks of Lake Nokoué with her mother awaiting the arrival of a boat taxi to ferry them out to Akosiwa's home. Ima trusted no one other than her mentor, Akosiwa, to shepherd her daughter through the rites of passage into Vodun. Urbi recalled standing on the banks of the lake with her mother and others waiting for the arrival of the ferry. When the boat arrived, the boat's operator refused to let Urbi aboard because no one else wanted to ride with a "ghost." Not until after much bickering-and her mother paying ten times the amount of the original fare-did the driver relent. The boat operator complained the entire ride. He swore his boat would sink because Urbi brought him bad juju. He said he would have to take a bath and wash the boat once he dropped her off to get rid of her cursed evil.

Urbi gazed upon the placid lagoon. She could not see the village, for it was shrouded within the mist. A low hum could be heard out over the water. It sounded like the motor of a boat taxi making its way to shore. In Bakulu's world, Urbi could not be certain. Although it looked like Lake Nokoué, this was not real. The sun broke through the clouds. Urbi was able to see beyond the shore out onto the lake. It took her a minute to discern what the source of the low, droning hum was. What came into view was a large cloud of tsetse flies swarming out above the lagoon.

As soon as she realized what it was, a fly landed on her forehead. The tingle of its tiny legs scurrying across her forehead sent her into a panic. Before she knew it, she was engulfed. Flies burrowed beneath her eyelids, infested her ears and nose, tickled the back of her throat as they invaded her nasal cavity and mouth. Urbi tried to remind herself this was not real. That did not stop the terror raging inside her. Her belly swelled from the thousands of flies filling her stomach. She tried to scream, but instead of her voice, a cloud of flies flew from her mouth.

Then they were gone. Urbi was no longer on the banks of Lake Nokoué. Instead, she stood on a beach looking out upon the ocean. She could smell the salt in the air. The sun's rays danced upon the waves, sparkling like diamonds. Wooden skiffs in need of repair lined the shore. On the horizon, fishermen were casting their nets out into the ocean. Their catch would feed the entire village that day. Urbi soon realized where she was. She was at the Gulf of Guinea outside of Ouidah. She looked behind her and saw the Point of No Return monument, a marker where many West Africans saw their native land for the last time after being led from the slave forts down the Rue des Esclaves to awaiting slave ships. There, they were put in canoes and rowed out to ships prepared to take them to a foreign land where they would be forever removed from their people, their culture, their religion, their gods. Some, fearing what awaited them on those ghastly ships, jumped out of the canoes and into the ocean shackled and bound, much more prepared to face death than slavery.

Urbi lifted her head to the sky to feel the sun's rays upon her cheeks. The sound of people caused her to look over her shoulder.

"Do you mind if we take a picture with you?"

From their accents, Urbi suspected they were German. She was not certain. They were definitely East Europeans. They did not wait for her approval. The couple gathered next to her and snapped the photo with a selfie stick. The disapproval on Urbi's face must have spoken volumes, judging by the way they profusely apologized and hurried off to rejoin their tour group. Urbi hated tourists. They looked down on West Africans. They came to their land and treated them like they were an oddity. Urbi imagined the stories the tourists told when they returned back home, tales of how they mingled with the "natives in the bush."

As children, Urbi and Ousman used to pick their pockets and snatch their purses in exchange for kashata, a sugary, coconut treat sold along The Rue Esclaves. Life was so much simpler back then. Rainbows were larger than life, and each day was an adventure. There was no such thing as Hunters. Her lack of pigmentation had yet to be a curse. Soon, her child-like naiveté would be replaced with a harsh reality that could no longer be hidden from her.

Urbi immersed her feet in the surf. The waves pushed granulates of sand in between her toes. Again, she had to remind herself that this was not real. It was a mirage. As another wave reached out and washed over her feet, Urbi closed her eyes and daydreamed about more pleasant times. Her thoughts were interrupted by the sound of people in hysterics. She opened her eyes to see people shouting and pointing. Some had begun to run.

Even before she saw the massive wall of water on the horizon, Urbi knew what was coming. The sheer size of the wave was terrifying. Her mind told her feet to run. Panic spread swiftly through the crowd as the water advanced. Urbi cursed her feet for being too slow. Self-preservation took precedence, which was clear in the countless people who were trampled and pushed aside.

The wave roared with the voracity of a freight train when it made landfall. "Oh, dear God!" Urbi screamed, as the water lapped at her heels. The sound of trees snapping like twigs and metal twisting filled the air.

"No!" Urbi said, as if her proclamation would keep the ocean at bay.

That would not be the case as a torrent of water swept her off her feet. Before she knew it, Urbi was riding a wave. She fought to keep her head above water, but the water stole her every breath. As life escaped her, something told her to relax, to let go. So rather than fight the raging water, she let it take her. She embraced it. She let her fears go. Urbi knew there was nothing Bakulu could do to her that had not already been done. As her world faded to black, Urbi took solace in knowing Bakulu would be joining her in death.

A MONARCH

L ight.
Was she in another one of Bakulu's dreamscapes?
The brightness of the light made Urbi fear she may have
crossed over into the Land of Invisibles. Yet, the smell of disinfectant seemed out of place.

Urbi opened her eyes to see she was in a hospital. She
needed to keep her guard up. She was not certain if this was
real or an illusion. Something rested in the palm of her hand.
Urbi looked down to see the amulet of Damballah, the pebbles
her mother had blessed to protect her. Even in death, her
mother continued to watch over her. Urbi squeezed the charm
and thanked her.

Urbi saw something moving in the distance. She peered
over towards the window to see a nurse trying to coax a
Monarch butterfly off the windowsill.

"How in the hell did you get in here?" the nurse said.

A Monarch butterfly did not strike Urbi as odd. What did
strike her as odd was the fact the windows were closed. In fact,

there were screens on the windows. On top of that, leaves sparsely populated the trees outside. It was either fall or winter.

Unless that Monarch sprouted hands and feet, there was no way it could've gotten into her room, unless it was not a butterfly at all. Urbi reminded herself that bakas customarily adopted the form of wolves, butterflies, and even infants to lure in an unsuspecting host. A baka such as Bakulu needed to mount. If that butterfly was Bakulu, Urbi wondered how the demon had thwarted her binding spell.

Urbi watched as the butterfly climbed onto the nurse's hand. "You're a beautiful little bugger. Something as pretty as you deserve to be set free," the nurse gushed.

"No!" Urbi said, but it was too late. The Monarch had already evaporated into a thin, dark mist.

Within seconds the nurse's eyes turned jet black. He looked over at Urbi and smiled. "Well, Urbi, it's been a blast. I wasn't quite ready to go back just yet. That's why I couldn't let you die. Nevertheless, I enjoyed our time together. I do recommend you brush up on your incantations. There is one very vital piece of the incantation you missed. Honestly, did you really want to be stuck with me for eternity?

"Don't worry, we'll meet again. I guarantee it. Right now, I'm going to go see what kind of mischief I can get into."

"No!" Urbi groaned.

The baka laughed, then strolled out of the room.

KINDRED SPIRITS

Urbi had failed to contain Bakulu. The baka had been set free on an unsuspecting world. It would take Urbi some time to recuperate from doing battle with the demon. Yet, she was at least alive. After Bakulu's departure, Urbi drifted in and out of consciousness. Lucid visions plagued her, remnants of Bakulu.

Finally, Urbi awoke to find Aaron at her bedside. "How are you?" she asked.

"You're awake. I can't believe it." He grabbed her hand and squeezed it as if to verify she was real. "Your brother went downstairs to the hospital cafeteria to grab a bite to eat. I'll go get him and tell the nurse that you're awake."

"No, don't leave," Urbi said. "How is it that they let you in the hospital to see me?"

"I am a doctor, Urbi. I really think I should get Ousman. He would like to know you are awake."

Urbi searched Aaron's eyes. There was truth to the old adage, that the eyes were the windows to the soul. She wanted to make sure she did not see Bakulu lurking behind them. She wanted to warn Aaron about the demon's escape. However, he knew nothing about the baka.

"Don't you think I should at least notify the nurse?" asked Aaron.

Urbi shook her head. "No, I want to rest."

"If you say so. You know you gave us quite a scare."

"Probably not as much of a scare as you gave your wife and friends."

"You are probably right about that."

"I see much happened to you while you were on the other side," Urbi joked. "What a beautiful new head of hair."

Aaron smiled, ran his fingers through his silver mane. "Yeah, a souvenir from the Invisibles."

"The divination tray, what happened to it?"

"Donna burnt the pieces of the divination tray about three weeks ago."

Urbi's displeasure at the news was obvious. "Did we do something wrong?"

"No," Urbi lied.

She could not blame Aaron and Donna for their ignorance in not knowing how to properly dispose of the pieces of the divination tray. Tradition stated that each shard of the divination tray must be buried separately. Burning the talking board did not properly pay tribute to the spirits that had passed through the tray.

"Did you say Donna burnt the divination tray *three weeks ago*?"

Aaron hesitated before replying. "Yes. Regrettably, you've been in a coma for close to a month. The physicians were stumped as to why your body continuously tried to shut down, or even why you had gone into a coma when you appeared perfectly healthy."

"There are some things technology and medicine cannot

detect. Three weeks, huh?" Urbi was not surprised. She had feared the demon might've wanted to keep her captive for much longer.

Even though they were alone, Aaron looked around the room to make sure no one was listening. "Donna told me that you pulled something out of me when I returned."

Urbi gazed up at the ceiling, recalling Lake Nokoué, the tsetse flies, the beach outside Ouidah, and the tsunami, all acts of torture dispensed by Bakulu. "Yes, I did. Sadly, I was not strong enough to keep it away from others," Urbi confessed. "That is a conversation for another day. How's your son?"

"Asher is doing fine. He made it through his crisis, thanks to you. The paramedics said whatever it was you had Donna give him saved his life. I am grateful."

Urbi waved off the praise. "It was nothing. I have plenty of the powder at the house. You can have it if you wish. How is Donna and your daughter doing?"

"Imani is doing fine. Neither her nor Asher remember much about what happened to them. Donna is okay."

"That's understandable, especially after what your family has gone through. And you, how are you?"

Aaron fell silent.

Urbi looked at Aaron and asked again, "Aaron, how are you?" Urbi sensed some unease. "Do you remember anything pertaining to your time on the other side?"

"I pretty much remember everything until the very end. The last thing I recall was falling towards my grandmother's light. I have no recollection of anything after that. I don't have a clue as to how Asher, Imani, and I made it back."

"Grandmother?"

"My late grandmother, Mother Dear, was there. She brought me out of Darkness."

"Are you certain?"

"I'm certain of it. However, I'm sure it came at a cost."

Again, Aaron fell silent. He hesitated before saying, "We're leaving."

"Where are you going?"

"Donna, the kids, and I have decided it is best we head back to D.C."

"You're going back?"

"Yeah, I came here today to say goodbye. It was the least I could do, regarding what you did for me and my family."

"So, you are going home?"

"It's best for me and my family. Everyone is a little leery about setting foot back in that house. We've been living in a motel since that night. We've put the house up for sale."

"That is understandable, given the circumstances."

"We have not been able to leave. The police refused to let us leave until they had concluded their investigation. They insist Donna and I perpetuated a hoax. We didn't think they would believe us. Hell, I'm not sure if I believe it. Nevertheless, we told them the kids came back home, which is partially true. The two detectives who were on the case, Detectives Mourning and Smith, are no longer on the case. Both of them have fallen deathly ill."

"Both of them?"

"Yeah, it's the weirdest thing. When I was on the other side, they spoke as if they were demons."

"That's interesting."

"The police department is considering charging us with fraud. Since the city is claiming Asher and Imani going missing was a hoax, they're threatening to stick us with the bill for all the hours put forth trying to find them."

"That sure is going to be one hell of a bill."

"Tell me about it."

Urbi was glad to see that Aaron could muster a smile. Again, Aaron fell silent. "Are you alright?"

Aaron looked Urbi in the eyes. "Is this real? Right here, right now. Is this real?"

"You know, I've been asking myself the same question since I saw you sitting there."

Aaron became solemn. "I ask myself that question every day."

As they sat there, the door to the room opened and Ousman walked in. He was delighted to see Urbi awake. He rushed to his sister's side. "I thought I had lost you. Losing Mama, then you, would have been too much for my heart to bear. How long have you been awake?"

"She awoke soon after you left for the cafeteria," Aaron said.

"And you did not come and get me?"

"I told him not to, Ousman," Urbi said, trying to shield Aaron from her brother's wrath.

Ousman grimaced. "How do you feel?"

Urbi was not accustomed to her brother fawning over her. "Other than feeling a little groggy, I am doing fine."

"Why is there no nurse in here? Did you not at least call for a nurse?" Ousman glared over at Aaron.

Aaron quickly pointed at Urbi. "I did not want him to," Urbi said.

"What do you mean you did not want him to?"

"I did not wish to be bothered. I wanted to catch up with my friend."

Ousman bristled. "Humph, they should have seen your vitals change, anyway, down at the nurses' station. You need a physician to examine you. I'm going to get one." Ousman frowned at Aaron on his way out.

"Don't pay him no mind. He's usually not this overly protective."

"Well, I can understand why he might be."

Ousman returned quickly with a battery of nurses and a physician in tow. Before Aaron could say a word, a nurse escorted him out.

DISCOVERY

U rbi was right; Aaron's transformation went beyond his new head of hair. Everything Aaron knew or thought he knew about life changed the instant he stepped into the void. Since his return, sleep evaded him. When he did manage to get some rest, he dreamt of Mother Dear. She was always on fire, screaming out in pain. Plenty of times Aaron questioned if he was doing nothing more than romping around in the playground of his own mind. A casualty of Missus Farmer and her trusty orbitoclast.

Picking up the pieces and going on with life after such an ordeal was hard. The incident exposed plenty of problems in his marriage that would be difficult to overcome. Not to mention, at times it was hard for Aaron to disconnect the Donna he encountered in the Land of Invisibles from the one he had married. On top of all of that, it wasn't as if they could simply go back to the way things were.

Seeking to truly understand what had happened to him while on the other side, Aaron suggested Donna and the kids head back to D.C. ahead of him. They preferred to fly back rather than drive cross country anyway. Aaron's excuse for staying behind was so he could oversee matters regarding the sale of the house. Yet, he truly hoped to find the answers to the many questions that perplexed him. Following their departure, Aaron spent countless days visiting with Urbi. They pieced together what happened to him while in the ancestral plane. Urbi spoke of her time with Bakulu after extracting the demon out of him. Aaron tried to recollect as much as he could about his time in Darkness. He explained in detail to Urbi everything he could recall, including his encounter with Nora. After listening to Aaron tell Nora's story, Urbi was certain he was the botono spoken of in childhood fables.

Despite their conversations pertaining to Aaron's experience in The Land of Invisibles, it did not quench Aaron's desire to understand. How was it that he was able to traverse between two realms? What is reality, and what is not? Or does everything exist in some shadowy gray area? Urbi informed Aaron the only way for him to find the answers to such questions was for him to travel to Ouidah.

However, Urbi was quick to warn Aaron, "People do not dabble in Vodun out of curiosity. As you have seen, this is how bad things can happen."

Also, traveling to Africa meant getting over his hatred of planes. Of course, that meant he needed to come to terms with other matters tormenting him.

CLOSURE

I t did not take any time for the house to sell. It sold in a matter of days. Aaron decided to conduct one last walk through to make sure they were not leaving anything behind. Pretty much everything was on the moving truck headed for Washington, D.C. And what wasn't on the truck was crammed into the trunk and the backseat of the car.

As he walked through the dining room, he found a small splinter of wood on the floor. He picked it up and examined it. He wasn't certain if it was a piece of the divination tray. He could only assume. He recalled Urbi telling him the proper way to dispose of the pieces of a divination tray is to bury them. So, Aaron held on to the piece of wood. If it was a shard of wood from the divination tray, he wanted to properly honor the souls that had passed through the tray by burying it. He scanned the living room one more time before walking out the door for the last time.

In the garden, Aaron dug a small hole with his hand and dropped in the piece of wood. He pushed the dirt back over the wood, patting the earth down firmly. He could not help but think of all the lives that had been altered by a piece of wood. He stood up and turned to leave, when he came face to face with Jennifer.

"Jesus! Can you please announce yourself rather than sneaking up on a guy?"

"Sorry, I didn't mean to scare you. I just came to say bye."

"Yeah, I saw on the news they caught the guy who murdered you."

"Yeah, about time. I thought about hanging around, but it's depressing here."

"So, where are you going?"

"I'm going to head back. I've gotten the closure I needed. It's time for me to join the others in The Light."

"I want to thank you for your help."

"No problem, don't mention it. I just wanted to say bye. Hopefully I'll see you again."

"I hope so."

Jennifer smiled, waved, then turned around and walked away. Aaron watched as she faded from sight. A few neighbors stared at Aaron oddly as they walked by. Aaron waved as he made his way to the car. Looking up, he saw the contrails of a plane in the sky. He stood there and marveled at the white streaks crisscrossing the heavens as the plane disappeared off into the distance.

ACKNOWLEDGMENTS

I must give special thanks to my muse, my wife, Tonya. You are the spark that ignites the flame. This would not have been possible without you. I want to thank my mother, Patricia Hampton, and my father, Preston Hampton, for instilling in me a belief that anything is possible, you just must be willing to work for it. My grandmother, Geraldine Quarles, and my late grandmother, Lassie E. Hampton, the two of you are the foundation in which all of this was made possible.

I must thank my friends and family who have been my nonstop cheerleaders and supporters throughout this journey. I must give much love to my daughter, India Hampton; my son, Phalen Hampton, my brother, Makeem Hampton, my sister, Danielle Dibba; my cousin, Ralph Redmond; my boys, Stephen Jones, Randy Brooks, John Jackson, Kenneth "Kenny" Johnson, Andre Redmond, Peter White, Loren Adams, Daryl James, and David "KJ" Johnson. I give much love to my father-in-law, Wallace "Jack" Jackman, for his unwavering support in everything I do. Most importantly, I want to give special thanks to my late mother-in-law, Lynda D. Jackman. You loved me and supported me unconditionally. You always pestered me as to when you would be able to read the book. I am so sorry that I did not complete it before you moved on. However, I assure you I will have a signed copy for you the next time I see you. Please know, your presence is missed.

I want to thank Marita Dingus for helping with your ideas

and knowledge of Vodun. I must thank Matt Ryan for being a true friend and helping me along this literary journey. I cannot forget Debra Beilke for the assistance with the French. Also, Brittany Foote for helping shape this novel in its infancy.

Finally, I want to thank my editor, Cecilia Kennedy, for helping me refine and sharpen my vision for this novel. Thank you!

RIZE publishes great stories and great writing across genres written by People of Color and other underrepresented groups. Our team consists of:

Lisa Diane Kastner, Founder and Executive Editor
Mona Bethke, Acquisitions Editor
Rebecca Dimyan, Editor
Abigail Efird, Editor
Laura Huie, Editor
Cody Sisco, Editor
Chih Wang, Editor
Pulp Art Studios, Cover Design
Standout Books, Interior Design
Polgarus Studios, Interior Design

Learn more about us and our stories at www.runningwildpress. com/rize

Loved this story and want more? Follow us at www.runningwildpress.com/rize, www.facebook.com/RW-Prize, on Twitter @rizerwp and Instagram @rizepress